SARAH MAYFIELD

JS Anthony

1

Sarah gathered her skirts and stepped out into the warm spring air. Her boot found the first toehold, a metal bar. The next step was a reach. She executed the drop perfectly, averting disaster once more at the awkward exit.

No one offered assistance and she didn't expect it. Any person bearing the slightest resemblance to a gentleman had last been seen a thousand miles back, before the Baltimore and Ohio, before the river. It didn't matter. Everything in the nature of a tragedy belonged to the life behind her. Everything bearing any kind of promise lay ahead. And even if at one of these stops she tripped and lay sprawled in the dust, it wouldn't be a humiliation because her two traveling companions showed no signs of noticing anything. They had problems of their own.

Sarah's hands stung, a remnant of the skull-pounding vibrations caused by iron wheels careening along severely rutted dirt tracks. A few steps brought the same sensation down to her feet. Her toes tingled in their narrow lace-up boots.

She considered the dwindling amount of time left and a moment of weakness overcame her. Maybe it would be far wiser to continue west over these rough roads, traveling right past whatever awaited her, even all the way to California. So many had already pulled up their roots and set out on the perilous but surely rewarding journey to that golden promised land.

Yes, the worrying voice in her head urged, a good idea, consider it at least, but her steadier self refused to entertain even the thought. Her own journey would end the way it had been planned to end. She revisited that image, still not knowing any more than what was contained in the creased pages of the letters she'd received. Over the long monotonous days of travel, she'd composed a face, a voice, the look of the surroundings, a meeting, the first shared words, then erased everything and started over, a different face, a slightly older one perhaps, a deeper voice, a less tentative greeting, better buildings. She knew she could invent a hundred different variations and everything would still be unknown, but it helped. She realized that, despite all her concerns, at least the longing for home had disappeared. The future was here, not behind her on the wide river she'd crossed or even farther back in the east she'd left behind forever.

Sarah looked down at the dust layered into every fold of her black traveling outfit. She shook out her long skirts and pounded the dust off her high-collared jacket and narrow sleeves. Small light clouds billowed up and off into the afternoon sunlight. The flat-brimmed hat had become a problem. She questioned why she was wearing it. Most likely because her proper mother long ago, possibly even in childhood, told her that was how a traveling lady dressed. Sarah reached up, took out the pins, and pulled off the hat, holding it in her hand as an afterthought, an accessory past its useful date. What she would do with it now, she didn't know, but the thought of doing something with it gave her momentary satisfaction, a useful task to perform, an easy problem to solve.

A voice from the curtained interior of the coach brought her back to the present.

"Mrs. Mayfield, will you kindly remove your maidenly form just a few precious feet one way or the other?"

And then there was this situation, definitely an annoying one, her companions.

"Sorry," she said. "How thoughtless of me. I was daydreaming."

"Not thoughtless at all, madam. Happy are those fortunate souls still acquainted with dreams."

Sarah watched as Dr. Morrison lowered his bulk out of the coach, feeling with his foot for the step he knew must be there, landing with a thud and a surprised look that he too had exited without mishap. Plainly speaking, Dr. Morrison was drunk and had been for quite some time.

"Might you know the way to the conveniences, my dear?" he said. "No, of course not, you've just arrived yourself."

"Would you like me to find you a cup of coffee?" she said. She knew the answer. This stage stop would be like the others, a plank table in one room, a rough bar in the other, with Dr. Morrison having no trouble making up his mind between the two.

"How sweet of you to offer. I believe in this instance however whiskey might be the better choice."

"I doubt it," Sarah said.

Behind Dr. Morrison, small Scottish Mr. Ford hopped to the ground and glanced around as nervously as an owl caught out in daylight. Dr. Morrison showed all the slovenly effects of his liquor-loving nature, unshaven, uncombed, shirttail out, dark suit stained down the front. Mr. Ford remained immaculate, a little dusty but still brushed and pressed. His starched collar sat firm under his chin, the thick tie knotted, vest buttoned, gold pocket watch in place.

The only item Mr. Ford no longer entirely possessed was his sample case containing the tools of his trade as a whiskey drummer. Mr. Ford harbored natural fears that unfortunately he couldn't conceal. These, he explained helplessly, came to the fore when traveling long distances away from what he considered to be civilization. This confession caused his listeners to wonder why on earth he chose such a profession, in an entirely uncivilized land that wasn't even his own. For this, there was no reason given. However, he was quick and eager to catalogue his fears, as if talking about them might take away their power over him. He panicked at the mere thought of lightning, whirlwinds, dust storms, hailstorms, rattlesnakes, vultures, guns, sheep, runaway horses, highwaymen and most of all, what he knew to be fearsome, marauding, death-dealing savages. He was also afraid of the dark. Dr. Morrison, spinning out ever more clever and fantastical tales concerning these fears to keep the little man

5

apoplectic, managed to co-opt and empty more than a few of Mr. Ford's precious bottles.

As Mr. Ford hurried in the direction of the conveniences, the good doctor, thinking to follow, stumbled. He grabbed Sarah's arm for support and exhaled, enveloping her in the harsh smell of spirits. She'd had more than enough. Good manners were no longer a welcome attribute.

"You reek, Dr. Morrison," she said.

He was beyond hearing the insult.

"It's the fresh aroma of God's fields, my dear," he said, leaning heavily on her till he righted himself again. "Rye and barley in particular."

"Now all of you please kindly get in there and eat," the driver said, climbing down wearily from his high perch. "We don't got much time."

The driver, Sam Oakley, pulled off his thick leather gloves, revealing rough, worn hands. The battered hat he removed left a dividing line like a fence across his forehead, deeply tanned underneath, pale white above. He slapped the hat against his trousers and more dust billowed up

The shotgun rider was already down in one leap and gone, gun on the ground beside him, head in the horses' watering trough. He was young and had proved himself to be fairly good with a rifle, but Sam sighed, knowing he was too restless to last long in the job. Then there'd be someone else he'd have to break in and share that hard seat with for all those miles. Sarah smiled as the boy came up spluttering and already refreshed. He reminded her of her older brother at that age, when he was still safe at home in Virginia and just as restless.

Beyond them, stables lined one end of a log corral.

"Come on, boy, we got work to do," Sam said.

"I know, I know. I'm coming."

As Sarah watched, a third person crossed the corral. Her thoughts flew to Mr. Ford, causing her to glance quickly at the open station house door. This person wore the same rough pants and worn boots as the others, the same faded shirt and jacket.

6

But there the resemblance stopped. His lean and quiet presence lent itself to the differences. His hair fell to his shirt collar, straight black and shining. When he reached up to push it back behind his ears, glints of silver showed at his wrists. His skin was warm and smooth. Sarah tried not to stare, but couldn't help herself.

He led a team of fresh horses behind him, speaking softly to them, while Sam and the young one unhitched the traces of the old team.

"Coming back with us, Elijah?" Sam asked. He had a name.

Elijah nodded.

"Heard of any trouble?"

He shook his head no.

"Well, okay, I got a shotgun rider, as you can see, least that's what he calls himself," Sam frowned at the boy, "but bring your rifle, okay?"

Elijah nodded again, one hand running down the neck of the lead horse to settle him. Sam struggled with the set of harnesses and Elijah stepped in to help.

"I'm being told we got a full house this last leg, so there'll be that kind of trouble," Sam said.

Elijah nodded one more time and freed the last horse.

Sarah realized that she hadn't moved. This change of horses drew her attention so strongly, even though she'd seen it repeated over and over again at every stop. She'd understood long ago that this was the only reason for the stops at all. Certainly no one cared if the passengers ate or relieved themselves. It was always all about the horses.

There was only this one person then who caused her to notice. She'd seen photographs of his people when they came through Virginia in delegations to speak to the senators and congressmen in Washington. Those were old men, however, the leaders, everyone said, the chiefs, wearing elaborate robes, feathers, beads, headdresses. She had never encountered anyone like him in real life before.

Well, she thought, and made herself look away. It was so warm that her piled-up hair stuck in damp curls around her face. She envied the shotgun rider his plunge into the trough.

In the station house, Dr. Morrison leaned against the bar, seemingly more for support than to strike a pose. Propped up on one elbow, he attempted to engage the bartender.

"Good to see you, Mr. Ryder," he said. He had to straighten a little, having leaned further than was necessary with the floor not so far away.

"I suppose I should say it's good to see you, too, Doc. To what medical emergency do I owe the pleasure?"

"The delivery of twins, I am proud to tell you, over in Dry Creek."

"Are you certain there were two?" Mr. Ryder said, then waved away the comment. "Never mind. I'm sure it was great hard work that's brought on quite a thirst and you'll be wanting your whiskey."

"A man of tremendous perceptive abilities, my friend. Quite remarkable."

Mr. Ryder poured the whiskey and wiped down the counter around the glass.

"Excuse me, sir," he said. "I've got to quit bartending to be the kitchen help after I get done being the cook."

Sarah took in the diners seated at the long table. Mr. Ford dug into his food, which Sarah stared at, puzzled. It seemed to be a plate of red beans and rice. Across from Mr. Ford sat a handsome woman and a straight-backed man. The woman wore a billowing skirt, a velvet jacket with lace at the wrists, a veiled hat and what Sarah thought might be real diamond drops in her ears. The man carried pearl gray gloves that lay now beside his plate at the table.

"Welcome to our humble lunch," the woman said. "Mrs. Addison Pruitt." She held out her hand for Sarah to shake.

"Now remember I do need some more of that celery," Mr. Ryder said, bringing another plate from the kitchen and setting it down in front of Sarah. "All I got left's the pepper and onions. Can't do it without the celery."

8

"I'll have it here next week," Mrs. Pruitt said. "Don't know how yet, but I will."

"And salt pork and sausage if you find it. What good's beans without sausage and I haven't got a pig walking around out back. If it's asking too much, I was just wishing."

"Did you make this?" Sarah said in astonishment. She sat down eagerly. The food was presented on a dented tin plate at a worn table, but was a far cry from the sinewy and unidentifiable stews at the few other stops where they'd managed the time to eat. Someone had suggested badger, someone else offered the possibility of possum or raccoon. Whatever it was, a day's worth of chewing didn't soften it up much. She'd swallowed a piece by accident and almost choked bringing it back up. From then on, she'd stayed with the dry rusks wrapped in her bag.

"I did," he said.

Sarah lifted the fork of tender beans, inhaled the wonderful garlic-laced aroma, and eyes closed, savored a mouthful.

"So good," she said. "Where did you learn to cook like this?"

"New Orleans."

"New Orleans?"

"Yes, ma'am, that's where all three of us come from, the beans, the rice and me."

"How did you get here?" Sarah's glance took in the unpainted walls and plain furniture, though there was, by some miracle, a painting behind the bar.

"That's a tale that doesn't get any better with the telling. I know, I've tried. All I want to say is that Mrs. Pruitt trusts me to do the cooking."

"I own the stagecoach stop," Mrs. Pruitt interrupted, smiling.

Sarah's eyes widened. She turned to the woman with renewed interest. Those *were* real diamonds.

"I'm sorry, I was so taken aback by the food that I forgot to mention my name," she said. "It's Mrs. Mayfield. Sarah Mayfield."

The stranger at the table watched this exchange. Sarah could feel his eyes on her, but he said nothing. His clothes bore the

9

same fine lineage as Mrs. Pruitt's, but his mouth was unfriendly behind the carefully clipped goatee.

"And since we're going to be spending some time together," Mrs. Pruitt continued, as if she could read Sarah's thoughts, "let me introduce you to the out-of-sorts but certainly dapper, wouldn't you agree?, gentleman to my left. This is my business partner and traveling companion, Mr. John Russell from New York City. You'll have to excuse his manner, he's with us under duress, couldn't pass up a good thing, but he's finding himself not too taken with our open spaces and harsh ways, not to mention dining on beans and rice. I guess they don't eat beans anymore in New York City."

Sarah noticed a flicker in Mr. Russell's eyes and wondered if the good thing he couldn't pass up might be Mrs. Pruitt.

"I'd eat beans every day if they were like this," Sarah said.

"We aim to please, don't we, Mr. Russell?"

Mr. Russell smiled faintly, lit a thin cigar and excused himself from the table.

"It's all very simple, really," said Mrs. Pruitt. "The railroad's coming through not very long from now. It'll take a while for things to fall into place, but I'm good at waiting. I've got a reputation, a better one this time, and money. I've got an investor. I've already got one fine hotel with a real dining room. We're not talking saloons and dance halls. That's for cowhands, trail riders, half-wits who can't spell their own names, most of them anyway. Railroad passengers come from big cities, not Texas. They expect more. And I'm going to be right there to give it to them. I've got an excellent hand to play, some very fine cards. One of them just walked out the door and one of them can cook a whole lot more than rice and beans, you just wait and see. I'm keeping him under wraps till I have my suppliers lined up and my second hotel ready. Then we will have us a time, won't we, Mr. Ryder?"

"I believe we will," Mr. Ryder said and pulled his towel out from under Doc Morrison's elbow.

10

"Guess we'd better get going," Mrs. Pruitt said. "Sam Oakley's usually shouting at people by now."

As they moved toward the door with Dr. Morrison in tow, the shotgun rider slid past them and sat down at the table.

"Heard there's food in here," he said. "And with the dustup going on out there, maybe I got me a chance to eat some. Mr. Barkeep, do you have a plate you can spare? Or hell, I'll eat out of the pot, just show me where it is."

Mr. Ryder, with his sympathy for youngsters, since he'd been one, brought out another plate.

"Better be quick, now," he said. "You're asking for trouble."

"I know, I know. If I could just please have a fork, I'll be done in no time. I'm so hungry I could eat an armadillo. You don't suppose he has a gun, do you?"

"This gentleman here?" Mr. Ryder pointed to the seat where the stranger had been. "Don't suppose so, no." He wiped his hands on his apron. "Least I hope not."

"Yeah, me, too."

Sarah and Addison Pruitt had both come to a stop outside the door.

Mr. Russell stood blocking the entrance to the coach. Mr. Ford, who had tried to board, but came back out as fast as he went in, now stood nervously wringing his hands. Sam Oakley stood with his hands on his hips, sizing up his opponent. Then he stopped and wiped his forehead with a handkerchief. The spring sun was already warm.

"I'm too old for this," he said to no one. "Just too damn old. I want me a cabin by a creek and a dog under the porch and some whiskey in a jug and that's it. Everybody leave me alone." He walked around, kicking up dust, then came back to the matter at hand.

"We are getting in that coach and we are going to Sweetwater," he said. "We can do that now, or in the middle of the night, but that's what we're doing. If you're a paying passenger, which all of you are, then this is what I got. This is the only way you're ever

11

gonna get there. And I'll tell you what, I'm so tired of how predictable this is. But go ahead, sir, have your say."

Mr. Russell drew himself up to his full height, his back ramrod straight, his posture suggesting there was rank and bearing in his past, soldiering of some sort. He ignored Sam Oakley and stared out over the green hills.

"I will say it again, even if you don't want to hear it, Mr. Oakley. I realize that I come from what might as well be another country. I realize that I might not understand the rules by which you govern yourselves. If there are any. Still, I don't consider it prudent for vulnerable persons," here he cast a disapproving eye on Dr. Morrison and then raised an eyebrow at Mr. Ford, "to be closeted with a member of a hostile race," now he fixed his gaze without any hint of compassion on Sarah and Mrs. Pruitt, "let alone travel in such company," now he concentrated on Sam Oakley, "for an interminable journey." Everyone breathed, hoping he was done.

"Not only a hostile race," he lamentably continued, "but one with recognizable grievances and," he glanced into the coach and then back at his audience, "weapons."

Addison Pruitt gripped her purse tightly and took one step backward, leading Sarah to understand that, though she knew full well what had happened, Mrs. Pruitt was tied to the money and could do nothing. But surely Sam Oakley could. Sarah waited.

Sam walked to the front of the horses to calm himself, running his hands along the harnesses as he went, muttering under his breath. Then he came back.

"Mr. Russell," he said. "I'm sorry you're from New York City. I never been there, but I understand it's a whole long ways from here. Which is the point. So you don't exactly know, begging your pardon, sir, what a hostile race is or nothing like that. Now let me tell you something. I got a shotgun rider, that young kid in there fool-like eating his fourth plate of them beans and where's his gun right now? He don't know. But I got me another shotgun rider, doesn't matter where his gun is, he can find it. Doesn't matter what he's got to shoot at, moving or not, he's gonna hit it. Doesn't matter how fast it has to be, he's that much and faster.

"And furthermore, Mr. Russell, this shotgun rider, he owns these horses we got pulling this stage. So if we want to get anywhere, we better stop this kind of protesting, if that's what you're calling it, or we're all gonna be walking to Sweetwater.

"Now I understand, cause of being where you're from, that you might not grasp this whole notion yet. But you will, being out here long enough, doing business out here as I see you're going to, and being good at, as I'm sure you will. But that individual you're claiming is from a hostile race, he's actually a friend of mine, and I'm counting on him to get us back there safe if there's any trouble besides what's going on here right now."

Sam Oakley took one last long breath.

"So, sir, if you don't mind, we're gonna board this coach and get on going before the sun goes down and we got even more trouble."

Beside her, Sarah heard Mrs. Pruitt exhale. Head bowed, she came forward, briefly glancing up at her business partner only at the last minute. Sarah could see other times and circumstances when that look would have been flirtatious, when it might have raised the hopes of lesser men. Now it was cool and deferential, like a careful woman. Or a high stakes gambler.

"It's all like he says," she said gently. "Elijah Blue owns the horses. He trusts the way my hands treat them, and for that, I'm glad. It's business, just not the way it's done in New York City, I guess."

Mr. Russell scowled down at her, not at all moved by her suddenly feminine and soft-spoken ways. The problem was that he'd been backed into a corner of his own making and now there were no options. He hated giving in to his inferiors. He hated it when there were no options. He threw down his cigar and ground it into the dust with the heel of his expensive boot. Grudgingly he moved to one side, looking as if he himself had eaten armadillo instead of the beans that he found disgusting enough.

Politeness, what was left of it, seemed to dictate that the women enter first. Sarah held onto the doorway and pulled herself into the coach. To keep matters from escalating even further, she took the seat next to the one they called Elijah Blue. In the quickness of her entrance, she caught only a glimpse of the same warm skin, black shining hair, a face turned toward the window as if the rest of them did not exist. She slid up against him, it was the only way they would all fit, and was uncomfortably aware of his stillness. She was surprised to find herself afraid of him.

Mrs. Pruitt entered the coach next and stationed herself against the opposite window. She, too, gazed out at the green hills, wishing the rest of them away. "Jesus Christ," she said to no one.

"No, wait, this won't work," she said, turning back to the problem at hand. She reached out to haul Doc Morrison with some difficulty past her as she slid under him into the middle seat. "Well, that was awkward," she said. "Just goes to show that chivalry's dead." Dr. Morrison slumped down heavily, causing the coach to tilt slightly in his direction.

Mr. Ford, gripping tightly to what was left of his sample case, backed into the seat next to Sarah and shut his eyes tight. Here was his number one living fear, separated from his own person by only one other human being, and a woman at that. Surely once on the road they would be attacked. Mr. Ford was weak. He would be the first to go. He pictured himself riddled with arrows, though there was not a bow anywhere in sight, and his bloody scalp of sadly thinning hair attached to a lance. Maybe he would be killed by a tomahawk, though nobody seemed to own one of those either, or staked out in the sun and eaten by ants, or vultures, or something. At any rate, he would die a horrible death and his dear mother in Scotland would never know what happened to him. Not that she would anyway. He wasn't very good about writing.

"Are you praying, Mr. Ford?" Sarah asked. She wondered if he was Presbyterian. She knew from experience that the Presbyterian God wasn't always very sympathetic.

14

"Shh, shh, shh," he stuttered, his bottles clinking.

Mr. Russell maneuvered himself in last, claiming his seat beside Mrs. Pruitt, at the farthest reaches from the hostile person on whom he'd laid his caustic judgment. Mr. Russell's face settled into an expression of pained endurance. For him, this journey could not end too soon.

Immediately, Sam Oakley slammed the door shut and shouted at the boy, who came running. They both swung up onto the high seat, then while Sam cursed, the boy jumped down and hurried over to retrieve his shotgun from where it lay by the water trough. Sam Oakley shook his head. He gave a sharp whistle, cracked the reins, and the horses galloped out of the yard, causing the coach to lurch forward sickeningly.

2

Silence hung in the air along with the dust, but in this silence were all the words John Russell had flung about so carelessly. It seemed as if everyone had been touched by the harsh sentiments one way or the other, and held them in mind. The only blank space was that concerning the thoughts of Elijah Blue, who had occasioned the sentiments.

The coach jolted back and forth, knocking the passengers against each other. The iron wheels sang on the hard road. The sound of the horses' hooves settled into a steady rhythm backed by the jangling of the harnesses. Sam Oakley's whistles and shouts punctuated the air at intervals. The sun arced across the sky and began its long descent. Doc Morrison snored unevenly.

Sarah felt caught between several poles. Mr. Ford fidgeted endlessly on her right. She feared that if he didn't calm down, he might actually break out in weeping and then what would they do? A small hysterical whiskey drummer on a coach packed with people having problems of their own was not something to look forward to.

Across the tight aisle, Mrs. Pruitt seemed bent on a distracting and close quarters inspection of the person opposite her, which was Sarah. Sarah felt her traveling clothes being appraised, her dark hair which had come loose again, her hands, her face, her figure, her less than stylish boots, the tapestry valise on her lap. She felt her color rising under such scrutiny and knew that was being noted as well, the flush in her cheeks merely indicating how embarrassed she was.

In order to evade Mrs. Pruitt, Sarah held her gaze down, even though this could possibly allow an assessment of her modesty or her lashes against her cheek. Mrs. Pruitt be damned! But with her eyes averted, Sarah came up against the third pole, not even taking into consideration Dr. Morrison's comatose state and John Russell's ice-cold presence.

The hand before her became of great interest, in small part because it was the only thing within the scope of her circumcised vision and in larger part because it belonged to the fearsome, silent Elijah. She thought the hand a good one, strong and steady. Above the hand, two taut bands of rawhide leather circled the wrist. Each was attached to a thick silver oval stamped with a design of some kind. She became so fascinated that she fought the urge to pick up the wrist, as if it didn't belong to a hostile person, and examine these objects from a closer viewpoint. Then she was horrified and at the same time wanted to laugh out loud, imagining the predicament that would cause.

She remembered that Mrs. Pruitt was watching, and tried to resume an expressionless demeanor. But the hand so close to her presented even more interest for the fingers being curved gracefully around the midsection of a rifle, the thumb resting easily against the backward sloping hammer. The polished wooden stock of the rifle was out of sight somewhere beneath her elbow. The end of the barrel showed, carefully lodged beside his right boot. As a result of the jolting and swaying in such crowded quarters, her many layered skirts had moved to cover all the rest of the rifle. She could see a tense event occurring, highwaymen approaching, the gun rising up in a swift soundless arc and taking her skirts with it, scorched holes being blown in the heavy dark material of her only traveling outfit, smoke rising from the burnt cloth. Again, she smiled without meaning to. Elijah Blue was not one to find such a thing amusing, she was sure. He had not moved, twitched, shifted, changed position. She couldn't tell for certain if he was even breathing.

Oh, Lord, she said to herself. Please remember that Mrs. Pruitt's watching.

And the afternoon was lengthening. Another reason to pause, come back to the present, forget small frivolous moments and return to the anxious goal of this journey, whose end was drawing unfortunately near.

17

There was no reason the silence couldn't last forever. It had in fact become comfortable and useful, a perfect way for everyone to avoid each other's company. Mrs. Pruitt became the reason, unhappy with silence and feeling betrayed by it, as if it were costing her a thousand precious moments when she could be seeking out information, gaining insights. How did one construct a promising future without information? And how did one get information when there was only silence?

"Mrs. Mayfield," she said loudly, jumping into the pool of steady breathing and surprising everyone. Sarah startled, so lost had she been in her own thoughts. Mr. Ford almost came out of his seat. Even Doc Morrison gained an upright position for a moment, his eyes nearly coming to a focus. Only Elijah Blue and Mr. Russell did not move.

And of course it has to be me, Sarah thought. She'd known it would be from Mrs. Pruitt's first deeply critical inventory of her person. Mrs. Pruitt would try to pry her open like a can.

"Yes, Mrs. Pruitt?"

"Call me Addison."

"I will do that."

"And may I call you Sarah?"

"Yes, you may."

A smile played across Addison's handsome features, then her brow furrowed and her eyes grew sharp. Not many lone women ventured this far without escort or belongings, a cookstove, china cabinet, children, husband. Schoolteacher was a possibility, though schoolteachers tended toward the more austere and drab, reaching for the excitement that had eluded them in their more ordinary lives. Women homesteaders brought their own animals and scorned social niceties. Dancehall girl? Hardly. Mrs. Pruitt knew breeding when she saw it, having forcefully acquired it herself when she realized what it was and that it hadn't been handed to her. Here, then, was a problem that she meant to solve.

Mr. Russell uncrossed his long legs and sighed. Doc Morrison began to mumble.

"You call yourself Mrs. Mayfield," Addison said, "but where is your wedding ring? I've noticed you don't wear one."

Sarah glanced down at her hands.

"No, I don't," she said. "My wedding ring is in a drawer back home."

"Why did you take it off?"

Sarah remembered the date and hour, winter dusk in her childhood room. The ring slipped off easily, as if it had been made for another finger than hers, as if it had been worn by another person altogether. She hadn't eaten in so long, that was the explanation, less flesh, the bony knuckle of her fourth finger barely holding the ring in place. She took the ring, just a sliver of gold but carefully engraved, and wrapped it in tissue. She laid the tiny knot of tissue in the blue box, tied the black ribbon around it, and put it in the keepsake drawer, along with the newly monogrammed flatware, and the locket and the precious letters filled with love and sadness. Her lace gloves went in the drawer also. She'd only worn them once. The roses would fade over time. Someone, someday, would open the drawer and find dry stiff stems, brittle petals that crumbled at the touch. The rest would remain. Into eternity, she had said to herself. Forever and ever.

"Because I didn't need it anymore," she said.

"Where is your husband?"

"He's dead," Sarah said.

Dr. Morrison came to consciousness. Mr. Ford stopped moving his lips in frantic supplications.

"I'm sorry," Addison said.

"So am I."

"I'm prying," Addison said. "It's my way."

"I understand."

"How did he die?"

"In the war."

Sarah saw her brother at the door alone and half dead. She heard her mother weeping as they brought him into the house. Her mother sat him down at the kitchen table, stroked his hair, pulled cool water from the pump. Sarah stood at the door again, waiting. Her father brought her back in and lit the lamps. He's not outside, her father said. He won't be coming home. She already knew that from the telegram. But the telegram was wrong, it had to be.

"He was in a prison camp in Richmond," Sarah said. "My brother found him. They tried to make it home, but he was too weak and he died. He's buried under an oak tree on a rise where you can see the sunset, or so I'm told."

"You're too young."

"He was too young."

"What was his name?"

"Jacob Webster Mayfield."

"How long were you married?"

Sarah stood in the county courthouse with her lace gloves and the family Bible. Jacob wore his dress uniform with the gold buttons and the sword. When he kissed her, his lips were soft. They fed wedding cake to the ducks in the river. She remembered laughing. She remembered being so happy, as if the blue sky had opened up and invited them both into heaven.

"Three weeks before he left," she said. And a year after that. But they had known it might not last. They had known he might not come home. She kept his dress uniform, wrapped in paper, but gave everything else back to his family. His mother was heartbroken. *So was I,* she thought.

"It's not an easy life out here," Addison said. "People die senseless deaths just like everywhere else. I just want you to know that, because there's always a stage going in the other direction if you want to change your mind."

"I won't change my mind," Sarah said. "I didn't want to live anymore with those sad memories."

John Russell gave no indication he'd been listening, but suddenly he spoke.

"I guess we all died a little in that damn war," he said. Sarah looked up because it didn't even sound like him, but his face revealed nothing.

The cabin grew quiet again, and stiflingly hot.

"Can you cook?" Addison asked, refusing to give in to sympathetic conversations, or let the silence settle in.

20

"Can I cook?" Sarah was glad to laugh. "What kind of question is that?"

"I was just thinking, trying to work some things out. It comes naturally to me, like other women work out how they'll feed their families or get their crops harvested before the rains come."

"I've been cooking for a while. Otherwise, we would have starved."

"Are you good?"

"I'm good, but what I learned leans mostly to the South." She'd been worried about this. Jace taught her many things before she ran off with the Confederate soldier, but not how to make sourdough or cut up a rattlesnake and she'd heard this might be useful knowledge out west. She could serve a decent fried squirrel though if she had to.

"Tell me something you cook that's wonderful."

Sarah laughed again. Addison Pruitt was interviewing her for a job, quite a lucky situation for someone just arriving in an unknown land. But she didn't need or want a job.

"Panfried oysters in Kentucky Bourbon sauce. I'll bet you don't even have oysters out here."

"I'll bet you're right. Canned sometimes, brought from back east, but that's not the same, is it?"

"Oysters," Dr. Morrison said. As he sobered up, he remembered that he forgot to partake of Mr. Ryder's fabulous lunch. "I had them fresh from the Chesapeake once. Quite a treat, if I recall correctly."

"It is quite a treat. I wonder if I'll ever have fresh oysters again."

"Maybe you won't," Addison said. "But that's what making decisions will do for you. In the meantime, Sarah Mayfield, would you like a job?"

"I'm truly grateful you would take a chance on me like that," Sarah said. "And under any other circumstances, I'd be honored to work for you. But I'm hoping I won't need a job. Or that I'll have an entirely different kind of job."

"If you're not going to work," Addison said, "then I guess you're not the new school teacher either. So I'm curious. Why did you come all this way? What is it that you're planning to do?"

"I'm planning to marry," Sarah said, and she wasn't smiling.

"*Marry*? Well, I have to admit, that's the last thing I expected. Who on earth are you marrying?"

"I hope it's all right to say."

"Why wouldn't it be?"

"Because what I've got so far are only three letters and I think they're meant to be private."

"Letters? Good Lord, Sarah Mayfield, I need a name. I could've sworn I knew every eligible bachelor in Sweetwater. It's not that big a town."

"You won't say anything?"

"Not if you don't want me to."

"Grady McGuire."

Addison's eyebrows flew up. Doc Morrison had a coughing fit, though it was unclear why. But what startled her most was that Elijah Blue's rifle hand moved.

A new kind of silence fell, one in which Sarah was very uncomfortable. Yes, she only had three letters, but you could tell a lot about a person by what they wrote. The letters Jacob sent her from the war opened up her heart. It was like hearing his voice, he was so gentle and kind, and thought about things in a different way from anyone she'd ever known.

The second set of letters moved her in another way. She would never have come, would not even have considered the idea for a minute if she'd not found the voice in those letters so appealing. The person writing those letters was not as smart as Jacob, and didn't know her, so couldn't possibly declare his undying love. But he spoke of his longings, fears, dreams in a way so honest and soul-baring that it also opened up her heart. She would never see Jacob again. She was putting all she had in the hope of starting over in an unfamiliar place and life tied to the sweet and sensitive author of those letters.

This silence hurt. Who was Addison Pruitt to raise her eyebrows? What right did Elijah Blue have to let one man's name move his hand? She remained stern in her resolve. She ran the meeting through her mind again with more happy details and an even better outcome.

Then out of nowhere a town appeared, turning the prairie into cornfields, pasture, fences, an outhouse, wash on the line. Sam Oakley reined in the team of horses, slowing them to a walk. It had seemed to take forever, but now the journey was so quickly coming to an end.

3

"We're here," Addison said, watching the livery stable go by. "Mr. John Russell will be so happy to find a first class establishment with a feather bed to sleep in and a nice bottle of wine to keep him company. And I can promise him that even though Mr. Ryder makes the best red beans and rice in any stage stop in this land, the hotel won't be serving beans and rice tonight for dinner."

Doc Morrison unhappily contemplated the fare he might receive at the boarding house across the street. It likely would be bread and butter and maybe, if he was lucky, soup. At least he had a bottle of whiskey hidden under his mattress.

Sam Oakley's booming voice brought the team to a halt. Sarah looked past Mr. Ford to the plain frame buildings and broad unpaved street. The sun slanted across the rooftops, creating deep shadows. From somewhere came the smell of wood smoke and meat frying.

John Russell reached for the door, glad to be free of these people. What did they know of the blessings of culture and cuisine, and how necessary those were to overcome, if not justify, the horrors of war? They knew nothing, living their small lives in a backwater town in this great emptiness. He was sorry for the young woman, Sarah Mayfield. But she had only suffered a loss, not the nightmare that went with it. He realized that he was not well, that his outlook had been forever changed, but that's what happened. He'd seen other men like himself, men who wished they'd been the ones to die. Thank God for the distraction of Addison Pruitt, whom he found vulgar but at least mildly amusing. And she wore diamonds well. She was a woman who could not be properly domesticated, not ever that, but who could certainly be transformed outwardly by well-placed diamonds.

Before the door opened, before the confusing logistics of the exit began, Elijah Blue spoke.

24

"He's out there, but he's passed out drunk," he said.

Sarah knew he was speaking to her.

"Who's out there?"

"The person in your letters."

She was insulted. "I don't believe it," she said. All eyes were on her.

"You don't have to believe it. He was in a buckboard in an alleyway this morning. I imagine he's still there."

Sarah had only one thing on her mind, to get out of the stage and as far away from these people as John Russell wanted to be. The letters could not be wrong. Human decency and tenderness could not be forged. And in any case, as her last proof, her uncle had made this journey before her, met the man, sent a telegram saying he approved. She wondered for the first time about her uncle.

Sarah stepped down from the stage and into the town that hopefully would be kind to her and accept her as one of its own. The young shotgun rider handed down her luggage, the heavy suitcase and the trunk containing what was left of her dowry, the small amount of silver and china. It was the same dowry she'd brought to her first marriage and never even had a chance to use. She'd told him in the letters she didn't have much to offer. He wrote back and said he didn't need for her to offer anything, he had too much of his own that he didn't know what to do with. This truth made up part of her uncle's approval, an abundance of resources in a land where those were sometimes scarce. But, caring less where resources might be concerned, she was instead charmed by the modesty, by what often sounded like humility. She prized that in a man, and felt it must surely be a good quality for a husband.

The inhabitants of the town went about their business, on the boarded sidewalks, in the street. Several horse-drawn carriages clopped by. Two women engaged in conversation while a small boy in suspenders hid among their skirts. A hay wagon pulled by oxen followed the carriages. A group of men stood in front of the barber shop smoking cheroots. A skinny dog lay in the nearby shade. There was no discernible figure hurrying forward to meet the passengers on the stage.

Sarah shaded her eyes, looking first down the street in one direction, past the hotel, a saloon, the dry goods store, another saloon, the post office, the cobbler, then in the other direction, past the boarding house, the court house, a third saloon, the barbershop and the jail. That was as far as she could see. It crossed her mind that there seemed to be a lot of saloons.

Sam Oakley took off his hat, perhaps moved by the obvious nature of her predicament.

"I can take your things and put them somewhere if you tell me where," he said. She didn't know where. What if no one ever came? What if he'd grown shy or had last minute doubts? She'd heard of that happening. But would he leave her standing here like this knowing how many miles she'd traveled under what circumstances and how many days? Would he really set her loose and expect her to somehow find her way in a place entirely foreign to her? No, she decided, the man in the letters would not do that. The stage covered a lot of rough ground under hard conditions and kept to a necessarily imperfect schedule. They were late. Who could stand out here all day in the sun doing nothing but waiting and being anxious? It was too much to ask. He likely went home and would come back soon to find her. Now the shoe was on the other foot, and she would be the one waiting and being anxious. It was a state with which she had a great deal of familiarity.

Then Addison was at her side. Sarah hadn't noticed where the others went. She'd been too confused, nothing was the way she'd thought it would be. While she wanted to remain steadfast and trusting, questions had arisen that couldn't easily be put back down. They weren't questions she wanted to think about. They weren't doubts she wanted to have.

"Do you have a plan in mind?" Addison said.

"I don't have anything in mind," Sarah said, though she would never have admitted this to anyone else. "I don't have any idea what to do."

"What kind of agreement did you have with these letters?"

"That he would be here."

"And what, you'd be married, just like that?"

"It seemed like we both had good reasons unless something happened." Sarah paused, thinking of what she'd just said.

"What do you know about him?"

"I know enough. My uncle came out here and met him and approved."

"What's your uncle's name?"

"Henry Leighton."

"Ah, yes. Henry. Now there's a man who loves whiskey and an all-night game of faro more than most."

"He does?"

"My point exactly. I'm sorry to tell you this, but I think you only have one option."

"What is it?" Sarah asked, knowing full well what it was.

"Leave your luggage here. We should probably take a little walk."

Sarah wanted to say no. She had a bad feeling. At least it was Addison who would be with her. Anyone could see that underneath the swept-up hair and fine tailoring, the woman was hard as nails. Addison Pruitt didn't back down from trouble, she thrived on it. Even more importantly, she could be relied on.

They passed the first saloon, called Jake's, and Sarah breathed a sigh of relief. But at the second saloon, The Pickled Beet, Addison stopped and appeared momentarily pensive, as if she were trying to decide how to approach this unhappy task.

"We can go into that alley," she said, indicating the open space between the buildings, "and face what might be there. Or you could think about it a little more if you want."

"He might be right then, is what you're saying."

"Who? Elijah? Mostly he only speaks when there's something to say. He wouldn't have got into that conversation any other way."

"Then you believe him?"

"I've never had a reason not to. Not ever."

"So you know him?"

"As much as anybody can. Except for Grady. Those two go way back together and nobody knows the whole story of how or why." When Addison saw the astonishment on Sarah's face, she added, "Maybe that wasn't important enough to put in a letter. Maybe it doesn't count for much after all."

"Is he really hostile? Does John Russell have any reason to be carrying those kinds of opinions?"

"Oh, John Russell can go piss in a pot for all I care. If he didn't have so much money, I'd be done with him. He's the moodiest son of a bitch I've ever known and way too particular for my tastes. You can't please him no matter what. But no, Elijah's not hostile at all, it's ridiculous to even think that. He's just his own person, goes his own way. So what's it to be, Sarah Mayfield? Understand that if we go in that alley, we'll be hunting for a buckboard and likely finding it."

"I understand," Sarah said. She composed herself, remembering how everything bad in life had already happened. Everything else was on the positive side of the ledger, regardless of what it was. "Let's go."

Together Sarah and Addison stepped off the sidewalk. The saloon's back door faced onto the alley. Over it a rickety set of stairs climbed to the second floor.

The buckboard sat outside the door, a sawn cedar box on spindly wheels with a spring seat, the grooved tongue resting on the ground. Involuntarily, Sarah put a hand on Addison's arm. Despite all the signs, she hadn't wanted it to be there. She had wanted to believe in the letter writer.

"He might not be in there," Addison said, but the tone of her voice suggested otherwise. Sarah resolutely started walking again. She went right up to the wagon, stood on tiptoe and looked over the side.

Inside, a somewhat disheveled person, good-looking in a boyish sort of way, was laid out on his back with his feet shoved under the buckboard's seat. Thick light brown hair fell over his eyes. In contrast, his face was very pale. He wore a brown

28

worsted suit with an open starched collar and a tweed vest that was only half buttoned. Beside him, a crumpled bouquet of prairie flowers had gone limp, the delicate colors fading in the sunlight. If it weren't for the fact that his mouth was open and he was snoring, he could have been at his own funeral.

"Oh, Jesus," Addison said, standing beside her. Sarah was staring, trying to take in this whole experience, how everything had changed. "Are you okay?" Addison asked. Sarah nodded yes. "Then Sarah Mayfield, meet Grady McGuire. He's looked better, I have to say. What do you want to do now?"

Sarah couldn't stop staring at him. This was the man in the letters. There was the hand that had gripped the pen so tight that the writing ran across the page like violent chicken tracks. She remembered thinking how nervous he must have been. Now she saw how nervous he actually was. The image in her mind of the first words, the polite small talk, the consideration of arrangements, the beginning of the rest of her life, all that had fled.

"I don't know," Sarah said. It was evidently her answer to everything.

"You don't seem to be completely put off or shocked, so I guess you're stronger than I gave you credit for. In that case, let's see if we can wake the dead."

Addison stepped up on the iron wheel and leaned over the wagon until she was within an inch of the head.

"*Grady shit-faced McGuire*," she shouted. "*Get the hell up. Your bride's here.*"

The eyes on the would-be corpse flew open. The letter-writing hands went to its ears.

"Stop, stop, stop," Grady said. His voice was hoarse. "What are you doing, shouting like that? You sound exactly like my mother."

"Your mother's been dead for two years."

"Sweet Jesus, my head feels like it's going to break."

"I'm going to break your head if you don't get up."

Grady squinted up into the light.

"Addison?" he said. "Is that you? I didn't know anybody could shout that loud. It's like you're calling the cows home right in my face."

"Grady, can't you remember anything?"

"I can remember lots of things. I just hurt is all. Everywhere. Did I puke?"

"Good grief. I don't know if you puked. Take that conversation somewhere else. Let's talk about the stage coming in."

Grady sat bolt upright, grabbed his head, and sank back into the wagon. "Oh no," he said. "What day is it?"

"It's the day the stage comes in."

"Addison, don't tell me, please don't tell me. Was she on it?"

"She was."

"And she's gone now, isn't she? Turned right around. It's okay. You can't hurt me. I just need to know."

"She's standing right here, Grady, waiting for you to meet the stage and take her hand and smile and say hello ma'am, pleased to meet you, and give her those flowers. Too bad none of that is going to happen."

Grady still had his eyes closed and had put his hands back over his ears, even though it didn't help.

"What do you mean, right here?" he said.

"Do you want her to say something? Sarah, say something."

"I can't," Sarah whispered.

Grady took his hands away from his ears. "All right," he said. "All right, all right, all right. Give me some room."

Addison and Sarah both stepped away from the wagon. Grady slowly sat up again, supporting himself on his elbows. Still slowly, groaning with the obvious pain of the whole endeavor, he got to his knees. From there, he managed to get a leg over the side of the buckboard, found the wheel with the toe of his boot, and with a great effort, heaved himself over the side and onto his feet. He kept his eyes on the ground while he attached his collar, buttoned his vest and smoothed out his suit jacket.

Finally, he dared to look up. He swallowed hard.

"You've already been introduced," Addison said. "I did that while you were still unconscious."

"I am so sorry," Grady said, meeting Sarah's eyes for the first time. "I can't tell you how sorry. This wasn't how I planned it. It wasn't how we talked about in the letters. I have them all, all the letters you wrote, I kept every one of them. I read them every day. And then when I knew for sure you were coming, I just got so, I don't know, so…"

"Shit-faced," Addison said again helpfully.

"No," he said, "that's not what I meant. I didn't feel good enough, I think. I'm never good enough, if you want to know the truth. And here you were, coming all this way, and it was just me at the end of the line, nothing, nobody. I felt like somehow, even though every word I wrote was true…I felt like somehow I'd disappoint you."

"It's amazing how whiskey takes away that feeling," Addison said.

"And every other feeling," Grady said. "But I have it all back now, in spades." He waited expectantly, but Sarah couldn't find anything to say.

"You've got to know," he said, "that I never intended for you to find me in a damn buckboard behind the Pickled Beet sleeping off a drunk. I got dressed at least, you can see that, and somewhere…" he gestured sadly at the buckboard "… in there, they're not good anymore, but I did have flowers. I wanted to do the right thing…" he said, and his voice trailed off. When it came back, it was small. "I just didn't."

"I came all the way from Virginia," Sarah said. Where he'd lost his voice, she'd found hers.

"I know."

"I expected that you'd be there when I got here."

"I know."

"We wrote that in the letters."

"I know."

"We said we'd be married next Friday, which would be a week. How do you feel about that now?"

31

"The question is, how do you feel about it?"

"Not good."

Grady nodded. "I know I'm the one that was passed out in the buckboard, but can I say something?"

"Of course," Sarah said.

"You're pretty. You said in your letters you weren't."

"It's in the eye of the beholder, I guess." Jacob had thought she was pretty. His name coming to her right at this moment brought tears to her eyes.

"Can I say something else?"

"Yes," Sarah said, regaining her poise. The man was maddening.

"I'm just trying to be polite. You tell me what you want to do and I'll do it, pay for lodging, haul your bags somewhere, get you set up however you need to be. I told you I got resources. And then maybe we can talk. Maybe we can use up some whole days and talk this thing out. But I got to tell you that right now I have to eat something or pardon me for saying, but I really am going to puke."

"For God's sake, Grady," Addison said.

"Go," Sarah said. "It'll be okay."

"It will be," Grady said. "I promise." He walked quickly past them out of the alleyway and back into the saloon.

"He won't start drinking again, will he?" she asked Addison.

"No. Not even he's that stupid. So I've got at least a temporary breakfast position open and I'm going to ask you one more time. Can you cook?"

"Yes," Sarah said, seeing how the pieces fit and she was lucky after all. "Yes I can."

32

4

Diego, the hotel chef, helped the day porter haul Sarah's trunk up to the second floor. Diego was not the largest of men and felt that he was going to die before they got to the top of the stairs. The trunk was surely loaded with rocks. But he was glad to have another set of hands suddenly appear, to have someone, anyone, take over the breakfast duties, if only for a week. Addison made many demands. She'd traveled to rich places, dined in the finest restaurants. Although this was still mostly a poor backwards cowhand town, she wanted her establishment to already be first class, for when the railroad came through. It was always when the railroad came through. No one could yet see that first locomotive, or even the tracks, those were still being made far off in the mountains, but that didn't stop her. She had everything planned out in her mind, including the acclaim Diego's food had been receiving, which was the point. He'd heard that Mr. Russell was buying her more hotels down the line, and that Smithy Ryder, sitting out there at the stage stop waiting for his vegetables to show up, would soon be a dinner cook and porter himself.

Diego knew The Russell Hotel was called that for only one reason. Mr. John Russell's supply of cash appeared to be endless. Diego had not listened to the rumors of silver mines in Argentina, privateering back east, illegal fur trading in Canada. Addison made it clear to her employees that, regardless of what they heard, the money only needed to keep coming, and they only needed to keep John Russell happy enough, if that was possible, to want to keep spending it.

Following Diego down the long hallway, Sarah received her first distinct impression from carpeted runners in a formal pattern of scarlet and green. Gold numbers and heavy brass doorknobs made a second impression. A hushed silence everywhere contributed to the feeling of luxury that had begun at the frosted-glass front doors.

Sarah felt great relief when she saw her room. Addison wasn't being kind. This was a bargain, a deal, a business negotiation, the first Sarah had ever undertaken. But thank God for Addison Pruitt. It was the second time in one day that she'd been saved by this unpredictable woman. Could she have managed on her own? Maybe. She had money enough saved and she didn't shrink from hard work. But these quarters were a gift, welcome breathing room until she could figure everything out.

Sarah smiled then as Diego, breathing heavily, stopped and shook her hand.

"Señora Mayfield," he said, "there are not so many with luggage that heavy."

"I was planning on dying here," she said.

"Soon?" he asked, alarmed.

"When I was old. That's everything I own."

"Feels like it. I want to tell you I'm glad you're here. I tried but I couldn't do it all myself, dusk till dawn. I'm good but not that good. I was so tired."

"I'm glad I can be of some help, but believe me, I'm here by accident and I don't know how long it's going to last."

"Doesn't matter. For now, I get up at noon."

"Are there are many guests?"

"Often, yes."

"Then you seriously must be good."

"I am. But now I have to go."

"One more question. There's never rattlesnake involved, is there?"

"Aiyee, Señora. I make quail and frog legs. I would not touch a rattlesnake with, how do you say, a twenty-foot pole."

"I just needed to know."

The room was small, the massive furniture barely fit, but to Sarah's eyes it was perfect. The curved bedstead stood against the wall, the bed itself piled high with layers of down. The way they do it in Europe, Addison had said. An ornate mahogany dresser held a porcelain washbasin and pitcher and a tall oil lamp. An imposing armoire wedged into one corner contained the rich aromas of cedar and cloves. The last valuable square footage was taken up with a high-backed rocking chair.

Sarah sat down in the chair and rocked. She got up and opened the trunk, running her hands over her grandmother's worn crazy quilt that was the last item to be packed. No, it wasn't the last item. On top of the quilt were Grady's letters. She closed the trunk.

The windows of the tiny room, framed by thick velvet curtains, looked out over the hotel's sprawling kitchen garden and then to the green hills beyond. The sun was just setting. Sarah sat back down in the rocker and listened to the symphony of a meadowlark's evening song. She was full of wonder that, when she was so tired and everything had gone so wrong, she still could experience such an incredible sense of peace here in this little room. Thank you again, Addison, she thought. I will repay you with the best I have to offer, I promise. And my promise is not Grady McGuire's. Mine will be kept.

<>

Sarah rose before dawn, as was her custom. Should she start cooking breakfast today? No one had told her as much. Better to be prepared than leave waiting guests hungry. She laughed, thinking she didn't even know where the kitchen was, or what supplies might be had. She was planning her first meal without any instructions at all and she'd never cooked for more than the six people in her family, seven with Jacob, eight when her grandmother had been alive. Somehow, she felt good about all of it.

She did, however, have a source of confidence. Opening the trunk and moving aside the quilt and the letters, she pulled out the odd-shaped linen-wrapped bundle. With this under her arm, she went down the dark stairs and into the back of the hotel. She lighted a lamp and found the kitchen, a large low-ceilinged room with cabinets, a pie cupboard, a long trestle table, a double-wide iron cookstove already banked with a glowing fire. Someone had been up before her, though she had no idea who that might be.

She unwrapped the cloth from the country ham. On the shelves she found the makings for biscuits. In the root cellar were the apples she needed. She'd make the coffee half ground beans, half chicory, the way Mr. Ryder made it, New Orleans style. His coffee had been delicious. A little hard cider wouldn't hurt. Her first breakfast would be simple and Southern, and if people didn't like it, well, that was what she had.

As she was setting the table with the flatware and glasses she'd found, Addison entered the room. She appeared fresh and ready for the challenges of a new day.

"You're here already!" she said. "I didn't explain anything to you. Lord almighty, I could have picked worse. And here you are setting the table before the crack of dawn."

"How many are there?" Sarah asked. She could be all business if that's what was needed.

"Twelve. The railroad men showed up again last night, greedy bastards, plus Fort Kendall is putting up those two colonels' wives. Then there's the Barrington men, made their fortune in mining supplies, Mrs. Brockman from Mexico who practically lives here in the spring and some crazy newspaper reporter from England who's traveling around the West. And never forget John Russell."

"Will you be dining, too?"

"Not me. I'm just a coffee kind of girl."

"Aren't you going to ask what we're having?"

"Nope. I've got good instincts. I hire well and let them be. No one's failed me yet."

"I don't intend to be the first."

"I trust you, Sarah Mayfield. Now I'm going out. I've got business to attend to and it's hardly light yet." With that, Addison strode the length of the still dimly lit dining room and out through the front door.

Sarah tied a large piece of flour sacking around her waist and set to work. Within no time at all, ham and bacon were frying in two huge cast iron skillets, apples were frying with onions in a third, the gravy was simmering, and biscuits were rising in the

36

oven. She'd made enough to feed more than twelve, but was already mulling over a week's worth of meals if she could find the fixings: hash, biscuits with sausage gravy, chicken-fried steak, brown sugar buckwheat cakes, potato omelets, fried mustard greens, stewed fruit, she was excited about the possibilities. Even batter-fried squirrel with onion and bacon could be an option, but probably John Russell would push back from the table and storm away from that one. This wouldn't be his food, or Diego's. She hated to think what Diego might make for breakfast if frog legs were on the dinner menu. It might not even be the railroad men's food, but that couldn't be her problem. This would be her food, what she knew and loved, what Grady McGuire's letters said he would love, too, damn him.

At a stroke of the clock before the appointed breakfast hour, a stout woman pushed in through the back door and hurriedly put on a white apron. Sarah paused with her wooden spoon in midair.

"You must be new," the woman said. "About time. I was getting worried that Diego was gonna fall asleep standing up and hurt himself on the cookstove. That Addison, love her to death but she's a slave driver."

"You work here," Sarah said.

"I do the serving, child, what did you think? Were you gonna do it?"

Sarah looked confused.

"It's okay," the woman said. "I never start at the beginning, which is my problem. Name's Elmira. I'm a failed homesteader, there I said it. Couldn't prove up my claim. Everything I planted died, my milk cow run off and the wolves got my chickens. Then it snowed up there in the Montana Territory for about a year. I live in the boarding house across the street and have a go with Doc Morrison now and again when he's tending towards sober while I think out what I want to do next. Is that enough or do you need to know more?"

"No, that's fine, believe me, thank you," Sarah said quickly. "My name's Sarah Mayfield. Sorry, I'm a little turned around at the moment."

"Which says Addison didn't tell you nothing. She's got to get better with the help, but she'll learn. One of these days she'll be the railroad hotel queen, and she's worked hard enough to deserve it. So do you think she's shucking that rich guy?"

"Good Lord, I don't know, I didn't ask, I mean I wouldn't." Who was this woman? Sarah found herself completely flustered. This wasn't the way people talked back east.

"Nah, I wouldn't neither, but I'd like to know. Wouldn't you?"

"No!" Sarah said, not even admitting to herself that she might have wondered just a little, though not exactly in those terms.

"Well, enough chit chat. Tell me when you're ready, cause I'm always ready. Do you do separate plates or home style?"

"What?"

"Never mind. Diego did separate so that's what we'll keep doing. Nice to meet you."

The twelve guests came to breakfast, ate all there was, and seemed to be pleased. At least no one came back to the kitchen with complaints. Just as Sarah was thinking she'd made it safely through one morning, John Russell appeared.

"Sarah Mayfield," he said.

"Yes, sir." She was the help now.

"I believe you're an aficionado of bacon grease."

"That's what I was trying to tell Mrs. Pruitt. I only know one way to cook."

"Interesting. Even in the biscuits?"

"Especially in the biscuits. It gives a flavor you don't get any other way. Some day, if you're so inclined, I'll make you a fruit pie and you won't find anything lighter than that crust."

John Russell didn't acknowledge the offer. He was still thinking.

"How did you make the coffee?"

"Half chicory, New Orleans style, the way Mr. Ryder makes it at the stage stop. I'll add hot milk tomorrow if you like." If there is a tomorrow, she thought.

"I didn't choose to eat Mr. Ryder's food. Or drink his coffee. You served hard cider."

"Gives a kick in the morning if one's needed."

"A far cry from more subtle breakfasts, say the English tea and toast."

"Definitely a far cry," Sarah agreed, wondering what her next job would be.

"And tomorrow?"

"I'm not decided yet, I have to investigate some."

John Russell took a cheroot out of his breast pocket and inhaled the pleasant aroma, but didn't light it.

"I didn't believe it possible, but I'm tempted to come back," he said. He turned, still holding the cheroot up to his nose, and walked out of the kitchen.

Sarah stood silent for a moment, amazed, then shook off John Russell and pumped water to heat in a large kettle for the cleaning up. Elmira washed the dishes while she wiped out the skillets and scoured them with salt.

"I tasted them biscuits," Elmira said. "Mighty fine. You're gonna do yourself proud. I been snooping around, give me five minutes and I'll find out what's what, and learned you just now got here. If it were me, with all that dust out there, first thing I'd be wanting was a wash. We can haul the bath basin upstairs if you want and I'll get the water heated."

At that moment, Sarah had never heard of anything more wonderful. "Elmira," she said, "there are no words. But I can warm up these last biscuits and fry another slice of ham."

"Works for me," Elmira said.

5

After her bath, with clean hair still curly damp and tied back, for the first time in a week wearing clothes she hadn't slept in, Sarah went back to the kitchen. She spent an hour taking stock of what was there. First the pots and pans, utensils, spoons, knives and cleavers, the bowls and platters. Next the intricacies of the double-wide cookstove, the iron pots in the fireplace, the outdoor spit. Then the foodstuffs. Every time she examined a shelf, opened a cupboard, explored another nook or cranny, she blessed John Russell's money. Someone had laid in any kind of ingredient a good cook could possibly ever want. Flours and meal sat in huge sacks. The root cellar was full. Seven different kinds of dried peppers hung from the rafters. Quarters of pork, venison and lamb filled the outside shed. She lingered longest over the smallest shelf. The coffee beans and chicory were familiar, but only the most blessed cooks gained the prized spices numbered here. She opened jars or packets and inhaled their contents, smiling. Exotic aromas of clove, cinnamon, ginger, nutmeg, allspice, cardamom filled the air. Next to the spices stood jars of raw honey and dark molasses, raw cocoa powder, a keg of salt, another of brown sugar, a jug of vinegar.

At noon, while Sarah was still in the kitchen considering her options, two things happened at once. Diego walked in the back door, from which Elmira had recently departed, and Grady McGuire walked in the front door. Sarah stood between them, the two opposites of her new life.

Diego spoke first.

"Señora," he said. "I don't see any table scraps, nothing to feed the pigs. You must have been a big success."

"Pigs?"

"Out back with the chickens."

"I've had one question about bacon grease, and I can't tell if that's good or bad."

"It's all very good, except for the hungry pigs. So tell me about this what you call Southern cooking. I'm from a very much different kind of south."

She handed Diego a plate of ham and gravy, ignoring the fact that Grady was standing in the doorway. She was glad he hadn't showed up so formally in his suit again.

"There were fried apples but they're gone and Elmira ate the last of the biscuits," she said.

"So rich," Diego said, pausing after every bite. "A different taste for me, but I like it."

"I imagine everything you do is new to me. What's your menu for dinner?"

"Crawfish bisque, wild duck, greens. I think maybe sponge cake with Mexican chocolate sauce. *Hola*, Grady. *Como estas?*"

"*Hola*, Diego. *Bien.*"

Now Sarah was forced to acknowledge him.

"It's noon, "Grady said. "I thought you'd be up by now."

Hadn't he been listening? He was standing right there.

"I cooked breakfast," she said. "I've been up since dawn."

"Cooked breakfast?" he said. "Why would you do that?"

"To earn my room and board. Addison gave me a temporary job."

Now he was horrified instead of just confused. But where did he think she'd slept?

"I told you I'd take care of you," he said. "I didn't write all those letters so you'd come way out here and end up being a cook. No offense, Diego."

"I take no offense."

Sarah considered that Diego would have no idea what this conversation was about, though in fact he did. He looked away politely and thought instead about how many crawfish he needed and how muddy the creek would be.

"Will you still talk to me?" Grady asked.

"Yes, I will," Sarah said.

41

Outside, Sarah watched while Grady dragged first one heavy chair and then another off the porch and around to the back. Apparently, a private conversation could only be had among the livestock. Rounding the corner of the hotel after him, Sarah took in the enviable dimensions of the kitchen garden. Here was a cook's paradise. Maybe it was her job to collect the eggs. She would do that as soon as he left. Then it occurred to her that she already had him gone. She wanted to do better than that, at least give him a chance.

He sat down and leaned forward. "This is what I meant to tell you yesterday," he said, "but I'll go ahead and tell you now." He sounded intent and sad. "Sarah Mayfield, thank you for coming all those miles and days in order to hopefully be married to me. You know from the letters what I'm offering, a home to call your own, and land, and sheep, cows, goats, chickens, geese, God knows what all's out there. Whatever it is, I can't do it by myself. I got help, it's just there's not a woman involved and there so needs to be. Nobody can cook, Jim's awful at it. I can't wash things so they look washed. There's a butter churn in the kitchen but who knows what to do with that? We got cornfields, hay, winter wheat, alfalfa, a kitchen garden that would be more useful for a small town than the four of us living there. The boy, Abraham, feeds the pigs, maybe he feeds the chickens too, I don't know, least they don't look starved. Don't get me started on the ledgers, who pays what to who, how many head of cattle, where the damn geese went, all of that. Like I said, and I truly mean my words with all my heart, I would give anything if you would be my wife."

Grady had told her all of this in the first place by putting down one painfully written sentence after the other in a strangled script that worked its way like bird tracks across the page. From his awkwardness came a sort of eloquence. What she heard in the letters, she heard in his same voice now, the troubles, the longing, the honesty, and underneath it, a better person than the one she'd seen so far.

"We don't know each other," she reminded him. This was true no matter what else happened. She watched the chickens scratch across the lawn while she acknowledged that if you went back to the words written in her own extravagant but legible hand, she'd already said yes. "Wasn't it always part of the plan, if you could actually consider us having one, that we'd talk till we were all talked out? How else could we go about this? No other way of beginning it makes sense." She wondered if the real beginning might also make it the end. She didn't want to admit such a possibility, but there it sat in front of her. She regarded herself as brave, not crazy.

"We'll start talking right now, then, is what you're saying," he said.

"Don't you think that's right? You did before."

"Do I think it's right? I don't know anymore. But I agree to it anyway. What are we gonna talk about?"

Sarah thought a minute. "Hard to say," she said. "But there were certain things in the letters that I found myself deeply curious about."

"Then you kept the letters?"

"Absolutely I did. They're in my suitcase, every one of them."

"I kept your letters, too. I told you that, didn't I? Read them every night. You write so beautiful, there were things that made me so happy and things that made me want to cry. They meant so much to me." He wanted to say that he couldn't wait till she got here, but obviously something had gone very wrong with that plan.

"Here's what we'll do," she said. "I'll get a turn to ask you and then you get a turn to ask me." Except about Jacob. Grady knew what he needed to know about that. Let war-killed husbands rest in peace.

"So since you're the woman, your turn comes first. That's how it's supposed to be, isn't it?"

Sarah smiled at the thought. The smile quickly faded. "Here's what I was most looking for," she said, "because you did write some about it, though not nearly enough. Will you tell me what there is to tell about your mother?"

Grady sighed and rubbed his forehead. That would come up right off. He'd tried to explain it in the letters, but his heart was never in it and he couldn't get the words right. So he left some parts in, took some parts out, and when he'd read it over, he could see that it made no sense.

"It's hard to get a grasp of it," he said. "But here's the truth. Even though she's gone, I spend every day thinking she'll be there about to say something and it won't be good. And I don't even really remember her."

"It doesn't seem from what you wrote that you liked her much."

Grady realized why he'd liked this woman from the start. She simplified things that were so complicated in his own mind. Did he like Ma? No. Did he dislike her? You couldn't dislike your ma, that wasn't even right. Did Ma dislike him? That was a whole other question. She didn't dislike him, he was fairly certain, but if he recalled correctly, she wasn't that taken with him either.

"You had to know her," he said.

"I guess I'm sorry I won't get to." A breeze whispered through the tall grasses and fluttered the leaves of the cottonwoods down by Jacks Creek. Sarah glanced up as the pigs appeared.

Grady sighed more heavily this time. "Do I really have to do this?"

Sarah nodded. He seemed at that moment very young.

"What do I tell you about Ma, let's see." He squinted, trying to form a picture in his mind. "She was tall and thin but strong. She had hair the same color as mine, all piled up like yours was yesterday. Sometimes she shook it out and for a minute, I never said this before to anyone, she was beautiful, and I believe that." He was proud that with all the bad times, at least as he saw it, he remembered that one small piece of good.

44

"She was a hard woman," he said. "Smart as anything, I guess, but hard. She started as a schoolteacher, came out from Kentucky, met Pa here and stopped."

"So they took a liking to each other."

"I didn't say that, for sure. They fought and cursed. Ma threw things. Pa went out and slept in the barn. The both of them were stubborn as mules and I think if there hadn't been three kids one right after the other, he would of took off right then. We slept under a pile of quilts and still there was nothing you could do to get away from the shouting. Pa wasn't as bad, but she was headstrong. Even the goats were afraid of her."

"But they didn't stay here."

"Those letters did make some sense then. No, Pa was smart and he wanted so much more than we had. Though we never met any of them, he said we came from good family back east. He'd tell us stories of how grand life could be, even though ours wasn't. He'd read books. Ma had, too, lots of them.

"Pa said people were finding gold in California. He'd read the newspapers. He ordered books and then he studied prospecting and geology and thought he'd figured out a thing or two. He wanted to go on his own to California, said he'd be back in a year, but Ma said we'd all go or none of us would go. Then we were like everybody else, headed out west, though it didn't seem like everybody else once we got out there in that big empty nothing, moving about as slow as you could move with all we owned, the three of us kids, the milk cow and everything, Pa's mare, trusting Pa knew what he was doing. Then Ma found out she was carrying Emma and she wouldn't go any farther. Pa located a spring not far from a bend in the Canadian so we'd have plenty of water. He gave Ma the shotgun. Then just like that he left, said he had to go on, there was no help for it, he'd come back as soon as he had gold and we'd live that grand life he talked so much about. He promised it wouldn't be long."

"When you've ever only known one place in your whole life," Sarah said, "it's an astonishment that people would think to pick up and move like that, not knowing exactly where they were even going." And yet, when she considered it, she had just done the same thing.

"It's even more of an astonishment when you have to live it. We slept in the wagon for a while, then Maybelline and me got to make enough adobe bricks to build a little one room house, but that little house had our big old iron cookstove in the middle of it cause Ma wouldn't have even considered leaving it behind, it was everything to her, we left a lot out to accommodate it. We brought seedlings, so she planted a garden but it took some time. We needed food, and we weren't about to eat the milk cow, so she got out her gun. She was scary accurate with that big old thing. We had prairie chicken and jackrabbit and Maybelline and me gathered what we could find, berries, greens down by the river, caught some fish. There was a barrel of cornmeal that we'd had ground before we left, I went with Pa to the mill, flour, beans, ham hocks, we weren't so bad off.

"We were lonely out there, but got along okay, I guess. We heard there were Comanches and that was a scare, but we never saw any. We just saw endless trains of wagons passing by. They always stopped so Ma could talk and find out any news there might be from back home.

"No harm come to us, I will say that. Ma only shot one man, fairly close up, a big old nothing but trouble buffalo hunter who took a fancy to her. He rode up on his horse all hollow and in need, said some things. I don't believe he thought she'd pull the trigger. Then Maybelline and me got to dig a grave and bury him. Nothing aids your advancement in life like burying a man in his flea-bitten buffalo coat still reeking of whiskey. Cora made the marker and carved his name in it. Since she didn't actually know his name, she invented one for him, but that was Cora.

"Then all three of us got to birth Emma and we did a good job, she came out fine.

"When Ma got up and going again, which was quick, she started the trading post. We were on the trail west and I guess it was a particularly useful way to do business. People dropped off a plow and picked up a rifle, brought in raccoon pelts and took away salt pork. Maybelline and me built that trading post, too. I never want to see another adobe brick as long as I live."

Sarah sat in the chair under the huge sky, listening. Grady's voice washed over her, a voice she thought she could get used to.

"What was her name?" Sarah said.

"Ma? Her name was Ellen. She built the business up good, started trading calico and books along with the plows and knives. People who got tired of being on the move stopped and ended up staying. There was water. There was Ma. Go down, you'll see. It's still a nothing town, bigger than it was anyway, but it's called Ellenville, Texas.

"Then one day an old preacher rode up in a falling-apart wagon pulled by two oxen as old as the preacher. I'll never forget that day. He asked for Ma by name. When she showed up, she was teaching school too by then, he said the big wooden box in his wagon was for her. 'What's in it?' Ma said. And the preacher said, 'It's the cookstove you wanted.'"

Ellen looked at the preacher and then at the box. Her one most important possession was her cast iron cookstove and everybody knew that. For a while, she didn't say anything, just stood there thinking. The preacher didn't say anything either. He was watching this thin, hard woman with her four children and considering the man who'd paid him a significant sum to bring the cookstove all this distance, even though he told the man he'd have to do some preaching along the way. The man had been mighty finely dressed and had a fancy lady on his arm.

"That box was damn heavy," Grady said. "Took me, Ma, Maybelline and the preacher to get it out of that wagon and into the house."

Ellen thanked the preacher. It wasn't his fault. She gave him a dollar and a side of beef. He sat in the wagon and raised his switch against the oxen to get them moving. He thought he understood and the sadness made him weary, but only for a mile or two. Then he got to thinking about the side of beef and having a big steak cut out and panfried for dinner. The Lord was good.

"We opened up that box with a crowbar to see what this cookstove was all about," Grady said.

"And there wasn't one?"

"No, there was, but it was just a big old tin campfire stove. It still had drawers for the wood or coal maybe, and you could use it if you had to, but it was mighty flimsy. The weight came from all those bags of gold."

Sarah closed her eyes. She could see Ellen, the worn dress and thin arms, the tiredness etched into her face.

"Your pa sent it."

"There was a letter inside. Ma sat down at the kitchen table and read that letter over and over again. Then she sat for a long time holding the letter in her lap. When she got up, she started making plans right there and then. She bought a wagon and a team of mules, sold the trading post, turned over the school, everything happened fast, least it comes back to me that way. She said we were going home. Maybelline and me looked at each other. We hardly remembered any other home and Cora didn't at all. And Emma was born right were we were standing. If Ma was talking about Sweetwater or Kentucky, or somewhere else, it was hard to tell. It was like she was burning up with this need to get going away from there."

"Tell me the next part," Sarah said gently. He'd written her about it, but not to explain, just to say in plain words what happened. She'd put his letter down then, thinking about mothers and their children.

"She said I wasn't going with them."

Grady stopped. A hawk soared in tight circles overhead. He watched as it turned and drifted down over the creek. Sarah waited.

"She told me I had some growing up to do," he said. "She said there was a cattle outfit heading north to supply some forts and they needed hands. Where was up north? What was a hand? I was fourteen. I didn't know anything. She took me over to the trading post and showed me a horse she'd bought. It was a good horse. It had a saddle and everything, even a rope and a damn bedroll. 'But don't you need me?' I asked her. And she said, no, she had Maybelline, which was the truth, Maybelline could do anything better than me. At least Maybelline made Ma wait till the two men came from the outfit to get me."

Grady stopped again. Sarah slowed her breath.

"That was the last time I saw her," Grady said. "She got back east this far, back to Sweetwater, found out it had grown into a town, called it home, and she and Maybelline built that place out there," he nodded into the distance, "with Pa's gold."

"I'm sorry," Sarah said.

"What I want to know is how the past can get to be past if everybody keeps on talking about it. Then it's not past at all, it's sitting right there in front of you. Doesn't seem fair, when it holds on like that. And I suppose your ma never left you anywhere." Grady ran his hands through his hair. "No, I apologize, that was not what I meant to say, hurtful things don't help anybody."

"It wasn't hurtful. You're right," Sarah said. "My mother never left me anywhere."

"Good. You talk for a while. I'm done. I'm not interested in the sound of my own voice anymore."

"I don't have stories like you do."

"That's the best thing that could happen to a person, to not have any stories. But you go ahead with what you know and I'll keep watch on the pigs."

Sarah paused, then began. Some of it, he knew already.

"My mother was born in Virginia," she said. "And lived there all her life like me. My daddy's a lawyer. They met at a church social. She mostly played the piano and wrote poetry. He liked to study history. There were three children that lived. Clayton's older than me, Miles is younger. Grandma came to stay when I was ten. We had a big old house with shade trees and four different kinds of garden."

"Did you own slaves?" Grady asked out of nowhere. Sarah was shocked by the question until she realized it was not untoward but honest. There'd just been a war fought over it.

"We didn't own slaves," she said. "We didn't have a plantation or anything like that, but Daddy abhorred slavery anyway, Mother, too. We were Yankees. We had a housekeeper, Jace, who did the cooking because Mother couldn't. Mother was a dreamer, her head always in some other place, and what's going on in a kitchen needs to be tended to. Jace took care of all the chores except the ones she made us do. She was stern. The boys learned to fish and clean game and spit a hog. I learned to cook Southern, which she could do like she was born to it, though she never would say where she was from. Nothing like that mattered, we loved her. Then right after Clayton and Jacob went off to fight in Tennessee, next thing you know there were troops coming up over the hill with torches. They burned the house down, we had to move closer to Washington, Mother was so afraid the boys wouldn't be able to find us and they'd think we were dead and Jace ran off with that Confederate soldier."

"Do you suppose the two of them got away?" Grady said. "He'd be a hunted man." Sarah regarded him with interest. He'd cared enough to remember the letters, and to listen when she talked.

"I'm only glad I don't know in case it was bad."

"You said you didn't move, but you did."

"You have to move when your house burns down. The neighbors helped us save what we could, loaded it all up in wagons. We didn't go any great distance, just far enough for Father, who was angry, to give his services to Mr. Lincoln. Our situation changed some but what was around us never did, same magnolias and rhododendrons, same warm days and soft blue skies, still Virginia." Sarah paused. "Mother died not long after Clayton came home, when the war was close to ending. And not long enough after that for his grieving to be respectable, Father married the widow who'd been the county clerk. It raised some eyebrows, made for some talk."

"Is that why you agreed to come here?" Grady asked. Sarah considered herself to be the straightforward one, but Grady was proving her wrong.

"Lord, I'm sorry," he said. "I don't have a place where my mouth can go until my brain catches up with it. I just say what's on my mind and it gets me in all kinds of trouble."

"I thought you'd just sit here and watch the pigs," Sarah said.

"I deserve that."

"But I appreciate that you're willing to ask the question. It's a fair one. I hope I was more running towards something than away from it. I'd just lost too much and that woman was the last thing I needed. It didn't make any difference what I thought, though. I wasn't the one that married her. Father, I have to say, seemed happier than was right."

"The thing is, whatever else he did, your pa didn't run off and leave your ma."

"No, he didn't."

"What makes someone do that, abandon an expectant woman and three children out in godforsaken Texas? Does all the contentiousness and sleeping out in the barn cause that to happen?"

"I wish I could say I knew, but I don't."

"And what makes a woman give up her son in that same damn Texas nowhere? I spent a lot of time trying to figure it out."

"Maybe you're not ready for the answer to come yet. Or maybe there isn't one."

"I suppose. Do you feel abandoned by this Jace of yours?"

"No," Sarah said, "but I don't know why. She did make us prepared. She raised us to be strong. That day, when the neighbors came on horseback shouting and said there were Confederates headed our way moving fast and they'd just crossed the river, she showed us the box she kept her secrets in. She never opened it, don't know what those secrets might have been, it was a little box. But she gave me and Miles a key and left another one for Clayton." Sarah reached down inside the collar of her dress and pulled out a key on a thin silver chain. "I'll never take it off," she said.

"You're lucky," Grady said. He wished his mother had left him anything personal, even just a letter. The land was

51

meaningless to him because it was still hers. Nobody could ever inherit it and do it proud. He was the perfect example.

"But understand, it's not my mother's key or my father's. It's from Jace."

"I see your point," Grady said, and grew thoughtful.

"Have you had enough for one day?" Sarah asked after a time.

"I believe I have. We made it through this one, didn't we?"

"I think so. Seems like it anyway."

Grady stood up and she stood up with him. "I'm honored that you've come all this way and I'm saying again that I hope you'll consent to marry me," he said. "I'm sorry about being drunk and passed out in an alleyway."

"In the end, it's not so bad. Gave me time to think."

"That wasn't my original plan."

Sarah laughed. "I've enjoyed talking to you," she said, and she saw that this was true.

"What will you do with the rest of your day?" he said.

"Walk around town a little, I guess. Get some eggs out of the hen house. Find out what a crawfish is and how you catch it."

"I'll be here at noon tomorrow," Grady said.

"I believe you will," Sarah said. She watched him walk away. He had the same easy gait that Clayton had before the war, and a thick shock of hair like Miles, and she found those small things a comfort.

6

Bean carried his homemade trap from the river in a cart. The sun was shining, the river smelled sweet and his fishhead bait still worked. At least a hundred crawfish rode disconsolately in the trap. He smiled. Diego would count out the money and he knew there would be enough left over after his investment to buy a bag of the horehound candy that he loved.

At the well, he set the crawfish in a large bucket and flushed them several times till the water ran clean. He left the cart at the back door and set the trap down on a towel in the kitchen. Diego turned briefly from the stove and whistled. But Bean knew he had another job to do. He went out to the woodshed and collected the ducks he'd hung there. Wouldn't be any shot in them to break the teeth of an important guest in the hotel dining room. These ducks were small, just little teals, but he had the truest aim of anyone, even the cowhands. When the cowhands were drunk they couldn't hit anything except each other. He realized people thought he was dumb, but he'd seen plenty who were dumber.

Sarah watched Bean come back into the kitchen, his arms full. One at a time, in a balancing act, he laid out twenty limp ducks on the worktable. Diego pulled a small purse out of his pocket. Bean drew a number on the worktable. Diego counted out coins. Bean nodded and smiled.

"Who is that?" Sarah asked, watching him go back out the door, loose-limbed and smiling.

"That's Bean, it's the only name I think he has," Diego said.

"What does he do for you?"

"Everything. I depend on him. He's different, I guess you can see that. I would give him a job in a minute taking care of this," Diego glanced ruefully at the ducks and crawfish. "But when he is in the kitchen, it's like the walls make his skin crawl and he has to go."

"Where does he live?"

"In town here with his sister. She takes in sewing."

"He doesn't speak?"

"No. Never."

"If he doesn't help you in the kitchen, then who does? You can't cook for that many people every night without some help." Sarah hadn't intended to stand around all day asking questions. She was hardly settled in and had work to do. But the room itself with all its aromas and Diego at the stove, not her beloved Jace, but an interesting and attractive person with his own very accomplished way of cooking, had drawn her in.

Diego was furiously stirring chocolate.

"Uh oh," she said, and laughed. "Who is she?"

"Señora, please, she is no one."

"She's got to be someone. I'm nowhere near capable of plucking all these birds and doing whatever you do to those crawfish by myself, though I'd definitely try if you asked me."

"Her name is Justine. She is very young, very much like Bean."

"She doesn't speak?"

"No, I mean, her family failed at everything, they have many children, hard times and no money."

"I expect I'll know her when I see her," Sarah said.

"Si, Señora," Diego said. "You are being hard with me, but maybe you understand."

"How young?" Sarah started to say, then turned toward the door. Sixteen, she guessed, or hoped at least that much, with an unruly mass of flaxen hair and long limbs. Poor Diego. But she had questions of her own.

Justine wrapped a large apron around her thin frame. Shy and blushing, she went silently and fiercely to work. Without a word of instruction, she started on the ducks. She scalded them, plucked them clean, and gutted them in sharp motions with a large knife she'd obviously handled before. Sarah stood with her mouth open. She felt rather than saw Diego grin from ear to ear.

54

"I can do some of this to help you," Sarah said at last. "But I don't know anything about those." She pointed at the crawfish.

The young woman seemed actually frightened. This was her work, Sarah thought. It meant food on the table. Diego intervened.

"Sarah," he said. "This is Justine." He had to get control of himself just saying her name. "Justine, this is Señora Mayfield. She is just arrived from in the east. She has come to make the breakfast in the hotel for a little while."

"But that's all," Sarah added quickly. "I can help if you need me, but I won't get in the way. Can I watch?"

The girl's face softened and she held out her hand. Her handshake was strong. Diego's attraction might not be as misplaced as it appeared.

Diego, finished with his chocolate sauce, moved on to the crawfish. Two large pots of water boiled on the stove. He hefted the trap, opened the top, and dumped half the crawfish into each of the pots. In minutes, he was straining the cooked crawfish back up out of the water in one pot and dumping them on the table while Justine did the same with the other pot. Mission accomplished, Diego went back to beating up the cake batter for his dessert.

Sarah helped Justine pluck and gut the rest of the ducks. She continued to be impressed by how quickly the girl worked, how deftly her hands moved. When the crawfish cooled, Justine showed her how to break off the tail, remove the legs and twist out the flesh, then dig the fat out of the head. Sarah picked up the girl's efficient rhythm. Soon bright red shells filled the stockpot and a mountain of sweet white crawfish meat graced the worktable.

"Onions and bread, please," Diego said over his shoulder to Justine. Sarah saw that he had filled two trays of tin molds with his batter. Justine nodded and headed for the root cellar. "And rosemary," Diego called after her. When she returned, Sarah stripped the rosemary, watching Justine's knife flash as it chopped swiftly through the onions. Then Sarah felt she had done enough.

"I leave you in good hands," she said to Diego, and knew this was in fact the truth.

"Thank you, Señora, for your help. I will bring you a dish. You see why you are a gift from God, here to make the breakfast. Even with one extra pair of hands, I could not do it."

"I think," Sarah said, "that one day soon you'll have a real breakfast cook." Justine, hands flying, was preparing the stuffing for the ducks.

"I am teaching her what I know," Diego said, flushing again, embarrassed to so easily be giving away his emotions. "She has the feel for it. For what is not familiar, and that is much, she still has good instincts."

Justine suddenly raised her eyes from the ducks. "I'm learning," she said. Her voice, though a young girl's, was as strong and steady as her hands. Sarah hoped she wouldn't some day break Diego's heart.

Sarah still meant to depart, there were so many things left to do. Yet she lingered, and knew why. The aroma of rich chocolate filled the air along with the pungent raw scent of the onions.

"Are the railroad men still here?" she asked.

"Si. There have been meetings all day. Also the wives from the fort and the English writer, or so I'm told."

"And John Russell?"

"And John Russell. One day he will stop thinking of us as peons, clods of dirt."

"He said that?"

"He doesn't have to."

"I need to ask one more question."

"Of course, Señora." Sarah knew that Justine was listening. She was not the sort to have wandering thoughts.

"About Grady."

"He is my friend."

"I know that. Is he everyone's friend?"

"I don't think in the way that you are meaning, no."

Sarah took a deep breath. "Does he spend a lot of time at the Pickled Beet?"

Diego knew she was serious in her questions. "I have to tell you, this I do not know. I myself do not spend any time at the Pickled Beet. I am here, working, day and night. The saloons are like a foreign country to me."

"And the Pickled Beet's only one of many," Sarah said.

"This is true, but he has a good heart, Señora, if that is what you're asking. He helped me when I needed help so much. And I am not the only one who could tell you such a thing."

"I was just wondering," she said. Diego knew exactly what she was wondering. He would never tell her the truth. Grady was his friend.

Sarah sighed and went out into the sunshine. She would walk to the creek, visit the chicken coops and not think about this again for a while.

7

Grady brought Sarah a present, a linen handkerchief embroidered along the edges with violets and permeated with the scent of roses.

"It was my mother's," he said.

"I can't possibly accept this," Sarah said, trying to hand it back. "We don't know each other that well." She couldn't see that hard woman owning something so feminine. But then who could judge? Hard women were likely not born that way.

"Just keep it for a while, till we settle things out. Maybe it'll bring me luck. Nothing else ever has."

"I shouldn't," Sarah said, but she felt softened by his words.

"Do you think she's watching? If she is, you'd do me proud."

"I don't think she's watching." The idea made her uncomfortable. "Surely dead people have better things to do."

"Or maybe they're just dead."

"Have you noticed nobody bothers to come back and tell you which it is?" She saw Jacob in dreams, but that was all. What she would give to hear his voice, speak with him one more time.

Grady laughed. "I like your way of looking at things," he said. He had spent considerable energy dragging the two chairs all the way out to the creek where there was shade from the cottonwood trees and no pigs anywhere. He gazed up into the leafy branches, still smiling, and thought that he was happy.

"How well do you know Diego?" she asked. He seemed suddenly wary.

"Why? Don't you get along?"

"No, there's no trouble. I like him very much. I helped him just a little bit with his crawfish bisque yesterday and he gave me some. It was perfection." She wished Jace could have tasted it.

"Sometimes he cooks me a beef steak," Grady said. "I eat it in the kitchen. Just the thought of crawfish bisque makes my mouth water."

"What favor did you do for him?"

He waited, working over the possibilities for an answer.

"What did he tell you?" he said.

"I asked him how much time you spent at the Pickled Beet. If that offends you, I'm sorry. Especially under the circumstances, it's my right to know."

"You could have asked me."

"The person in the buckboard doesn't get to answer that question." Grady winced. Maybe not that happy. Not yet. "He said he didn't frequent saloons, but he stood up for you because you were his friend and you did him a favor."

"I gave him a horse. He needed one to get to Mexico. His wife was expecting."

"His wife?"

"She lives there, with his family, her family, everybody in some little town. You know, home."

"Why doesn't she live here?"

"I guess because she doesn't want to. That may seem peculiar to you, but with what Ma and Pa went through it doesn't seem peculiar to me."

"Did you get your horse back?"

"The horse? Oh, no, I didn't want it back."

Sarah turned over the puzzle in her mind.

"What is his wife's name?" She had no idea where the question came from. For some reason, it seemed important to know.

"I don't remember," Grady said quickly. "Isn't there something else we can talk about?"

Now he was depressed. Nothing in his life made any sense. All of it would only cause hurt and problems for whoever got involved.

"We could go back to where we were yesterday," Sarah said. She still held the image in her mind of a frightened boy with his bedroll and rope heading out in the Texas morning away from everything he knew and into a life he never saw coming.

"We could. I don't know why I ever thought we wouldn't."

59

"I know I can ask unfair questions so forgive me if I do that, but did you cry?"

"Not sitting on my horse with two cowhands who'd just come to get me for a job. But at night I did. Then one night I didn't, I was finished with it. Maybe that's what Ma wanted. You cross that line and you're not the same person anymore. There's no more crying. You just do other stupid things instead."

"What was it like being a cowhand?"

"Hot and dusty and boring. Then for five minutes it could scare the living daylights out of you, lightning out on that flat prairie with no shelter or a big river to cross and you couldn't tell how deep until your horse was swimming in it. Then hot and boring again, unless it turned cold and you froze. Cows stink. They're dumb and slow except for the ones that are ornery and fast and you've got to watch out for them. The food's the same every day, bad, and you don't even care, you eat it cause you're so hungry. The ground's hard to sleep on, you get soaked when it rains and there's rattlesnakes. Sometimes, when you get away from the cows, it's so quiet you can think you're the only person left alive on this earth and after everything else, that's not always a bad feeling."

"But you got good at it."

"Is that what I wrote? How generous of me but that's not right. I learned to live with it. Took about a year, but I graduated from behind the cows to in front of them, which is a mighty big improvement, no more stench and dust in your eyes and throat and mouth all day. I could rope a cow if it stood still, which they don't do very often. I did have Ma's aim with a rifle, I will say that."

"So that's all it is, moving cows around?"

"That's all it is. Find a herd down south, drive it up north, try to get there in one piece." It was a life she couldn't even understand.

"What happens to old cowhands? Do they ever come back home and settle down and raise a family?"

60

"Besides the ones that got killed, I only know what happened to two cowhands and that's me and Elijah."

"Elijah?"

"Elijah Blue."

"Who rides shotgun on the stage and owns the horses?"

"That's him, but how did you know that?"

"He was with the stage I came in on. Do you know of John Russell?

"There isn't anybody in this town who doesn't."

"He refused to get on the stage when he saw there was what he called a hostile person riding with us. The driver had to have a big conversation about it and got very angry. And Mr. Ford, the whiskey drummer, was shaking in his boots. But Addison, do you call her Mrs. Pruitt?, set everything straight and we all got on and managed to live with each other till we got here."

"I don't envy Elijah what he puts up with, but those things don't bother him at all."

"But you know him."

"Spent every one of those Texas days beside him."

"He was a cowhand?"

"Same age as me. He doesn't talk much about it, it's a long story anyway, but he had white parents and they understood how it was going to be so they sent him out into the world to learn some things. He got enough experience in doing that, no doubt. But the thing is, being who he is, he was better than anybody out there to begin with. While I was still eating cow dust, he was five miles up ahead scouting. He doesn't laugh about much, but he laughed about that. When I finally worked my way to the front, him and me were a team. Only thing I ever learned to do, shout at cows enough when he said to so they got running west instead of east or north instead of south."

"Are his parents here somewhere?"

"No. His ma, I liked her so much, Dell, she had a ranch in north Texas. And his pa, Conn, he was her second husband, married her late, so now they had the ranch together. Elijah and me wintered over there, working the ranch, and times in between

61

we took jobs in Mexico. The last time we went home, that's funny, I call his place home, Conn was dying. He was an old cowhand himself and a Texas Ranger once and a bunch of other things, so it was maybe his time, but still. When he went, we buried him out next to a peaceful grove of aspen, that's two I've done if you're counting, and then his ma went a month later. So that's three. Dell had a son but he was dead, so Elijah inherited the ranch, but he didn't know what to do with it. He sold off the cattle, closed up the house and we came east together. Maybelline sold him some of Ma's land for his horses and that's where we are today. End of story, hopefully."

Sarah suddenly thought of a question that set her back a little. "Does he live with you?"

"He doesn't live with anybody. He moved into an old homesteader's cabin out there by the river and that's what he calls home. Sometimes we sit around a campfire, like the old days when we were kids in Texas, and I talk about how I wish things were different but he never does. Now I've told you more about Elijah than he'd likely tell you himself."

"Does he know people in town?"

"Course he does. If you're asking are there more John Russells in this world, maybe, but Elijah's easy about just walking away. And he knows things they don't and never will. Now I've said my piece. Your turn."

"I told you everything. I can't think what else there might be."

"Would you talk about the war? I didn't see any of it and for that I'm thankful but we wondered about it plenty. Only reason any of us out there had cattle to run was because of the forts needing to be provisioned. Otherwise, cattle-running was finished for the time being. It was all about the war. And there you were seems like in the middle of it."

"Well," Sarah said, "if that's what you want." She thought for a moment, to find the words. "War's as hateful as slavery," she began, "and there wasn't a place on earth where it was more hateful than Virginia. The legislators decided one thing but the people sometimes decided another and it was hard to tell which side anybody was on. I was young when they started shooting at each other, I guess the same age as you when you went to Texas. And when they were done, there was nothing left but death and destruction, houses burned, cornfields trampled. Just the graves alone, there's a whole countryside full of them, who knows for sure who lies in them but the Confederates had to be buried here, the Yankees over there, still fighting when they're dead. Our own family didn't hurt for much except food sometimes until the Confederates pulled back from up north, just trying to get home. I don't know if we would've fed them, I don't know what Father felt about that, but it didn't make a difference in the end. They were so tired and angry when they crossed that river that I guess it was easier to just burn us out.

"If you could have seen them," she said. "Most were too young and they had nothing decent, not food or boots or uniforms, using old squirrel rifles that didn't even shoot straight. They had torches, which I guess did better."

Grady couldn't imagine being a soldier, being shot at by someone with a cannon. It was hard enough being a cowhand with rattlesnakes and ornery bulls everywhere you went.

"Was it different in Washington?" Grady asked. Washington seemed like London or Paris, an important place he'd heard of but would never get to see.

"Washington had to keep its mind on the Confederates just like we did, waiting for them to break through all the armies and burn the city down. Meanwhile, all we did was wait for Clayton and Jacob to come back safe from Tennessee. Father didn't come home some nights because he was working so hard for the government. Grandma didn't live to see the end, she died that spring. Miles entered law school in the fall and I kept on thinking about Jace and cooking and praying.

"It's a wonder," Sarah said, "that anybody won that war. What they mostly did was to kill all the husbands and sons. If people had listened to the Yankees or what was right even, but I guess that's too much to ask."

63

And then Clayton was there at the door, exhausted and alone, his uniform torn, his horse lame, with a story to tell that no one wanted to hear.

"Starting over might not be so easy after all of that," Grady said.

"If you'll remember, I just came about a thousand miles, an uncomfortable amount of them on that damned stagecoach. If that doesn't tell you something, then I don't know what does."

"I mean, can you leave him behind?"

"Jacob? No, I can't leave him behind. He's here with me right now, but he's quiet. Do you see me wearing my wedding ring? I made a choice that I have no intention of regretting and this is my life now. I cook breakfast at the hotel in Sweetwater, so far anyway, till John Russell gets tired of bacon grease. I spend every afternoon with Grady McGuire discussing the possibility that our marriage contract might yet be negotiated. We tell each other things. Whether they help or hurt I don't know."

Grady nodded. "I hear what you're saying," he said. "Tomorrow then?"

"I'm more than willing," Sarah said.

"But not noon," Grady said.

"What's wrong with noon?"

"Will you accompany me to dinner?"

"What?" Sarah was completely thrown off balance. "Dinner where?"

"Dinner here. I've been told there's more important guests and oyster stew on the menu…"

"From cans!" Sarah said.

"Well, all right, it's Diego so it'll be good, won't it? Most importantly, he's making beef steak and I bet there'll be some sort of good sauce and a heap of grilled onions." Grady closed his eyes. "I can taste the onions," he said.

"Sounds like if I said no you'd go anyway."

"I wouldn't. It's too nice a place for someone like me if I was to be there on my own. I haven't got the right kind of conversation."

Sarah couldn't make the idea work in her head.

"Won't it be strange?" she said. "Me eating dinner in the same dining room where that morning I served up breakfast?"

"Every time you say that it gets me upset again. You aren't here to be the cook. You're from the east, you're pretty, you're educated, you have manners, you've got every right to eat dinner there like any other guest. Besides, Addison likes you."

"How does she feel about you?"

"Depends on what day it is."

Sarah hesitated, but decided not to pursue that answer.

"Will you please go to dinner with me?" Grady asked again.

Why not? What could it hurt?

"Yes, I'll go. I'll meet you here," she said. "And anyway, as far as your position is concerned, you're a landowner and that's all anyone needs to know."

"Right. I keep forgetting. I am the sole proprietor of the Ellen McGuire Memorial Eternally Annoying Sweetwater Ranch."

8

The dinner had gone well, Sarah thought. She was back in the kitchen before dawn making pork chops for breakfast. She loved the sharp, tangy vinegar she'd found in the pantry. It would go perfectly with the greens. And yes, John Russell, she said to herself, they would be stewed to a delectable finish in bacon grease. Who could cook without it? She'd kept the hard cider on the table since he'd specifically requested it on the second day.

She stepped out the back door and picked up the bucket of warm milk. Bean had already been there. Maybe she would pour cream over the wild berries he'd found for her. She looked up in time to see the sun just edging the horizon, a small fiery dome.

As she moved around the kitchen, still needing the light of the fire and the cookstove, Sarah remembered again all the wonderful things about Diego's dinner. His oyster stew was magical. She defied anyone on the Chesapeake with a plate of freshly shucked oysters to do better. His grouse fell apart at the touch of a fork, tender and savory. What seasonings gave the squash pie such a deep warm flavor? She'd have to ask. The filet of beef, running with juices, was like no meat she'd ever tasted. Cowhands like Grady growing up only got to eat beef on the run, when it was tough and sinewy, before the cows stopped moving and fattened up on the rich grass of the plains. Again, her heart went out to Grady. It was as if he'd died and gone to heaven. He even experienced rapture over the simplest of desserts, sweet sugar meringues.

The dining room had such a different aspect at night. The round tables were set with the starched white clothes that the proprietor of the Chinese laundry delivered every afternoon. Sarah had carefully inspected one of the floral patterned dinner plates. The name was there on the bottom in faint blue script, Spode, the same dinnerware her grandmother had brought from England. Sarah liked the pattern. It was simple, like the silver and wine glasses, fine in a way that would please sophisticated guests but not frighten those less acquainted with the offerings of wealth.

Once more, Sarah admired Addison Pruitt's instincts for proper business. The dining room spoke of elegance and immaculate attention to detail. The wood floors were polished to a high sheen, reflecting the light. The flocked wallpaper seemed fresh, like a bouquet of roses, in the glow of the oil lamps. There was even a chandelier. If you closed your eyes, you could find yourself in another country, which is likely exactly what Addison intended.

In the slowly fading evening, the windows of the dining room held images of the candlelight on the tables and Sarah had wondered who, walking by, might wish themselves part of such a lavish assembly. Or simply be hungry at the end of everyone else's fine spring day. She wondered if Bean stood out there somewhere in the gathering dusk. When Elmira came to clear the plates, Sarah kept hers. In the morning, if she could find him, Bean would get what she had saved from her dinner.

They ate and conversed, mostly with the English reporter and the colonels' wives. Once the subject came up, the reporter coaxed Grady into talking about Texas and cattle drives. The wives sniffed and asked insulting questions, though Grady seemed not to be aware of their condescension. Sarah glanced up from her food when the writer asked if anyone had connections to members of the tribes. Grady stayed silent. She was glad. Elijah Blue's life was not for sale.

Now Sarah basked in the contentment of the kitchen. The pork chops, breaded and seared, were baking in the banked down coals of the oven. After she sliced the potatoes, chopped the onions, and set them to slowly frying, there was, for the time being, not much else to do. She sat out back on a bench and listened to the waking birds. The chickens fluttered all at once like an explosion out of the coop and she smiled.

Everyone had told her the west would be different, and they were right. No land could be more beautiful, more lush, than the green of Virginia. But here, there was a quieter beauty, one that took some getting used to, one that slowly made its way into the heart. The grasses that stretched out to the horizon bent in the wind, changing in their movement from pale green to gold. In their shifting range of hues, the wind could be seen, not just heard. And then there was the sky, a vast bowl of light unencumbered by obstacles in every direction. The weather announced itself across that huge expanse half a day before it actually arrived. Clouds billowed up in formations that sailed majestically by. Their progress, their changing shapes, could be watched for an hour before they were lost to sight.

Sarah had only ever been as far behind the hotel as the creek where Bean caught the crawfish. The branches of the cottonwoods dipped down and trailed in the water, leaving patches of cool shade. It was a longer walk along the path, Diego told her, to where the creek met the south fork of the Antelope River. A river spoke of good fishing, so likely Bean knew the currents, the eddies and quiet pools, as well as he knew his own hands. She would have to go out there some day and make the acquaintance of the river for herself.

Some day. That was the problem. In order to get that far into the future, she had to make some decisions in the here and now. There were two questions she needed to ask herself. One was how she felt about Grady McGuire. The other was, could she marry him and perform all the wifely duties that came as rightful expectations regardless of what she felt about him. At the thought of the second question, she laughed out loud, then became alarmed at such a response.

It occurred to her that she should likely be doing some hard thinking on the matter instead of just ignoring these aspects of the situation.

Did she love him? she asked herself. No, of course she didn't. How could anyone love another person after knowing them but a handful of days? He's not the type of person I would love anyway, she told herself, then stopped again. Where had that come from? Was it true?

She knew that, in a way, it was true. Grady very much resembled her brothers in his looks and boyishness, in his humor and good-natured, if not entirely optimistic, approach to life. He was completely unlike her brothers, however, at least as she saw it, in seriousness of purpose or accountability.

Once they were married, would she be the one in charge? Sometimes it sounded as if that's what he wanted most out of this union. Someone to take care of him, pay the bills, oversee the hands, find out how many goats they had and determine who was feeding the chickens. Cook. Wash the clothes. Churn the butter. And then what would Grady spend his time doing? It was a question she meant to ask him. Though none of this was entirely foreign to her. She wasn't afraid of hard work and his letters had made quite clear his reasons for wanting a wife. She remembered regarding his forthrightness as appealing, no secrets kept, and she had answered those letters in the affirmative, saying, Yes, I can do this. I want to do this. At the time, she'd felt exhilarated. It was a whole new life. Now, she wasn't so sure.

One last question lingered, the difficult one. I will not think about this, she told herself. But she had to. She was not a flirtatious Southern belle at the ball, when there had been balls, having no idea of the difference between girlish ideas of romance and the real world. She was a young woman with a sad past that had very briefly taught her both the wondrous and vexing aspects of married life. The point was, did she want to experience both those wondrous and vexing aspects with Grady McGuire? Or, in the absence of consensus on that first question, *could* she? Oh Lord, she thought, I am not even ready to go near this. In her mind's eye, she saw Grady pulling off his boots, his face alight with hope. Her brow furrowed. Her hands clenched. She shut her eyes tight. She had assumed this would be easy. Women managed it all the time by a variety of means. She'd been told as much anyway. She realized that she was deeply ambivalent on this aspect of the venture.

Shaking off the entire subject, which had completely unnerved her, Sarah stood up. The slanting rays of morning sun cast long

69

shadows across the garden. The sky brightened as the last stars faded. She thought, let's not do this again anytime soon. In the chicken coop, she reached into the nesting boxes and one at a time gathered a basket full of eggs. This life suits me, she thought. I like it right here.

The potatoes and onions were browning nicely. She washed the berries with cool water from the well and heaped them in a large crockery bowl. As she was pulling out the plates to set the table, wondering where Elmira was, Diego walked in the back door.

Sarah shaded her eyes. Light streamed in from the east.

"Diego?" she said. "The sun just got done rising. What are you doing here?"

"I was fooling myself thinking I could sleep till noon."

"But don't you have something else to do? You'll be right here the rest of the day."

"I'll visit the stores later, buy some supplies. I wanted to try out another of Señora Mayfield's breakfasts."

"That's crazy talk," Sarah said. "I'm flattered, I can tell you that, but all I know is what we cooked at home. It wasn't high class or worthy of advertisement." It was just good. She touched the key around her neck.

"I hear people talk," Diego said. "But I would want to come anyway because this is my home and I like having you here."

"Thank you," Sarah said. She felt deeply embarrassed. She didn't deserve any of this. Everything had been an accident. "I'll give you what I have. Today it's pork chops. Maybe not what everyone eats for breakfast but Virginians have their way."

"I know it's pork chops. I can smell them."

"I found some very fine vinegar in the cellar to use with the greens. Can I ask you, where did it come from?"

"Do you like it?"

"Very much. It's so unusual."

"Bean makes it. I don't know out of what. Wine but also there's fruit. It's hard to decide what it is you are tasting exactly and of course he doesn't say."

70

"Bean?"

"He is his own industry. He cooks up things. I told you his sister takes in sewing. They live poor but between them I think, being quiet and working hard the way they do, they would probably have enough money to buy the town."

Sarah's jaw dropped. "Your dinner last night was so good, every part of it," she said, "that I saved half for Bean. I thought maybe he'd be hungry."

Diego laughed. "That is kind of you. He is many things, some of them strange, but I doubt that one of them is hungry."

Diego sat in one of the chairs at the kitchen table. He liked the feeling of sitting in his own kitchen instead of working. He liked the smell of baking pork chops even more. When Elmira bustled in, late as usual, she did a double take.

"Like old times," she said as she grabbed a stack of plates.

"It's not even a week," Diego said. This was in truth why he had come. Little worry messages traveled through his head, creating a noise that wouldn't stop until he got to the bottom of his dilemma.

"Seems like forever," Sarah said, concentrating on the greens. "But in a good way."

"Do you think it will be forever?" Diego asked.

Sarah frowned at the uncertain note in his voice. Then she understood.

"Ah," she said. "You know more than I thought you knew. You're Grady's friend."

"Si. I got the flowers for him. Anything after that I am not responsible for, but the flowers were lovely. I made sure."

"Then I wish I'd tried to revive them."

Elmira returned for the starched napkins and silverware.

"I'll start the coffee if you want," she said. Sarah had showed her how to make it. What had once been Sarah's exacting standards were now also John Russell's. She didn't envy Addison. He was far too much work.

Diego leaned back in his chair and waited till Elmira went back to setting the tables.

71

"You want to know what I'm going to do," Sarah said.

"I'm happy that you are here, Señora. I told you that. It makes my life easier. And better. And I am always glad to learn new things."

"But I'm supposed to get married on Friday."

Diego kept his eyes on the table. He knew that was the plan, but this was none of his affair.

"Is that completely mad?" Sarah said. He shrugged. What a gentleman. She knew he wouldn't dream of offering up his true opinion though it wouldn't be hard to guess what that opinion might be.

Suddenly Addison was at the door leading from the dining room.

"I smelled delicious coffee," she said. "Do you mind if I join the party?" She wore a brown silk striped dress, a large gold and pearl brooch at her neck and a dazzling array of rings on both hands. The brooch alone must have cost a fortune and the dress was as handsome as anything Sarah had ever seen a woman wear. She took a china mug from the shelf and filled it with her French dark roast and chicory blend.

"Wonderful," Addison said. "Thank you. What's the topic of discussion?" She had a sharp eye for tension, one of her endearing traits. Diego was not about to take her on but Sarah felt up to the challenge.

"I'm supposed to marry Grady McGuire this Friday," Sarah said.

"And Diego wants you to stay here and help him out by cooking your lovely breakfasts. So what are you going to do, my dear?" Addison said. She sipped her coffee. "You know, by the way, that the job is certainly yours as long as you want it."

Diego studied his hands, which bore the inevitable scars from hot pans and sharp knives. Part of him longed to speak up. The other part would never allow it.

As no one said anything, Addison again filled the space.

"A woman should keep her options open," she said. Did they think she would ever actually consider marrying a man as irritating as John Russell? Did Sarah not recall that her own delicate intended had been passed out drunk in a buckboard? These were the things she wanted to say, but other people's lives were theirs to live as they saw fit. She could only interfere so much.

"I know what I have to do," Sarah said. Addison waited, hands folded. "I made a promise, and regardless of what's happened since, I'm going to keep it. I'll marry Grady McGuire on Friday." Friday was two days away. Forty-eight hours. Sarah opened the oven door and pulled out the heavy pan of baked pork chops. The rich aroma filled the kitchen. "That's why I came here, that's what I said I would do, and I'm not going back on my word." And a wife was supposed to get up and cook breakfast for her husband, not a whole hotel, though she considered that her mother never got up and cooked anything for anyone. Now that she thought about it, her mother didn't sleep with anyone either. But none of that had any bearing on the present.

"Bravo," Addison said loudly. "I'm happy for you." She put down her empty mug, having poured the coffee quickly down her throat. With that pronouncement, she got up and left the kitchen in a sweep of rustling silk.

"That woman is impressive," Sarah said, the admiration showing in her voice.

"Truly," Diego said.

"Like a hot iron wearing jewelry," Elmira said, coming back in through the door that she'd been afraid to open. She began collecting the cream and coffee sugar, bowls of salt, pepper grinders.

"Not that bad," Sarah said. "It's not hidden with her, that's all."

"But for you, Señora," Diego said. "Are you certain? Have you decided that this is so?"

"I am certain. Would you like coffee?" she asked.

"I would," he said.

She poured a mug, gave it to him and sat down at the table.

"I loved someone," she said. "I lost him in the war. I want my life to be different now. And it will be." Diego watched her.

73

There was concern in his eyes. "Easier away from there. Not so sad," she said. "Different and better." Better at least than living with her father and the former county clerk. Grady had been right on that point. And sleeping in a room with Jacob's uniform.

"I will help you in any way I can," he said.

Sarah knew that was the truth. She studied his face, wondering.

"How did you come to be here?" she asked.

"It's not very interesting, Señora." And it wasn't anything he would be telling her anyway, interesting or not. "I should go now. I should find Bean. Half of my menu depends on what he is gathering or catching or shooting. I owe him for much of what is good in the dinners."

"Would you like breakfast first?"

Diego had been standing, poised to leave before the conversation turned in some other difficult direction. He sat back down.

"I would very much like breakfast."

"Do you have a horse?"

"A horse?" Though he was exceptionally pleased to experience someone else's cooking, he just wished this pretty woman that he liked very much would put the pork chops on a plate and stop asking questions. Now he didn't even know what she was talking about. "I had one once, Señora, but I don't anymore."

Sarah gave up. There was no way she could ask him if he had a wife.

9

Grady appeared again at noon. They hadn't even discussed it at dinner. She'd just assumed he would be there. He was definitely a creature of habit, and anxious, though surely with good reason. But she was beginning to realize that every time she was convinced she had the upper hand, it turned out that she didn't.

This time was no exception. He'd arrived in a buggy. The horse stood in the broad street, docile-looking. The black carriage with its spindly wheels and covered top had room for two people. Sarah couldn't even begin to fathom what was happening now. She was used to having a plan, expectations, an understanding of how things would be.

"What is this?" she said.

"Do you like it? I bought it this morning."

"I was talking about the whole idea, but you bought a carriage this morning? Why?"

"To take you out and show you the ranch. All I had was the buckboard and I don't know, it didn't seem..." His voice trailed off.

"We're going out to the ranch?"

"Wouldn't you like to?"

"Yes, very much. You just caught me by surprise."

"Sorry. I'm like that, impulsive I guess. But it's important to me that you see it, to understand what you'd be getting into. If, that is..." His voice trailed off again.

If, that is, I say yes this one more very important time. Sarah knew she'd made up her mind, but saying yes again would make it real. She didn't know if she was ready. There were butterflies in her stomach and she couldn't quite catch her breath. She wished the buggy held more than two people. She would ask Addison to excuse herself from her crowded schedule and come along, adding some clear-eyed support to a tenuous expedition.

"Are we going right now?" Sarah said.

"That's what I was thinking. If it's all right with you."

Sarah was completely flustered. "I'll get my shawl." What she needed a shawl for, she didn't know. The day was warm. Maybe there'd be dust on the road. Did she need a hat? Not likely. Where was the ranch? How far away? She had no idea. Should she bring food? She'd made bread that morning and there was a wheel of hard cheese that Diego bought from one of the traders. Some wild plums, maybe.

Then she took herself in hand. Calm down, she thought. Get a shawl but that's it. Get in the buggy. Sometimes she felt like Jacob was nearby, helping her out. This was not one of those times.

Grady took her elbow and lifted her into the buggy. It was the first time they had touched. Nothing came of it. Sarah was only worried about catching her skirts in the wheel. He went around and climbed up into the other side, seating himself easily next to her in the shadowed hollow formed by the buggy's roof. He did have pleasing features, made young and sweet by his unruly hair. The cuffs of his sleeves were rolled back in the heat. As he took the reins and flipped them to signal the horse, she watched his hands. They instantly brought back the memory of Elijah Blue. Though Grady wore only one, it was the same thin rawhide bracelet with the silver medallion. Sarah sighed. She was exhausted. There were too many questions and she couldn't ask them all.

<>

The dirt road out of town was broad and well worn, used by travelers heading west. Within a few miles, however, Grady turned off the road and onto a track running south through the tall prairie grass and headed in the direction of the river.

"Wait," Sarah said.

Concerned, Grady reined in the horse. "You're still coming, aren't you?" he said.

"Yes," she said. "I just wondered if the top goes down. I want to see everything." All of it, she thought, the immense prairie, the wildflowers blooming, the hawks overhead, the clear blue sky.

Relieved, Grady leaned behind her and folded back the canopy. He flicked the reins again and the horse settled into an easy trot.

"So you like the look of this country?" he said.

"It takes some getting used to, but yes, I do. Don't you?"

"Tell you the truth, I don't think about it much."

"Maybe that's because you were born here, no need to think about it."

"Maybe. It's just all got confusing. Being born here is one thing, being alone here is a whole other thing."

"I'm sorry," Sarah said. She knew what it was like to be alone.

"I'm sorry, too," Grady said. "That's why I'm glad you answered my letters. That's why I'm glad you're here."

Sarah took a deep breath and self-consciously turned to the view passing by. The sun shone down, golden and warm. Insects buzzed. A cloud of chittering sparrows rose and dipped in flight. A breeze shifted the grasses like currents in a stream.

"Are we close?" Sarah said. She couldn't hide her nervousness.

"We are," Grady said. "But don't worry. There's no one there. You'll have as much time as you want to look around, see what you think." He thought about Ellen hovering. Hopefully she'd stay in a closet somewhere.

"She's not there, you know," Sarah said.

Grady startled. "What?" he said.

"Your mother. She's not there."

"Did you read my mind?"

"I could tell what you were thinking, I guess. Maybe it's what I'd be thinking." Again he understood why this woman was the one for him.

"No, I know she's not there," he said. He wished he believed that. "I'll show you where she is."

The track led to a grassy lane bordered by a long white fence. Sarah's heart began to beat faster.

"This is it," Grady said as they drove under the reaching branches of a solitary elm and into the open courtyard.

"Oh," Sarah said, one hand flying to her heart. The sight took her breath away. On the outskirts of Sweetwater, small cramped houses sat squarely on their plots, a cow tied up, chickens pecking in the yard. Groups of these houses formed the outlying community. Some grew into rectangles with the addition of a kitchen or a storage room, a second fireplace, a porch, a barn. None in any way attained the proportions of the house that Grady lived in.

It was not a mansion. In Virginia, there were mansions of classical design with columns, wings, circular staircases, ballrooms. But that was Virginia.

This house rambled in a less formal way. The first floor was wide, made of clapboard, with many windows, two doors and a deep porch that ran the whole length. The second floor sat easily above the first, a visually satisfying mix of peaks and dormers. Several narrow stone chimneys defined the roofline. There were two rockers on the porch and a cat in one of them.

"What?" Grady said. "It's not what you expected?"

"Not at all," Sarah said. What had she expected? She didn't even know. Something garish maybe, a Virginia mansion exploding with complicated turrets and gables, circular porches and gilded towers, what someone newly rich with gold might construct. Something out of a catalog or a glossy brochure, fit for a king but completely unsuited to the land on which it was built. How wrong she had been.

"It's beautiful," she said.

"Do you really think so?" Grady felt that he should look at the house with new eyes, Sarah's eyes.

"I do. You have a cat."

"I hate that cat."

Grady got down from the buggy and went around to the other side to help Sarah out, but she wasn't ready. She had to take it all in. Behind the house along the winding path through a meadow was the barn. A two-story gray structure with wide doors and a

78

loft opening, it contained the same perfect sense of belonging as the house. A group of horses grazed beyond the fence. On the other side of the barn was a small flock of sheep.

"Grady," Sarah said. "It's got everything."

"Yes," he said. "I know."

She held out her hand and he helped her down.

"I need talk to your mother," she said. "I have to tell her how wrong I was, how insulting. What did I know? Now I see, she would never have wanted turrets."

"Oh, Lord," Grady said. "This is what happens."

"It is?"

"It's what I'm living with. First, why not, we'll go and talk to my mother."

Sarah felt caught in a waiting trap, a tug of war between mother and son. She followed Grady around the side of the house and down a slope toward the river. Underneath a cottonwood tree was a headstone.

"This is her," Grady said. "Anyone you see in the house is only your imagination."

"You mean a ghost," Sarah said. "I don't believe in those. I just wanted to pay my respects. I need to do that." This was so thoroughly Ellen's house. Grady had been right. Sarah felt she almost had to introduce herself, ask permission, or there would be thunder and lightning when she walked through the door. If she'd been able to visit Jacob's grave, she would have simply talked to him, told him what was on her mind. That's what she would do here, sit and talk to Ellen. Grady backed away. Sarah sat down in the grass, wrapped her arms around her knees and talked. She told Ellen how sorry she was for the hard life they'd had to lead. She told her how wrong she'd been about the house, how beautiful it was, how much she loved it. It was harder to say if she loved the son, but she felt that Ellen understood. He's a good man, Sarah added, and believed with everything in her that Ellen must know that, too. Then it was done.

"We can go on now," Sarah said to Grady when she reached him.

Grady just shook his head.

Sarah was still nervous walking up the broad steps to the porch. The cat leaped up and bounded off the chair, disappearing swiftly through the banisters and into the grass.

Grady opened the wide front door and stepped aside. Sarah paused. It seemed too momentous, to cross that threshold. She had to will herself forward. Once in the entry hall, she breathed more easily. No going back now.

The room to the left was a long parlor. Oriental rugs in deep burgundy hues covered broad-planked wooden floors. The furniture was simple but obviously expensive, tufted pale rose upholstery, cherry wood occasional tables, a grand piano, a games table, leather ottomans, a carved mantle over the large fireplace. Sarah moved her gaze slowly around. Oil paintings hung on every wall. They were all of the prairie and the river. She could not for a minute imagine Grady living here.

Sarah drew her shawl around her and shivered a little.

"Quite incredible," she said.

"You could call it that. Next."

Grady slid open the pocket doors on the other side of the hallway.

"Why do you keep these closed?" she said.

"Why do I do anything?" he said.

Sarah stepped into the room and drew a sharp breath.

"Good heavens," she said. At every turn, she found another challenge to the image in her mind. Here was the library. Dark glossy bookcases completely lined the room, every shelf filled in with volumes ranging across the entire spectrum of size and binding, a collector's paradise, the spines old and worn, new and stiff, some leather bound in sets, others intricately etched. Where rose upholstery dominated the parlor, here cream settees sat by the window for better reading light along with several big cushioned wingbacks. A writing desk stood alone, it's pigeonholes immaculately empty.

"Did all these books belong to your parents?" Sarah asked.

"Not a chance," Grady said. "They owned maybe ten books each and traded around for the rest of what they read."

Sarah made some swift calculations. "It seems like there might be ten thousand books here," she said. "Where on earth did they come from?"

"You're asking me?"

"No, I guess not."

"Keep coming, there's more." Grady led her down the broad hall. "You've only seen one parlor," he said. "Every respectable house needs two. This is the back parlor."

"This one's green," she said, noting the less formal, more cushioned seating and large pedestal table with its proper quotient of ladder-back chairs. Candles had burned down in the chimney hurricanes on the mantle. The tall windows looked out on the fields.

"Don't stop now," he said.

Across the hallway, the formal dining room held an impossibly long table surrounded by what Sarah counted up as eighteen chairs flanked by a long gleaming breakfront and a matching credenza with a marble top. Over the credenza hung an imposing primitive oil painting of a cow.

"Anyone you know?" she asked, nodding at the cow.

"Hard to say," he said. "I've known so many. But here, we've reached your favorite part of the house."

A wing jutting out from the back of the house held the expansive kitchen. It had the appearance of exactly what she'd worked in to feed a hotel full of guests. Here was the double cast iron cookstove, the generous open hearth, the long trestle table, the pantry, the supply cabinets, the myriad pots and pans.

"Oh my Lord, you could take in boarders," she said, laughing.

"Go ahead and laugh. You're right, I could. But don't forget, I have to live here."

"No, I didn't forget. I understand what you're saying."

"And this is for bathing." Grady opened a paneled door onto a warm, roomy space outfitted with racks of towels, a gilded mirror, a hammered metal tub sitting on the floor and its own small fireplace. Before Sarah could begin to contemplate the luxury, Grady was back to being the guide. "Next, on to the second floor," he said.

Sarah started having trouble breathing again. Back and front staircases met at the landing and continued up into a hallway that wrapped completely around the stairwell. At the top, Grady began at one end and worked his way around, opening one door after the other. All the rooms fit in under the eaves with slanted ceilings and varying combinations of charming dormers, window seats and lovely views. All the beds were four posters piled high with down duvets and a mountain of pillows. Each room held its allotment of armoires, sitting chairs, vanities, lavatories, swagged draperies, richly hued carpets and huge mirrors.

Grady stopped. Sarah suddenly had a coughing fit and fixed desperately on the idea that she was coming down with something. "Some are larger than others," he said. "Are you all right?" His expression was earnest. "You could pick whichever one you wanted, you know, for...you...or for us."

For us. The words made her want to run screaming down the stairs. If that's your first thought, she told herself, then you really are in trouble. But there was something else confusing on her mind as well. There were no personal belongings in any of the rooms. They were all neat, tidy, every object in its place, no clothes strewn around or open books lying on a bedside table. No hairbrushes, boots, pocket watches, nightclothes, nothing that would suggest a person lived in any of them. They all stood ready as if awaiting guests, whoever those might be. She realized that the only sign of inhabitants she'd seen were the burned down candles in the back parlor.

"Grady?" she said. "Which is your room? Where are your things?"

"I was afraid you'd notice that. The truth is I don't have a room in here. Not anymore."

"What? Are you saying you don't actually live here?" Sarah felt completely at a loss. Apparently she'd been right when she couldn't imagine him in this house.

"No, I'm not saying that, not exactly. Let's go downstairs. I'll show you."

Returning to the kitchen, Grady led her out the back door. "I'll get to it," he said, "but we might as well keep up the tour." He approached an obvious though unusually large outbuilding and knocked on the door. "You can never tell," he said, which made her frown even more. When no one answered his knock, he opened the beautifully finished door onto the privy with its arched ceiling, high windows for light and three seats. The reasoning behind the three seats left her completely baffled.

Beyond the huge kitchen garden, Grady pointed her in the direction of the other outbuildings, the bake house, smokehouse, spring house, gargantuan hen house and the two-story barn.

"Grady," Sarah said. "Is there anything you don't have?"

"Not that I can think of. Maybelline told me Ma hired this architect sort of person from back east to build it all and seems like he just kept saying, How about this? and she'd say, Sure, and he'd say, How about this? and she'd say, Sure. The one and only answer is that there were a whole lot of bags of gold in that tin stove. Probably it's all mixed up with something to do with Pa but that's none of my concern. Maybe it wasn't Ma's concern after a while either. It was just, we got this gold, let's do something with it."

"Have you ever heard from him?"

"Pa? I never have."

"I'm sorry."

"I'm not so certain I am, but thank you."

"I'm still waiting for the last piece."

"I know." Grady sighed. "Come with me."

Over the rise behind the barn was yet another out building, low and long with a peaked roof and square windows, more homespun, less ambitious.

"What is this?" Sarah asked.

"This is where the hands live."

"What hands?"

"We don't have as big a concern as we used to, but we still needed hands to manage everything. Listen to me, saying we. Who else do I think is here? Riding the herd is one thing, but there's also just taking care of the general livestock, the gardens, the field crops, that requires somebody. The damn sheep take up enough time just by themselves. And don't get me started on the geese."

Grady opened the door onto a room full of bunks with a hearth at one end and a potbelly stove at the other. Each bunk owned a small upright closet. Four of them were open, revealing clothes. Underneath four of the long down-covered iron bedsteads were rows of boots.

"What are you telling me?" Sarah said.

"We have two full-time hands since I cut down the herds. I'm doing it again. I have two full-time hands. They're not really hands, they're my friends. Names are Jim and Booker. Plus the boy, Abraham. They sleep in here." Grady waited. "So do I," he said.

Sarah's mouth fell open. "But why?" she said. "You have that whole big house to sleep in. You have all those rooms to choose from. That doesn't even make sense."

He held up a hand to quiet her. "Now wait," he said. "It's complicated. And we do use the house. Jim cooks. He's awful at it, I told you that. His cooking's worse than out on the trail if that's even possible. We eat in the kitchen. Sometimes we play cards in the back parlor. And when we're moving the cattle, then Bean comes out and takes care of the rest."

"Bean?" What am I getting into? she thought, finally alarmed. "Grady, this is not exactly what a marriage is made of, you sleeping out in the bunkhouse, Jim whoever doing the cooking, Bean doing whatever he does."

"I know," he said, "but that could all change. I told you in the letters what I was thinking. But Friday's not here yet. We've got one more day to talk, don't we?" This had been the hard part. He kept thinking if he could just get past this, then it would be all right.

"We do have one more day to talk. But no more unplanned excursions," she said.

"No more, I'm done," Grady said.

Sarah was so glad she hadn't brought the bread and cheese, the plums. She loved the house and wanted to go back and talk to Ellen again. But she also needed to be away from Grady. He was right, he had written everything to her, if only in so many words. She had only listened to the parts she wanted to hear, impressed by how honest he was, how endearing in his way, and kind. Who was Booker? Who was Abraham? She had a feeling she would be finding out, but not today. The ride back into town was silent.

10

Addison slipped into the kitchen before dawn wearing a mother-of-pearl day dress trimmed in black and only a few fine pieces of gold.

"Coffee yet?"

"Will be soon," Sarah said.

"Only eight for breakfast. The railroad men have taken themselves to Denver."

"Is that good or bad?"

"Everything's good where the railroad men are concerned. They'll be back a week from Tuesday."

"Did John Russell go with them?"

"No, my dear. John Russell finds that certain aspects of the climate here suit him. He'll be staying a while. Likely he'll devote most of his time to buying things. It's fascinating, hardly makes sense, but the more money he spends, the more he makes."

Sarah busied herself with breakfast. She had Jace's recipe for buckwheat pancakes with the thick gravy that accompanied them, along with rich syrup and butter. Bacon and sausages were frying, the eggs were waiting to join them in the pan, stewed fruit warmed in its cast iron pot. Everything was as she wanted. Now she was going to ruin it.

"Are you ever going to marry him?" Sarah asked, pushing back curls damp from the heat of the cookstove.

Addison laughed. "Who, me?" she said. "Never."

Sarah had the question on her mind. She bit her lip and plunged back in.

"Will you live in sin then?"

Addison's eyes flew wide open and now she laughed even harder.

"Depends on who's calling what a sin," she said. "But I know that doesn't answer your question. First, I'm not living with anybody. That's not the way I do things. And second, what's good for me isn't necessarily ever good for anybody else. I have my reasons for what I do, but other people should have their reasons too, and theirs'll be different from mine."

Sarah nodded. Addison knew exactly what she was talking about.

"Thank you," she said. "Now I've got another question."

"Fire away. But first, is the coffee ready yet?"

Sarah poured the steaming aromatic brew. She handed it over.

"Thank you," Sarah said again. "I mean it. For everything." She took a deep breath. "I'm marrying Grady McGuire tomorrow. I haven't changed my mind about that. He doesn't know it yet, so there's no plan. But when there is a plan, would you stand up with me?"

Obviously Addison had been taken by surprise, this keen woman who wasn't surprised by anything.

"Don't make me get all emotional. I hate when that happens. Of course I'll stand up with you. Let me know when and where and I'll be there. Are you sure you know what you're doing?"

"No, not at all."

"Well, at least you're aware of that. That's half the battle. Maybe the rest will come easier."

"Maybe," Sarah said, thinking of a house where no one lived and nights that might be long.

At noon, Grady stood in the doorway as was his habit. Sarah had just finished boiling down fruit for jam. She smiled. He'd brought a bucket full of blueberries.

"First of the season," he said, holding them up.

"I'll make morning custard," she said. "That was very thoughtful of you."

"Bean picked them."

"Naturally."

"Don't know if you've noticed, but it's been about to rain all morning."

"So sitting out back might not be a good idea is what you're saying." She'd almost been looking forward to it.

"Do you want to eat in town? Maggie's Saloon serves a noon meal on Thursdays. It's always the same, chops, boiled potatoes and pie, so that's what you have to be hungry for. And there's no cigars allowed, so that makes a difference in the atmosphere, too."

No more unplanned excursions, Sarah had said. Now this. There must be ten saloons in town and after what had happened, she'd vowed she'd never go in any of them. She didn't even know what a saloon was like inside. But she found herself curious, about the saloons, about the whole town. Damn him.

"Is a woman welcome?" she asked.

Grady looked at her. "What?" he said. "You've heard those wild west tales. This isn't Abilene. There aren't outlaws spitting on the floor and pulling out their guns. Especially not at Maggie's."

"Is that where you go to eat?" she said. As opposed to the Pickled Beet where you obviously go to drink.

"Of late, I'll go anywhere there's a meal." Grady glanced out the kitchen door. Dark clouds loomed on the horizon and a wind was coming up. "Not to encourage you one way or the other, but you'd best make up your mind cause that storm's nearby."

On the one hand, Sarah didn't like going back on such a vow to herself, not even in a town like this where men sometimes tipped their hats and ladies mostly smiled. On the other hand, she wasn't back east anymore.

"Are there dancehall girls?" she asked.

"No, no, no, no, no. No dancehall girls. I can take you to one of those places if you want." Grady started to say something, but thought better of it. "This is Maggie's very respectable Thursday lunch. There's a piano player in the back. He's Irish and everything he plays is so damn sad that sometimes people pay him to stop, so that's quite a racket he's got going. Chops and boiled potatoes, that's all it is."

"But there's a bar."

"There is a bar. Trust me. This is Grady McGuire. It's okay for a woman to eat a boiled potato in Maggie's Saloon. The judge's wife eats there all the time."

His argument put her over the top. The first light drops of rain pattered along the windows. Sarah pulled off her apron.

"I'll be back," she said. Grady sat down. He'd briefly forgotten how women were. He put his head in his hands and prayed everything would go right.

Sarah returned with her face washed, her hair piled up and held with tortoise shell clips, and an ivory brooch pinned at the neck of her blouse. She wrapped a finely woven shawl around her.

"I'm ready," she said.

Grady shook his head. It was the noon meal, taken by workingmen and farmers, in a saloon.

Sarah found that she was excited to finally see the town. She realized that she'd been entirely focused on Addison, Diego and the Russell Hotel's kitchen for the entire time she'd been here. Beyond those boundaries, she knew the creek, the kitchen garden and the hen house.

What were all these storefronts? Who were all these people passing by and nodding hello? She knew instinctively that the patrons of the hotel were not the ordinary citizens of the town. To them, though she'd sat amongst them, she was a servant. Out on the sidewalks, hopefully she could be anybody. With a sudden stab of pain, she realized that no one, likely ever again, would recognize her as Jacob's wife or even his widow. That person was gone. It was what she had chosen, but sadness overcame her anyway.

The air grew humid. The rain continued to fall lightly, making patterns in the dusty street. Grady showed her the dry goods store. Sarah felt pulled inside. He ushered her back out. The noon meal was only served for so long. They passed the post office with its passage through to the telegraph office. This place she knew. She had sent a letter to Miles and Clayton when she first arrived. The seamstress hung out a sign advertising her skills as did the shoemaker. Steam billowed from the door of the bustling laundry. Bloody haunches dripped into sawdust in the butcher shop. Then came the alleyway, the Pickled Beet, the Fish

Head Saloon, Shearson & Day attorneys at law, the Sweetwater Bank and Enterprise Services, and all too soon, Maggie's Saloon.

Sarah wanted to see more. The original town seemed hastily thrown up, board buildings with cheap windows, staircases that leaned, roofs that sagged, signs already losing their legibility, though sturdier buildings stood out here and there among the makeshift ones. Such a sharp contrast could be drawn with the solid stone and brick authoritarian architecture of Virginia, many decades older, seemingly wiser, yet not nearly so fascinating. Sarah could already see the beginnings of the march of progress, when bankers would outnumber cowhands and the shoddy buildings would all disappear. When the railroad arrived, John Russell and Addison Pruitt would be there to meet it, dressed in their fine silks and furs, their hats and gloves, with their retinue of prosperous acquaintances. And where would she and Grady be? She almost asked the question out loud, it was so strong in her mind.

All of that remained to be decided, the details of a very unclear future, for her, for him, for both of them. Today, Sarah Mayfield knew where she would be at least, in Maggie's Saloon having chops and boiled potatoes.

Outside, the rain came down harder, churning the dust in the street to mud. Inside, the long narrow room was snug and convivial, humming with conversation. A dozen or more mismatched tables filled the space from the door to the wall where a fire burned brightly on the raised hearth. Gray light filtering through the windows dissipated in the crackling flames. A narrow bar in the front room stood empty and gave off more the aroma of burnt coffee than bitter ale. The less populated back room held a longer bar worn smooth and black along its edge. A few men played cards. A battered upright piano stood alone in the corner, no pianist in sight. Sarah was disappointed. She wanted to hear the Irishman's sad songs.

But still, here she was, actually inside a saloon. She inhaled the tangy richness of wood smoke, grease, leather, sawdust. Almost all of the front tables were filled with men, some in dark suits, others in homespun woolen pants and jackets. Grady had been right, women, mostly dressed in black, occupied several of the middle tables. Maybe one of them was the judge's wife.

"See?" Grady said. "I told you it'd be okay."

"I can't believe I'm here," Sarah said.

"This is where I brought your Uncle Henry."

"Uncle Henry?" Sarah was completely taken aback. "He was here, too?"

"What do you mean, here, too?"

"Addison said he was gambling and this doesn't look like a place for gamblers."

"Oh, that. He wanted to see the sights, all of them. And you sent him, didn't you?"

"I didn't send him." Sarah tried not to comment. All of this had not made her happy. "My father sent him," she said. "When I told him about the letters." Henry and her father, brothers-in-law, did not get along, but Henry was the one with time on his hands and a yearning for excitement. Of course he'd go out west and determine the credentials of this possible suitor. Of course he'd inspect the situation with his educated eye and report back. Sarah had felt like a girl whose elders were negotiating a bride price to be measured in livestock.

"How much did he gamble?" she asked.

"He was an all-nighter, but he was also slick with the cards. I figure he went out of town richer by a degree or two than when he came in."

"He was supposed to be taking the measure of your suitability as a husband, and that would be, by the way, a husband for me, his kin, his flesh and blood, not playing cards."

"He saw Ma's house. Without meaning to say too much, I think that's when he got favorable to me."

Sarah sighed. It was hopeless and none of it mattered anymore anyway.

"Let's eat," she said. Grady offered the remaining tables for her to choose from. She took one close to the fire and immediately shed her shawl. Rain began to beat steadily on the windows and the wind came up to a low roar. A wet blast accompanied every new patron through the door.

"There'll be more of a crowd settling down till the storm's over," Grady said.

"But how does it work, how do we order?"

"Just wait, sit down in a chair. That's the way Maggie runs her business, food's on if you want it, show up and you've got it."

"I'm happy," Sarah said, and realized with a start that at least for this moment, she was.

"Good," Grady said. "I'm not used to making people happy."

Another time, Sarah would have taken up the remark, but for now she decided to let it go. "But we do need to keep talking."

"If you could only know how my stomach knots up every time you say that, like right before a rattler bites you in the leg."

"That's terrible. But we do."

"I know," he said.

"Do you have something left you wanted to say?"

"I didn't have anything I wanted to say in the first place."

"Grady."

"Okay, no I don't."

"No questions either?"

"No questions."

"Then it's my turn again and it's been hard to keep from asking. Why on earth do you sleep out in the bunkhouse?"

Grady wished Maggie would hurry up with the chops. "I told you there's not an easy answer to that," he said. "I'll try. It's all I can do." He ran his fingers along the wood grain in the table top, trying to think through the way to go about it. "Maybelline wrote me a letter," he said. "Took four weeks to find me, we were down in Mexico. I told you Maybelline and me are close in age, close in our thinking, built all that adobe together, birthed Emma, not to mention burying a man without instructions. But mostly she's the person I won't ever be. The letter said Ma was dying and I should come home."

He read the letter twice, first quickly, then more slowly to let the words sink in. Then he handed the letter to Elijah, got on his horse, went out into the cactus country and didn't come back for a week.

Maggie arrived. She set a metal platter in front of each of them, and a large tumbler of wine. She winked at Grady. Sarah glanced quickly down at her plate, though Maggie was of an age not to care and happily wider than she was tall. Venison chops lay in a ring. Parsley butter melted over a mountain of boiled potatoes.

"Elijah and me were both sick of cattle," Grady said. "I asked him if maybe we were done with Texas and he said maybe we were. Locusts had got everything there was to eat anyway. He packed up Dell's things, closed up the house and we said goodbye forever to the Canadian, the Red, the Brazos, the Trinity, all those rivers and all that dust. We took the horses though.

"Last thing," Grady said, "Elijah put a sign in the front yard that said: *Contagion*. I told him there wasn't one dumb cowhand or renegade Kiowa out there who would know what that was even all about. Didn't matter, he said, it was just a word that might keep out the jackals."

Grady had already eaten half his food. Sarah took a long swallow of the wine. It left a sharp edge on the tongue, biting almost, but went down quickly after that, soothing and warm. She needed something to ease her nerves. The week was catching up with her.

"We took our own sweet time," Grady said, "cause the horses needed it and I did, too. I just sort of knew Ma would be in the ground before I got there. Maybe I was praying for it. We herded the horses on out to fenced pasture then I came up those steps for the first time and found Maybelline sitting in the front parlor waiting like there'd been no time gone by, like everything was just yesterday, us in Texas, Pa leaving, everything. Funny thing is there were trunks piled up in the hallway, which she didn't account for.

"We ate in the dining room," Grady said carefully. His hands were shaking. He hoped it didn't show. "We sat at Ma's long table and Ma had hired herself a cook named Beatriz who sat down at the table and laughed with Maybelline, and no one accounted for that either, specially when we'd never had us a cook before and sometimes in the past we didn't have all that much to cook anyway."

Please don't ask questions, he thought. "Cora'd grown up," he said. "I practically didn't recognize her and they even had to introduce me to Emma. Last I'd seen Emma she had little tiny shoes and a rag doll under her arm. They all stared at me like I was a ghost and stared at Elijah because of who he was and they couldn't quite believe that either."

The rain continued to beat on the window. A log burned through and sparks flew up the chimney. Sarah felt the wine going to her head.

"What was it like being home?" she asked.

"It wasn't home, that's the thing. I was in a place I'd never seen before. The town hadn't been an actual town when we left, now there were storefronts and saloons and a big hotel. Ma had land and cattle and four chimneys and a damned three-seat privy with a window in it. But there was more to come. Maybelline put down her fork and said, We've been waiting on you, Grady. I told her I knew that, but I had to take my time about coming and I was sorry I missed Ma, though I wasn't. And she said, no, that wasn't what they were waiting on. Cora's getting married, she said. Now you're here we can set the date and you can give her away. We'll have the wedding in the church out at Bishop's Meadow. It's what she wants. Then I put down my fork, too."

Grady didn't know about a church out at Bishop's Meadow, or even that there was a Bishop's Meadow. He bought a suit, put it on, and gave his little sister away to a rich Texas businessman who seemed way too old for her. Cora told Grady she missed being out there in Texas, missed him, missed everything.

Remember when Ma shot that buffalo hunter? she said. Remember when Pa sent the gold? He wanted to shake her and say, Remember when he left? Remember how we had nothing? But he could see that Cora looked at it a different way and they did have Ma, she was what saved them. I don't have anything to give you, he told her, and she said, You just gave me what I wanted most. You came home.

Sarah slid the remainder of her lunch across to Grady to finish since the food on his plate was gone. As soon as she did, a new plate appeared in front of her, covered with one gigantic slice of berry pie. Someone had refilled her wine tumbler as well.

"Then things got confusing," Grady said. Sarah was fairly certain they were already confusing. "Ma had a whole damned army, ranch hands, farm hands, a gardener, an old woman who didn't do anything but the dishes and the laundry. Seemed like there should be somebody to help you get out of bed in the morning. Maybe there was and I just missed it.

"Elijah didn't come again after that first night, he had no need of comforts. The bunkhouse didn't suit him because he mostly likes being alone, so Maybelline told him about the empty homesteader cabin down by the river. That suited him fine. Still does. On rainy days like this one, he used to come up and sit in the library and read Ma's books. I kept pointing out to him that was a comfort, he didn't listen.

"So anyway, I'm getting back to where it got confusing. There were trunks in the hall again, this time a mountain of them. We're sitting at the dining table eating dinner on china and silver like we're born to it, *and the cook was still there, he thought*, and Maybelline says she's just been waiting, giving me a little time, here's what she wants me to know, she's leaving, too. Now I know I shouldn't have feelings about her doing whatever she feels like doing cause in the end I did whatever I wanted to do like not coming home, but that hurt. I was just getting used to her again. She's all I remembered of being a family. She said she had a promise of engagement to a lawyer in San Francisco and she was taking Emma with her. Personally, I thought she was going to look for Pa."

Sarah was trying to eat more pie and drink less wine, but it wasn't easy. She understood now why the judge's wife took lunch here. All she had asked was why Grady slept in the bunkhouse.

95

"Don't be restless," Grady said. "In this weather, there's nowhere to go anyway. And I'm getting to the point. Then Maybelline moved the china out of the way and laid a survey map on the table. It was of Ma's property. Then she put Ma's will on the table. She said Ma gave all of us enough, no one need ever worry, but I got the land and the house. Before I had time to understand what she was even saying, she said it was too much land. This is Maybelline, like Ma only better. She said right out that before I took it over she'd be offering to sell a certain amount of acreage to Elijah, just like that, and for how much, which wasn't anything but a dollar. And she showed on the map what she was talking about, the part that would be good pasture for his horses, she'd thought of everything."

Grady took a small swallow of wine and shook his head.

"Don't know why Ma left the whole damn thing to me," he said. "Except maybe to cause me more irritation, like poking a hurt squirrel with a stick, and in that she succeeded."

Sarah waited, but there didn't seem to be any more. Then suddenly the Irishman began to play, adding a series of dirge-like minor chords to the sound of the driving rain.

"Grady," she said a shade too loudly, "why do you sleep in the bunkhouse?"

"It's like this," he said. "There was just too much of everything." Again, his hands were shaking and he'd barely touched his wine. "That was Ma, have a pile gold so you could own more and more and work harder and harder till you managed to get yourself dead. I didn't want any of it. It was this embarrassing larger than any other goddamn thing property out there by the river and built for what reason? Pleasure? Don't think so, not Ma. Revenge? More likely. Get rid of it, I kept telling myself. Revenge is no good reason for owning anything. And then one piece or another at a time I did, most of the hands, some of the herds, till I was down to what's left, which is still too much, the herds anyway, and Jim and Booker, thank God for them, and Booker's boy Abraham who actually likes taking care of the pigs."

Grady thought he had to be truly careful here. He couldn't be the least bit light-headed. He had to consider every word.

"I was like Elijah," he said. "Not made for down quilts, porcelain wash basins, breakfronts with china in them that nobody's ever gonna use, a big old polished piano that nobody's ever gonna play. This was Ma's house, Ellen's house, not mine." He paused, as tense as he'd ever been. "So I moved into the bunkhouse and it made me happy and I've been there ever since."

"The telling of that took forever," Sarah said.

"I know."

"I think I'm drunk."

Grady breathed a huge sigh of relief.

"Honey," he said, "you don't even begin to know what drunk is."

"So what do we do about tomorrow?"

Grady pushed back his chair, scraping it more loudly than he'd wanted to, and stood up. Conversation stopped. Everyone in the crowded room was suddenly watching, as if they'd possibly heard something and knew what might be coming. Maggie came out of the kitchen, a dishrag in her hands. The Irishman's fingers paused over the worn keys.

Grady moved to the side of the table, in front of the hearth, putting himself out of most people's view so that they had to crane their necks as he dropped to one knee. Then there was a rush of anticipation and a collective intake of breath.

Sarah fully intended to panic. This was actually happening. She had to do something. But then the room started to spin.

"Sarah Mayfield, will you marry me?"

"I need to lie down," she said and put a hand over her eyes.

"Sarah," Grady said with studied patience. "Will you marry me?"

"I think so."

"For God's sake, will you just say yes?"

Sarah prayed to God, Jacob, Miles, Clayton, and Jace. She opened her eyes. There were briefly two of Grady and she knew this was not good.

"Yes," she said.

"Give me a time."

She held up two fingers and her head went down hard on the table as the muffled noise of cheering and applause wrapped around her.

11

"Sarah?" Addison shook her gently. Sarah awoke with a start. Bright sunlight poured into the room. She reached up a hand to shield her eyes.

"Do you know who I am?" Addison asked. She was sitting on the bed now.

"How could I not know who you are?"

"Does your head hurt?"

Sarah put a hand to her head, puzzled and then it all came rushing back.

"Oh God," she said.

"I should have warned you. You're just not used to it. Maggie spikes her wine. Nearly everybody does, she just doesn't always do it very well, uses the hard stuff. I expect you didn't notice till it was too late."

"I was nervous. But I did wonder about the taste. And about the judge's wife being there."

"Every Thursday without fail. Wonder why. But if I'm going to stand up with you, you've got to be standing up yourself. There's hot water coming and a dress would be a good idea. You do have one picked out, don't you?"

"I'm getting married."

"You are."

"When?"

"Two o'clock is what I hear."

"Is everyone talking?"

"Of course, but in a nice way. It's romantic. They're happy for you, but those that know him are very happy for Grady. He carried you all the way back here. By the way, you have a black eye. Not a bad one, not a real shiner. Do you want a mirror?"

Sarah sat up and stared into the pearl-handled mirror Addison took from the dresser. She only remembered the rain and the pie. Could it get any worse?

"Should you ask me what time it is?" Addison said.

"What time is it?"

"Noon."

Sarah almost choked. "Do you know where we're getting married?" she asked meekly.

"City hall, such as it is. Justice of the peace. Grady said you'd approve."

"I guess I do approve." That was strange. "And now I have to pack up my things, don't I?"

"Yes, you do," Addison said. She paused, one hand on the door, "but in case the wedding night doesn't go so well, I'll keep this room open for you."

"The wedding night," Sarah said. "Well, I can't possibly do that."

"Do what?" Addison said and was still laughing as she went down the stairs.

< >

Sarah washed then put on the simple gray satin taffeta dress she'd chosen for the occasion. She clasped her grandmother's locket around her neck over Jace's key. Carefully, she removed her belongings from the drawers and wardrobe and folded them into her trunk. She brushed out her hair and piled it up while staring at the ornate mirror on the wall. She sighed at the pale image staring back at her. The black eye didn't help. She felt cotton-mouthed and slow. Everything hurt. The sun was too bright. She remembered her uncle and wondered if a secret fondness for liquor might run in the family.

Downstairs, she quietly entered the kitchen. Diego still heard her and turned from the stove.

"Ouch, Señora," he said.

"I fainted and hit my head."

"Stick to that story," he said.

"Oh, no," she said. "Everybody really does know."

"Have you seen the size of this town? Congratulations, Señora, on your good news. I wanted to make you a wedding dinner, but Grady said no."

100

Sarah went over to Diego and put her arms around his neck. Because he knew of these things, he held her and didn't comment when she cried into his shoulder.

"I just needed to cry one more time. Will you call me Sarah? Please?"

"Of course, Señora. Will you make me pork chops again?"

"Whenever you want them. Am I doing the right thing?"

"You know it is not for me to say."

"But if it were for you to say?"

"You are asking the wrong person. I am not a believer in fairy tales."

"Not even for yourself?" She thought of Justine.

"Not even. Time will tell what happens, no one else. You smile, you hope, you do the best with what you have, that's all."

"I agree."

"Good. Now sit down and I will cook you some eggs because that is what I do. You are very pale, *mija.*"

Sarah smiled and he had to look away.

<>

Sarah's trunk and valise stood out on the porch. She peered into the hallway at the grandfather clock. It never told the right time, but the hands did hold a position halfway up to two.

Addison emerged from the interior of the hotel wearing a cinch-waist suit and gold ear bobs. Sarah considered that she looked smart and confident, much more promising as a prospective bride.

"Deep breath," Addison said. "Think lovely thoughts."

"I can't. My stomach's in knots," she said.

"Mine would be, too," Addison said. Sarah narrowed her eyes. This was the woman who was supposed to be her comfort. "I'm just saying. But then maybe I'm thinking of John Russell, not Grady McGuire. No, I'm thinking of both of them."

Sarah ignored her and started walking along the storefronts. I'm strong, she told herself. I'm calm. I'm my own person and can do what I want. In part, that's what this was about, doing what she wanted. Taking a risk, a chance. That's what Jace had

101

done, for love, or at least it had appeared that way. Sarah wouldn't be making this leap of faith for love, not yet anyway, but for all the tomorrows she saw in her mind's eye and the promise in them.

"I can do this," Sarah said.

"Yes you can. This is the easy part."

"You're not helping me, you know."

"It's always good to be tested a little."

"On your *wedding day*?"

"Sure, why not. But we're here. Are you ready?"

Sarah felt that if she said no, Addison would have her heading in the other direction so fast they would be a blur, two women with skirts flying. Clearly Addison didn't actually believe in marriage at all.

Give me strength, Sarah prayed, and wondered briefly if she'd already used up her supply of that commodity in other times, for other reasons.

Addison opened the door to the courthouse and they stepped into a reception room with a small desk and short hallways leading off in three directions.

"Clarissa," Addison said to the elderly woman sitting at the desk. The parrot in the cage next to her flapped his stubby wings and small feathery bits drifted to the floor.

"Addison. Nice to see you. And this is the bride."

"It is. Clarissa, Sarah Mayfield. Sarah, this is Clarissa, the judge's wife."

Sarah was instantly mortified. "I'm dying a thousand deaths," she said. Of all people. But then honestly, who did she think might work at the courthouse on a Friday afternoon? Why wouldn't it be the judge's wife? "I'm mostly not a drinker."

"We all know that. But then Maggie's wine does sneak up on you. Makes for a good Thursday no matter what, but sometimes it's just a little raw. Sweetheart, you got the good stuff. And men like Grady, honestly, I don't think they even notice. But we've got more important things to do, don't we?" She smiled, her etched face beaming with all the emotions attendant to a wedding. "They're in there," she said and pointed to her left.

"They're here already?" Sarah said.

"Yes they are and they're waiting for you."

Sarah grabbed Addison. At least she could count on an arm for support. There should have been more to this, more milling around and small talk before the main event.

"My, my," Addison said. "Seems quick. I thought we'd at least have a chance to converse with the parrot." The parrot cocked his head, listening, then attacked the bars of his cage with his sharp beak.

"I can have him whistle Here Comes The Bride if you like," the judge's wife said.

"Fascinating," Addison said. "Would it cost?"

"Oh, no. He does it for free, loves to."

"How nice."

Sarah realized that Addison was giving her time to stop hyperventilating.

"We can go in now," Sarah said.

"We could always run instead." There it was again.

"I came a thousand miles. If I was going to run, I should have done it way back there somewhere. I'm good."

"Pinch your cheeks," Addison said. "The color might offset that eye."

Always helpful, Sarah thought, but at least she wanted to laugh instead of cry.

And then they were in the judge's chambers. Sarah took in the three men standing there and tried to appear as if she were something other than completely stunned.

The chambers were high-ceilinged, with a minimal amount of furniture, ornately framed portraits, a chair rail over paneling, nothing out of the ordinary. Narrow windows faced the street. The judge had outfitted himself in black robes and was busy positioning himself next to the corner of a large desk. A vase of flowers stood on a white pedestal. The parrot started to sing in the other room, then was cut off with a squawk.

Grady wore a suit and vest, a starched collar, shined boots. He'd slicked down his hair and combed it to one side. His boyishly handsome charm was only partly undone by his anxiety. A half-smile lit up his eyes in a hopeful way. He held a bouquet of lilies that was obviously meant for the bride, though he hesitated giving them to her when he saw the look on her face.

To Grady's left stood Elijah Blue, the person who had occasioned the look. Elijah also wore a suit with a high-necked vest that buttoned up to a rounded band of shirt collar at the top. He held his hands folded easily in front of him, though his back was straight and his face said nothing. The narrow bands of rawhide and silver showed at his wrists. His eyes, when he looked up, were a clear shade of gray.

Sarah couldn't understand why she hadn't seen this coming. Who else would stand up with Grady? Well, anybody, she reasoned. He seemed to know the whole town. And yet this was the one person she'd never expected to be here. In the first place, what she remembered about Elijah was his glance focused steadily outside during that long ride, his immoveable demeanor, his intense silence, his utter disregard for those ostensibly in his company.

In the second place, although maybe she'd got the wrong impression, nothing she'd heard about this person gave even the slightest hint that he would be present on such an occasion. In fact, all Grady told her proved the opposite, that the friendship they shared was private and no one else's concern.

She'd sat next to Elijah Blue for hours and never even heard him breathe. She'd only felt him jump, his rifle hand move, at the mention of who she was, this hapless woman from the east, Grady's intended.

I need to think about that for a minute, Sarah said to herself, wishing she had a minute. What made Elijah Blue start, this person who didn't seem to flinch at anything? But then Addison was taking up time for her again, brushing invisible lint off Grady's suit as if she were his mother, discussing some unclear legal point with the judge, holding her bejeweled hand out to Elijah, who took it, saying nothing.

Sarah felt uncovered, exposed. Elijah was the watcher among them, the one who saw everything. She dreaded the moment when his eyes would move from Addison, whom he regarded with familiarity but no opinion, to her own injured face and half-baked schemes. The resolve she'd built through these last long days was gone. Getting drunk was the last straw. She felt that if Addison weren't here to hold her up, she would sink to the floor in a small pool of nothing. That idea became instantly appealing, to disappear, vanish into thin air, end up somewhere that didn't have so many complications and difficulties.

She should leave these good people and go home. They weren't her people anyway. She didn't share their history or know their rules. She'd lived an entirely different life that likely ill-suited her for this one. The trouble was, she had no home left but the room in Addison's hotel and now she'd just moved out of that small safe haven with its velvet curtains and dear rocking chair by the window.

"Sarah!" Grady was saying. She got the feeling he'd already said it several times. Now it seemed like he was shouting.

"Yes, I'm here," she said, and felt herself flush. More distraction from the black eye, more fodder for Elijah. "Addison's here with me," she said, reaching out for Addison's arm again.

"I can see that. Have you met Judge Cousins?"

"Hello, Judge," Sarah said, shaking the judge's hand.

"And Elijah?"

Do I have to? Do I have to? No, she decided, she did not. She could see that there would be no reminiscing about the rifle and the stagecoach. She nodded in his direction and he nodded back. It was enough. She couldn't be accused of being rude, only silent and apparently that was his role anyway.

Then the Judge was speaking, saying things in the way of preliminaries, instructions, cautions, all the while moving people around until they were standing in the right place, Sarah beside

Grady, Addison and Elijah on either side, all facing forward. Addison carefully undid Sarah's grip on her arm. Grady took Sarah's other hand as if it were china, or an explosive of some sort.

Sarah closed her eyes and prayed again to her list, from God on down. She listened to the judge's voice droning on in the room. She heard the words as if in a dream. She was insane to be doing this, she knew that now. Then something was being asked of her. She opened her eyes.

The judge looked at her sternly. "I said, 'Do you take this man to be your lawful wedded husband?'"

"Oh," Sarah said. "I do." So easy in the end, such simple words, uttered with hardly any thought at all.

Grady was asked the same question, repeated the same words and then was turning over her hand. What now? she wondered and realized with another shock that it was time for the ring. Grady slipped on the gold band and she stared at her hand as if she'd never seen it before. Why had it not occurred to her until just this very minute that there would be a ring? Her face threatened to crumble.

Grady glanced frantically at the minister for those last important words.

"By the power vested in me, I now pronounce you man and wife." It was done. "You may kiss the bride, if you want to."

Wait. Sarah tried to turn to Addison for help but Grady got there first. Before she could take evasive action, he leaned in and kissed her unyielding mouth. Then he quickly withdrew. He'd had enough experience with women to recognize a dangerous situation when he saw it.

When Sarah looked up again, tears were streaming down her face, Addison was smoothing her skirts, Grady was giving money to the judge, the parrot was whistling Dixie and Elijah Blue was nowhere in sight.

12

The buckboard surged along the wide dirt track pounded hard from the constant movement of horses' hooves and wagon wheels. Sarah was thankful to Grady for having brought her out here before, even if it was an unannounced occasion. Now she knew what to expect, what would be in every room, how the house would feel. She didn't need to be wary or ask any more questions. The only thing she had left to figure out was how to be Grady's wife.

"I wish we had something else to ride in," she said.

"I suppose I could've bought something, but I'd already bought that buggy."

"I know, I'm sorry. It's just…"

"I understand, believe me. I didn't start out so good, but I'll try really hard to make it up to you."

"Diego said you wouldn't let him cook dinner." Sarah was a little concerned about this. She wondered what Grady did have in mind. Also, he hadn't consulted her feelings in the matter. After all, she thought, she was the bride.

"To be honest with you, although I love Addison and she's been good to me, I'm afraid of her."

Sarah laughed. "To be honest with you," she said, "I'm afraid of Elijah. I never dreamed for a minute he'd be there."

"He may not seem like that'd be his place," Grady said. "But I wouldn't ever have wanted anyone else to stand up with me."

They rode in silence for a while. The buckboard creaked and the horse's harness jingled. Sarah considered again how much she loved the wide, endless sky.

"There," she said suddenly and put a hand on Grady's arm. A jackrabbit with towering pink ears bolted out of the fields in front of them, stood stock still and almost vibrating with alertness, then in two huge graceful leaps disappeared again into the tall sheltering grass. "How beautiful," she said.

"I never looked at a jackrabbit that way. It was always, there goes dinner."

"We used to set traps and cook smaller rabbits. The jacks were too big and wild. But it does remind me of something."

"What's that?"

"I want to be an independent woman."

Grady stayed silent. All he could think of was that he'd somehow turned his wife of less than an hour into his mother. It was Ellen sitting here on the buckboard beside him when before she only haunted the house. Now apparently she could get outdoors as well. It was too much.

"You haven't said anything," Sarah said.

Grady nodded and waited. It could only be something bad. Why hurry along the telling of it?

"It's what you wanted, isn't it?" Sarah said. "Someone to take on the job of running this place? I'll do that, but I need to have a say, I need you to talk to me and not just make decisions on your own."

Grady was mystified. "Is this about something in particular?" he said.

"Maybe I wanted a wedding dinner. Next time, ask me."

He felt relieved. He just had to be careful, but it wasn't that complicated after all. Asking first? That, he was pretty sure he could not mess up. He flicked the reins and the horse broke into an easy trot.

<>

They had to choose a room. Sarah was aware of this. They were married. Grady couldn't bring up her luggage until she'd made the decision. He didn't care. The house was dead to him, a feeling he wanted very badly to get over.

Sarah finally picked the wide room at the back with the double armoires. The windows faced east for the morning sun. She liked the deep blue patterned carpets, the mahogany four-poster bed, the long window seats. She pictured herself sitting there when everything else had gone wrong, taking solace from the brief glimpse of the river through the cottonwoods.

Grady left her to unpack. Sarah fell deeply into the act of placing her dresses in the armoire, her camisoles and shifts and stockings in the drawers, her hairbrush and tortoise shell clips on the bureau next to her small velvet-lined jewelry box. Grady's letters, what to do with them? She had a hopeful reason for wanting to keep them. She slid them under a layer of shawls.

Then Grady was in the room again, taking up all the space with his earnest energy. Sarah sat on the window seat and watched as he put his own belongings in the other armoire, his pants and jackets, his shirts and woolens in the other bureau. Nothing could be more intimate, she thought. The wedding ceremony was for the ages, providing the piece of paper containing both their signatures, along with Addison's and Elijah's, sworn to by a judge. This moment, however, confirmed them as truly wedded to each other, sharing a small space and dividing it up in such a personal way, finding a place for each of their possessions.

She might as well continue the process to which she had surrendered. She reached for the book she'd been reading and placed it on the left nightstand. Grady watched her, only slowly understanding the implications. His relationships with women had never included getting to choose a side of the bed.

"I'll have to go down to Ma's library and find a book," he said solemnly. "I haven't got one."

Sarah smiled just a little. "It's okay," she said. "You don't need a book."

"No," he said. "I do."

<>

The day had been exhausting, but tension still filled the air.

"I have something to show you downstairs," Grady said. Sarah found herself incredibly grateful to get out of the bedroom. She followed him down the staircase that led to the back of the house.

"Are you hungry?" he said over his shoulder. The sun was still high above the horizon, but the staircase had fallen into shadow and Sarah realized that she was famished.

"Yes," she said cautiously, wondering what might possibly come next.

As they passed the dining room, her eye caught two place settings at one end of the long formal table. In the kitchen, a basket stood on the butcher's block.

"I wish I didn't need your help," Grady said, "but I do." He lifted the cloth tucked over the basket and uncovered the makings of a delicious supper. It was all very familiar.

"Diego," Sarah said.

"He put it in the buckboard. I guess since we wouldn't come to him, he came to us."

Sarah blinked back the tears. She had friends here. That knowledge was the best wedding present anyone could give her.

"Are we going to eat in there?" she asked Grady, indicating the dining room. She felt as if these moments were of great importance to him and she was willing to go along. If it absolved her of responsibility for the outcome, allowing her to simply go through the motions, so be it. In the process, she seemed to be providing him with at least a temporary small amount of happiness. Surely, for a new husband, this was not too much to ask.

"Find serving plates," she said as she lifted out Diego's offerings. There was cold roast pork and sardines, boiled eggs, fresh-baked bread, butter, vinegar and a bottle of wine. When all the items were artfully arranged, Grady carried them to the table. He poured wine into two crystal goblets. Sarah didn't resist. He put her at the head of the table. She didn't resist that either. She watched in bemusement as he lit the tall taper candles. His hands were trembling. She was touched. And Diego's food was excellent. He could cook down the scale of grandiosity as well as up, make the plainest of repasts into a feast with his touch. She felt lucky to know such a person.

There was no old woman in the house anymore to do the dishes.

"Leave them," Grady said when they were finished with the meal. He'd allowed himself a glass of wine. Sarah had allowed

110

herself two and was thinking about a third. Instead, at his insistence, they walked out by the river. As the sun set on one horizon, an almost full yellow moon rose on the other, a magical moment. In the gathering dusk, Grady took her hand, then stopped and kissed her. It wasn't the same as what she had known, nothing ever would be. She acknowledged that and kissed him back, gently, caring for him, trying to make it right.

<>

In the moonlight, Sarah rose carefully. Grady lay beside her, sleeping as soundly as the dead. She crept downstairs in her nightgown. The house was solidly built. Not one board creaked. In the library, she lit a lamp and walked slowly along the bookcases, looking at the titles but not seeing them.

She considered that they had both brought a case of nerves to the undertaking. Hers drew her back, startled, tentative, unsure. His propelled him forward in a headlong anxious rush, clumsy and awkward. She had felt foolish afterwards, gathering the bedding tightly around her in the sudden stillness, pressing silent tears into the pillow.

Here would be her sanctuary. She pulled a book randomly from the shelf and sat down to read about the history of Egypt. When the sky began to lighten, she silently climbed the stairs and slipped back into bed.

In full sunlight, she cooked breakfast for Grady. He sat at the trestle kitchen table waiting. Sarah was glad at least that his emotional needs didn't include eating every meal in the dining room. The two of them seemed pathetic in there, taking up a mere fraction of the space.

Sarah shook the cobwebs from her mind and tried to think how to go about this in yet another unfamiliar kitchen. Grady smiled expectantly.

"I'm afraid I have to put you to work," she said.

"I'll do anything," he said, and she knew this was true.

"Can you please load kindling into the smaller side of the range and get it hot while I go out to the hen house?" She hesitated. "How many chickens do you have?"

111

"I don't know, fifteen? Twenty? Wait, maybe it's more like thirty."

"And is there anything in the smoke house?"

"There's lots, I think, sausage, hams, those kinds of things."

"Do you know where I'd find cornmeal?"

"No, but I could go looking for it."

"Grady, I think you've got enough food put up here for years to come and I was taught how to cook for a family. Would Jim and Booker, whoever they are, like to have me cook breakfast for them, too?"

"Well, it is our wedding morning."

"We can have all the wedding mornings we want some other time."

"I think once you get them in here you're not gonna get them back out. But I see what you're saying. Can Abraham come, too?"

"Who's Abraham again?"

"Booker's son, the one who for whatever damn reason likes taking care of the pigs."

Sarah knew she must have been in odder circumstances in her life, but she couldn't think of any. She went out to get the eggs and would gladly have lived in the architecturally pleasing hen house with its shutters and domed ceiling. The chickens were out on their morning foraging, so she had their nests all to herself. An arm stuck into a pile of straw here and there easily turned up a basket full of brown speckled eggs. The smoke house yielded a fine ham that would almost be good as the one she'd brought from Virginia. Who produced this bounty? she wondered. Who orchestrated such a vast array of plenty? The cook, wasn't Beatriz her name?, must have been quite accomplished. Sarah reminded herself to ask Grady where she'd gone.

"Got it," Grady said, and presented her with the cornmeal. Quickly she mixed up a simple batter and slid the pan into the roaring oven. Some chopped onion, bacon and hard cheese would make up the eggs. The sliced ham was soon frying in one pan, sliced apples in the other. She brought up a jug of hard cider from the root cellar. If it was good enough for John Russell, then surely it would be good enough for the people who'd stood by Grady when he seemed to need them.

Sarah turned to find Grady setting the table and gave him a broad smile. He was trying. She put her favorite mix of coffee on the stove so that the aroma would fill the kitchen, and nodded to him.

"I'm close to ready," she said. "Bring them in." This was her life beginning again. She decided she would be fine with all of it, no concerns, no regrets. As of the moment when she signed the marriage papers, she was in possession of a house, a husband, fields, a stately chicken coop, sheep, a cat, cornfields, enough smoked hams to last a lifetime. I will be happy here, she told herself. I will.

Jim, Booker and Abraham entered the kitchen cautiously, obviously not knowing what to think. Their own life had more recently been confusing. They were the only hands left. Ellen, who'd hired them, was under a headstone out there by the river. Maybelline, in some ways tougher than her mother, was gone for California. Grady, that was a whole other story. They loved Grady, but the situation with him had not been easy. Now he was married to a woman from the east who'd answered his heartfelt letters, they were grateful for that, and here she was the first day inviting them into breakfast.

Sarah looked up from the eggs. Jim, loose and rumpled, regarded her cooking with an interested eye. Booker, a strong and careful man, was black. His son, Abraham, was not. Sarah smiled at the towheaded, blue-eyed boy, carefree and cheerful in his nature, possibly twelve years old, she thought. Why didn't Grady ever present her with one thing that was simple?

"Sit," she said. She was the mistress in the kitchen again. As they followed her direction she noticed that all of them had wet hair. They must have washed their face and hands at the pump before coming in and she was touched.

Sarah set a piled-high plate in front of each of them, including Grady. She poured the coffee into mugs and the cider into tumblers, skipping Abraham, though from what she'd seen out here, he'd likely been exposed to all sorts of things of which hard cider was the least harmful. Then she remembered that this was her breakfast as well, and sat down with her plate at the head of the table.

"Please eat," she said. "I'm Sarah."

"Mrs. Grady McGuire," Grady said.

"That, too. I came from Virginia six days ago, by buggy, train, riverboat and stagecoach. I have two brothers I love very much. One of them hasn't been well since he came back from the war. So tell me about yourselves."

The two men watched her while they quickly forked up their breakfasts. The boy ate as if he hadn't seen food in a week, which was likely only to do with his age.

Jim coughed, picked up his fork, put it down again. "These are mighty fine fixings," he said.

"They are," Booker said.

"Can I say something?" Abraham added.

"Of course, you can," Booker said. "When were you ever quiet?"

"Well, I didn't know. But Mrs. Grady, these are the best eggs I've ever had in my whole life that I can remember."

"It's true," Jim said. "About them being the best eggs. But on the other side of the conversation, begging pardon, but were you a Yankee or a Confederate?"

"You understand in Virginia this was a terrible question if you needed an answer to it," Sarah said, "but we, my family that is, were always Yankee, never anything else. My father worked for Mr. Lincoln."

"Good, cause Booker and me were with the Northern Army and it'd be bad if you was Confederate."

"Yes, ma'am," Booker said. "Guess we'd have to shoot you."

"After we ate," Jim said.

"What he's been trying to say," Booker said, "is we were out of Fort Ellsworth. I did the scouting, he did the cooking, though there were some regrets around that."

114

"Where are you from originally?" Sarah said.

"I'm from Missouri," Jim said, "but that's a whole long time ago."

Booker's gaze was level and direct. "I'm from Virginia, myself," he said. "In a way."

"I'm sorry," Sarah said. "For all of us. I didn't…we didn't…"

"No need," Booker said. "I've been free for a long time, got me a life. Me and Jim, we've seen some things."

"And this is your son?" Sarah said.

Booker put his hand on the boy's head. Abraham smiled as he cleaned the last bits of food from his plate.

"This is my son, name is Abraham."

"That's a serious name for someone who smiles so much."

"He's the one who chose it."

"I don't pretend to understand," Sarah said. "I'm just glad he's here. I'm glad you're all here."

"We're much obliged, ma'am," Jim said. "You done us a good turn."

Sarah was incredibly pleased even if it was only breakfast. "Here," she said as they prepared to leave, scraping the last remnants from their plates, draining the cider. "Take what's left."

She heaped the leftover slices of ham, cornbread and fried apples into a pan and handed it to Booker.

"Take care of him," Booker said, nodding at Grady. "It's about time. He could use it."

Grady felt like Booker had been easy on him, patient, kind, never said a word when he could have said so much. Living with these three in the bunkhouse, except for when Abraham won at cards, was almost as good as having Elijah for a brother.

"Not true," Grady said. "I'm fine."

"Now you are," Booker said. Then they laughed and the three went back to their home forty yards away across a low ridge.

Sarah felt the satisfaction of what might someday be a home. She wondered, after all the hardship years, why Ellen had built such a grand kitchen, then hired someone to cook for her. The kitchen was where Sarah most wanted to be.

"Are you all right?" she asked Grady.

"I owe them," he said. "I can't ever forget that. They took me in when they didn't have to do that."

"But Grady, isn't the bunkhouse yours?"

"It's Ellen's bunkhouse. And they liked her whereas they weren't always so fond of me."

Sarah frowned. She was missing something.

"Speaking of which," Grady said. He couldn't comprehend why he kept going in such perilous directions. Quickly, he moved to a safer topic. "I wanted to show you the ledgers, get that started."

"Already?"

"Just to get you acquainted, maybe."

In the library, Grady hastily pulled down the thick stack. Sarah shrank away from the pile.

"Give me a day or two," she said. She was so tired.

Grady sat down by the window where she already saw herself dreaming and she took the massive desk chair instead, moving it away from those intimidating black binders.

"Tell me about Abraham," she said.

"You mean where'd he start out at?"

"Something like that."

"Far as I understand it, he was born into a group of religious wandering around out there in the desert. And his Pa didn't believe in sparing the rod or the child. Booker says he came across them too many times when he was out scouting for Comanche and had angry words with the father. Then one day Abraham showed up at the fort with a horse and a bedroll and said he was looking for Booker. Young as he was, he knew he wanted to move down some other road. Or maybe his Pa kicked him out, moved him down some other road himself. No one ever seemed to know for sure, though maybe Booker does."

"Why is he called Abraham if that's not his name?"

"Booker said his given name is Theophilus and when he decided to get himself another life, he wanted a new name, too. So he asked Booker who was the most important man there was besides Jesus Christ since you couldn't go around calling yourself that."

"He named himself after Mr. Lincoln." Sarah said.

"He did."

"That's very brave."

"I guess. Now if he'd only stop winning at cards. But everybody does have an affection for him, even Elijah. Which reminds me." Now he was completely back on track. "Next thing is to get you a horse."

Sarah was instantly awake. "What did you just say?" she said.

"A horse. You need one. Everybody needs one. I've got to show you the land, the fields, you've got to get from one place to the other where a buggy doesn't go. This isn't like in town."

"Sorry, I'm not going near a horse. Ever."

"What are you talking about? It'll be your own horse. You're that woman now, remember? You can have any horse you want."

"I hate horses."

"That's the craziest thing I ever heard. How can you hate a horse? Lord, I wouldn't have given up my first horse for anything. She's out there in the pasture, still with me, old as dirt."

"That's you. I'm different."

"In what way?"

"I'm afraid of horses."

Grady stared at her, then laughed out loud. "Oh my God, you can't even be saying that. Sarah, it's a *horse*. Didn't your pa ride? Didn't your brothers ride?"

Her father and brothers did ride. Men didn't go around in buggies all the time, that would be strange. Her father had tried to accustom her to the gentlewoman's way of riding, but something bad happened every time. She fell off. She lost her hat, her gloves, her riding crop, the reins. She was stepped on and kicked. Even sneezed on, which was a godawful mess. Twice in a fall she broke her arm. Now that she considered it, it wasn't that she hated horses, it was that horses hated her. And for that reason, she *was* afraid of horses. Who knew what they were thinking? Even being in the buggy with Grady was uncomfortable. Every

117

minute she anticipated a scare, a runaway, a problem of some sort. In her experience, horses were totally unpredictable and therefore to be avoided whenever possible.

"Grady, don't push me on this. You don't know what I've been through. There's got to be some other answer."

"And what would that be?"

She knew she could be stubborn. "I'll walk."

He laughed again and shook his head. "Okay, I'll ride out to the range and wait for you to show up. It'll only take a week." Then he grew more serious. "Listen," he said. "I've got all this to offer you. I want you to be a part of it in every way. It'll be us in it together. That's what I wrote you and I counted on what you wrote back. You even said yesterday it's what you wanted."

It was true, that's what she'd said.

"Here's what the answer is," Grady said. "It'll be simple. I'll send you down to Elijah. This is what he does. This is who he is. He knows everything there is to know about horses."

The look on Sarah's face turned from startled to horrified.

"I know," Grady said. "You're afraid of him. I understand that, but it's just cause you don't know him."

"I sat next to him on a stagecoach for half a day and he had a rifle and he never even moved."

"There's that part of him, but it's his job. I spent all those years with him and I can tell you, he's all kinds of things. First off, however, he's the one can find the right horse for you and get you on it. I don't know that he'd accommodate just anyone that way, but he'd do it for you cause now it's you and me."

Sarah wished he would stop saying that. She wondered what time of day it was and if she could go back to bed yet.

"I'm so tired," she said.

"Go up and lay down. I'll tell him you're coming later on."

"I'm sick."

"He won't mind."

118

13

Sarah woke refreshed and had one moment of contentment until she realized where she was and that it was still the same day. Then she instantly had a headache. And there was another night coming up. She splashed water from the basin on her face and piled up her hair again in front of the mirror. She was very pale but at least the black eye was fading into yellow.

Downstairs, Grady had the buggy ready by the front door. He smiled when he saw her.

"Feeling better?" he said.

"No," she said. "Worse." She wondered how he could be so cheerful when in her view everything lay before them and all of it was daunting. How would they ever get to know each other? How would she ever make sense of all those ledgers? Was she really responsible for every last creature living here? And a thousand acres to boot? How large was a thousand acres? She had no idea. Except apparently you could only find out if you were on a horse.

Grady was still smiling. "You'll get the hang of it," he said.

Get the hang of what, she wanted to ask, but felt easier letting the question go. Grady helped her into the buggy and she sat back, deep in her black mood, like a woman going to execution. At a turnoff a mile down the road, Grady stopped the buggy. If he wanted to kiss her again, in the middle of the afternoon, she wouldn't let him. But instead he got out, came around and lifted her down from the seat and deposited her in the dust. She felt like a statue that had just been put in its place.

"Yes?" she said. She worried that she should have brought her handbag, a bonnet for the sun, or a handkerchief at least.

"There's the path," he said, indicating an opening in the field that led, like every path seemed to lead, toward the river. Far out in the distance were tree-shaded buildings that might be stables.

"I'm walking?"

"It's not that far. I thought you liked to walk."

"I'm going alone? You're not coming with me?"

"It's better if I don't. I'd just get in the way. Elijah's waiting for you and he's very serious about these things. I know I'd say something that bothered him or interrupted what he's trying to do."

"What's he trying to do?"

"Get you the right horse."

"And how do I get home?" Home, she'd just said it.

"The whole point is to ride your horse back, I think."

She wanted to raise her voice, remind him in no uncertain terms how she felt about surprises, scream at him that they wouldn't survive if he kept doing this to her and may not survive anyway. Spontaneity was one thing, it had a time and place, could be charming and lovely. But a lack of order or regard drove her around the bend and that's about where she was right now.

Anxious and tense, she headed off down the path, listening to the jingle of the harnesses fade as Grady drove off. She hoped he had stopped smiling.

The warm breeze moving in the grasses calmed her somewhat. The sweet rise and fall of birdsong settled her even more. She watched a hawk circle low overhead, so graceful and intent, its prey likely scurrying for shelter somewhere nearby. The path was well-worn and yet she noticed a blanket of tiny yellow flowers at its edges as if, left alone, nature would reclaim this human byway in an instant.

After a walk that seemed far longer than it had appeared, Sarah emerged from the shielding grasses and found herself standing at the edge of a clearing. The low structures were in fact stables, but there was not a horse in sight, only Elijah sitting on top of the corral fence in the sun, waiting for her. All her calm fled. Did anyone realize she'd just gotten married? Didn't they know what that already involved without adding on this?

Well, she reflected, Elijah at least knew about the marriage because he'd been there. And he hadn't changed nearly as much overnight as she had. She wanted to tell him not to look at people so hard, it made them uncomfortable. She wanted very badly to turn and run.

She regained what little composure she had and kept walking up to the fence posts of the corral. She shaded her eyes, squinting up at him against the sun.

"I don't want a horse," she said.

"I heard," he said. He seemed to know more about her life than she did. She waited, but the two words weren't followed up by any more words.

"What now?" she said.

"Nothing now. If you don't want a horse, that's your decision."

Sarah thought she might just have found herself in the position of having to ask if she could have a horse. She refused to be in that position. She walked resolutely away from the corral, back onto the track and into the prairie grass, moving as fast as she could, finally breaking into a run. Halfway out to the road, she suddenly stopped. It was coming, she could feel it, the whole burden of everything. She'd had time to cry before, but didn't. She'd had hope back then at the beginning, and now there was a little less hope. Not a whole lot less, but a little less. What had she expected? More, she told herself. Irrationally, ridiculously, more.

She put her hands up to her face and the tears rolled out from underneath her fingers, dripping down her chin. She sat down in the dust and her chest heaved as the tears turned into huge, racking sobs. Get it all out, she thought dimly. She'd done the first important crying long ago. This was the rest of it, the second wave, coming and coming. She put her head down on her knees and considered that maybe this time the crying would never end.

Then there were boots in her vision, ones she'd become quite familiar with on that last long stretch of the journey. Oh, Lord, it would never end, not the tears, but the humiliation.

Sarah didn't look up, but she did abruptly stop crying and tried to wipe her wet face with her hands. A handkerchief would have helped, but too late for that now. If she tried to get up from where she was, with all these skirts, it would entail the awkwardness of getting on her hands and knees. How could she possibly survive that?

Elijah held out his hand to her. She took it and he pulled her up to a standing position. She tried drying her face on her sleeves but that didn't work either. Here she was, with nothing left.

"What *now*?" she said.

"I've been where you are," he said.

"Married to Grady? I don't think so."

"Not that. But Grady's right about one thing. You don't need a horse, but out here it's better if you have one. And I'll tell you something strange. If you let yourself fall in love with one, you will. I'll show you."

Sarah felt as if she'd just had the Declaration of Independence read to her. It was more words than she ever thought she would hear from the silent one on the stagecoach. All the way back along the narrow path, Elijah leading while she followed, he talked in a calming voice about horses, explained about horses, and she listened. As they came out into the open spaces surrounding the corrals, Elijah stopped. She knew her eyes were red and puffy and she was still sniffling.

"Remember what I said," he said. "I've been where you are." He seemed unfazed by everything about her except her clothes.

"Is that what you'd wear?" he asked.

"It's all I have."

"Have you ridden before?"

"Many times, when I was young. I had brothers. It was always a bad experience. I broke my arm. Twice." And that was only the half of it.

He clearly didn't know what to make of that statement.

"I'll give you Emma's horse," he said. "You couldn't find a steadier, kinder animal. It was hard for her to give up this horse."

"What if they come back?"

"By then she'd likely be ready for a different horse."

"Different how?"

"A little more headstrong, a little more wild."

122

Wasn't Emma a child just like Abraham? But before she could frame a response, he was asking more questions.

"Do you ride sidesaddle?" he asked.

"Yes."

"Good, because I don't have one. You'll have to manage with those skirts."

Sarah had had enough. She was resigned to her fate. "Just bring me the horse," she said.

"It's better," Elijah said evenly but without judgment, "if you come to the horse."

Sarah went to the horse, which was in one of the back stalls of the stable, munching on hay, a fine-boned bay with a blaze on her forehead and huge brown eyes.

"Touch her," Elijah said.

Falling off horses was traumatic every time but touching them was easy. Sarah ran her hand from between the horse's ears to its nose, once, then several times. The horse whinnied softly.

Elijah opened the stall. Sarah followed him in, her skirts trailing through the fresh straw. Elijah ran his hands down the horse's neck. The horse shivered and turned her head in his direction. He ran his hand slowly down the length of her shoulder, down her leg to the white stocking at the top of her hoof then along her back and her flanks. She trembled.

"Now you," Elijah said.

Sarah repeated what she'd seen him do and felt the horse move under her hand, respond to her touch as she had to his. It was an odd sensation, one she hadn't ever experienced before.

"Do you hate this horse?" Elijah said.

"No," Sarah said, and realized instantly that this was true. "What's her name?"

"Tess."

"How old was Emma when she had this horse? Eight? Nine?"

"You have to start somewhere."

Elijah led the horse out to the corral, where she stood patiently while he saddled her. Then the moment had arrived.

Sarah sighed deeply. She tried several times to get her boot into the stirrup but her skirts kept getting tangled up. There was nothing else for it. Elijah formed a stirrup out of his hands and boosted her up into the saddle the way her father used to do. I'm regressing, she thought. Soon I'll be too young to be married.

It felt unladylike sitting astride a horse this way, though young girls in Virginia did it all the time, sometimes even riding bareback. Her father's stable of horses were sleek animals, some trained to the chase. The sidesaddles came from England. Though they weren't rich, they weren't poor either and she should have been accomplished at this horse-riding business long ago.

"Get all this out of the way," Elijah said, indicating her skirts. He shook his head. When her boot finally appeared underneath the layers of hem and petticoats, he adjusted the stirrup, then went around and fitted the other one the same way.

"How do you feel?" he said.

"Shaky."

"Is it familiar to you, being up there?"

"Yes. That's why I feel shaky."

"Has it really been years?"

"Many. There's nothing wrong with a buggy and someone else to drive it."

"But you sit well. Seems like it's natural to you."

She laughed. Nothing about horses was natural to her. They were always too big, too tall, too broad, except for the ponies, and she'd even fallen off one of those. Or maybe that was the one that she'd saddled herself and the saddle fell off. Ask me to cook something, she thought. I can do that.

"We'll walk," he said, "but this won't take long. And be thinking about whether this is the horse you want."

He gave Sarah the reins. Taking the horse by the bridle, he walked her in a large, slow circle around the corral. Sarah could feel the rhythm of the horse in every part of her. It was easy to adjust, to move in the same rhythm. And the horse was beautiful. As she settled into the slow pace, she realized this was true, she thought this horse beautiful. Impulsively, she ran her fingers through the thick mane. They were going around the corral for a second time when it occurred to her that Elijah wasn't with them anymore. She looked back in a panic and saw him sitting on top of the corral fence. The horse felt her movement and started to turn in that direction. Without thinking, Sarah laid the reins lightly against the horse's neck and guided her back onto the right course.

Why was it so easy now when it hadn't ever been before? Sarah couldn't think of an answer, except that this time around it seemed she had no options. Apparently Grady was not going to get out the buggy every time she needed to go into town and see Diego, let alone check up on the south forty, wherever that was. She'd had enough interaction with a variety of good and difficult horses over the years, however, to know that this one was not only gentle but very well trained.

Pleased with herself, Sarah came back around the corral and noticed immediately that Elijah was no longer even there. Instinctively, she signaled with the reins and Tess halted. Was this some other game or ploy to catch her out, make her feel helpless? Would she have to sit here in this corral all day not knowing what to do? Before she had time to work up feelings about it, Elijah reappeared leading a second horse, which he mounted in one fluid motion. From the saddle, he leaned down and opened the corral gate.

"What are you doing?" she asked, only a little alarmed.

"I'll show you the trails."

She tried calling out to him, "What do you mean, *trails*?" but he had already headed down the path she'd come in on. He seemed so sure that she would follow. She gave a moment's consideration to taking a stand, but where was the use in that? She held the reins the way she'd been taught by her father, asked Tess for forgiveness, and led her where Elijah had gone through the tall grasses. He was far enough ahead, damn all the men in her life, that she had to urge Tess into a trot. She was amazed that it worked. She was equally amazed at how comfortable it felt, as if she'd known this horse all her life, which was surely not the case.

125

Elijah was waiting where the path met the road. She was grateful to him for his respect, but just briefly aware of the steady watchfulness in his eyes, as if he knew everything because he saw everything. She couldn't think about that now, however. She had to fully concentrate, or completely let go, she couldn't decide which. Whatever else happened, this had to work.

"It's this way," he said, and nodded in the direction leading away from town. Then, as she somehow knew he was going to do, he brought her up alongside, gave her a look that said nothing, and with her following his lead, eased his horse slowly from a walk into a trot and then a cantor. Then they were flying down the road at a gallop and her hair was coming loose everywhere, her skirts ruffled and blown, her hands still conscientiously light on the reins. She wasn't laughing, she was definitely terrified, but there was the thrill to it all that she'd forgotten, those miraculous times when she hadn't fallen off.

Miles down the road, they turned into a meadow full of wildflowers and game trails. The one Elijah chose ended predictably at a clearing above the river. They were far from town and Jacks Creek. The river was broad here, bordered with low-hanging willows, the current still running fast from the spring rains.

"This horse suits you if you want her," Elijah said. "You move the same way."

"I want her," Sarah said. She knew in her heart it was true. "This is the first time I've seen the river."

"It's a good one."

"But isn't it very different from Texas?"

"Not as different as you'd think, but that's what I meant."

"So you learn to live with it."

"Or you go home."

"I can't," she said. "There is no home."

Elijah stared out into the trees. "There's always home," he said.

A window had opened and just as quickly closed. As Sarah watched, Elijah glanced back at her again and swung easily down from his horse. She realized with a sinking feeling that they weren't finished yet.

"Stay with me," she said to Tess. She gathered her courage, then in one great effort swung her leg over, dragging her skirts with it, held onto the saddle for dear life, released her foot from the stirrup, and slid down to the ground. "Ha, ha," she said, beaming, still holding the reins. Elijah never hesitated. He climbed back on his horse.

"You're doing this to me," she said.

"I am."

"My hair's all come undone," she said, brushing it back from her face.

"It's that dress you should be worried about."

"Stop watching," she said.

While he led his horse down along the bank of the river, she struggled with the task of getting all the fabric out of the way, then managing the foot in the high stirrup, then lifting with all her might, untangling the other leg, getting it over the saddle, pulling on her skirts until her boot found the other stirrup. How long had that taken? She didn't want to think. She was sweating and her mother had always told her a lady didn't do that. Then again, it was doubtful her mother had ever gotten on a horse by herself in her whole entire life.

"I'm ready," she called out, though ready for what she didn't know.

Elijah walked his horse back up from the water.

"Are you confident yet?" he said.

"No."

"Then it's better to keep going."

They rode farther along the meadow till it joined the road again then headed west along wire-fenced acreage filled with grazing cattle until they came to where the wheat fields began. Elijah slowed so that she had to slow with him. He faced one way and then the other. Sarah communicated gently with the reins and Tess obeyed her every move. Heading back through the dust they'd churned up, Elijah quickened the pace, covering ground swiftly but not racing full out.

He pulled up suddenly where the tall grass began and the path veered off.

"Now?" he said.

"Better, anyway. Much."

"Then we're done."

"But how will I get home?"

"On your horse?" he said.

"Just like that? I take her with me?"

"Just like that."

He waited, but she didn't seem capable of saying any more.

"You've taken care of horses," he said.

"Yes."

"Is there something else?"

"I don't know. It just seems so fast. Won't she be upset? Won't she be lonely?" Grady likely wouldn't understand if she had to sleep out this first night with her horse in the barn.

"It's a horse. And that's where she came from, Ellen's stables."

Just having him say that name unnerved her. She'd had a few moments when she almost forgot about Ellen and the fact that this was her property, her land, her house, and this had been one of her horses. But now this one's mine, Sarah thought. And she's beautiful. Elijah had made a wise choice.

"I love this horse," she said.

"I told you," he said. And then he turned his own horse away and was gone, leaving Sarah sitting on Tess in the bright light of high afternoon. She was dizzy and had to breathe in the fresh sharp air until she felt steady again. Then she laughed. Here I am, she told her old self, out in the wild west with a husband and a library and thirty chickens, though she bet it was more like fifty, and a horse that apparently is all my own. Her old self would not have believed any of this.

She lifted the reins every so slightly, eased Tess into a trot and headed along the road to where the green fields and white fence

128

began. The property of her husband, or her husband's mother, or at least somebody she had some sort of relationship with. She slowed, walked Tess up to the house and then past it to the barn. Tess whinnied as if she recognized her surroundings and Sarah was ridiculously overcome with affection. Wait till I fall off this horse, she thought, and this will all go away. Until then, she wanted to savor it.

The saddle was a problem. It was heavy. But she remembered how to loosen the cinch and release it, how to undo the bridle. She led Tess into a stall, hoping it was a good one. She hadn't ever been in the barn before and didn't realize how many horses there were, with the milk cows down at the end. Tess whinnied again and set up a sort of soft chorus. Sarah went into the stall, heedless of her skirts, and rubbed Tess down, warming her sweat-chilled hide. When she was done, she walked out to the root cellar, gathered a handful of softening apples and fed them to Tess one at a time. She was her eight-year-old self, before life happened, all hopeful and happy.

She came into the house through the kitchen door and stopped. Then she laughed. Grady stood at the broad cookstove peering into a pan on the top. A huge fire roared in the oven.

"What on earth are you doing?" she said.

"Cooking dinner for us."

"But what are you cooking? It looks like a conflagration."

"When the coals die down, I wanted to try my hand at making some biscuits. It was the one thing I used to be good at. And I was figuring to fix some greens." Grady looked up from the cookstove and actually saw Sarah for the first time.

"Good Lord, what's happened to you? Your hair's sort of incredible. And you're full of dust. Honey, shouldn't you go back outside?"

"Grady, I have a horse."

Grady let go of dinner.

"I forgot," he said.

"Where I was?"

"No, how good Elijah is.

"You figured it would take weeks?"

"At least maybe more than one day."

"I have Emma's horse."

Grady nodded his head thoughtfully. "That would be the perfect choice," he said.

"She's out in the barn."

"I'll go out and take care of her."

"I already took care of her. I rubbed her down and fed her apples."

Grady regarded her with surprise. "You got accustomed to it fast for being so against it."

"I know. It makes me happy."

He came over and hugged her despite the dust. "That's the best news I've had in a long time," he said.

Dinner turned out to be Grady's biscuits, Sarah's greens, onions, fried ham and gravy. There was wine. Sarah insisted on it.

They ate in the dining room again, at the end of the long table. Grady lit the candles and the room glowed in the gathering darkness. Sarah had changed into a clean dress and brushed out the tangled curls of her hair. Grady thought she glowed as well and he said so. Sarah tried to duck the compliment.

"I never thought I'd have a horse," she said. The idea briefly occurred to her that having a horse might end up being better than having a husband.

14

In the morning, after more awkwardness and another sleepless night spent in the library, Sarah found that she could hardly wait to get out to the stable. Why was this? It was just a horse. Yes, she told herself, but this was a horse that didn't hate her. Now she and Grady could go out riding together and he could show her his land.

As Sarah approached the barn, she heard the distinctive, annoying sound of bleating goats. Following the path around the barn, she discovered an enclosure full of nanny goats and their noisy kids all being kept in line by a funny-looking dog. Abraham was leaning over the fence watching them.

"Whose dog is that?" she asked him.

"I don't know, everybody's I guess. His name's Petey. He's mostly for sheep, but when the goats are in here he takes care of them too."

"Where did Booker and Jim go?"

"They're out moving the herd."

"And you're not with them?"

"I got chores. We're butchering a hog today."

"And you'll be doing that?" He was so young.

"No, not me. Booker says I'm not ready yet and since he's pretty much right about everything, I guess I'm not ready yet."

"I wouldn't think so." And then she had to tell someone who wouldn't laugh at how foolish she was.

"I have a horse," she said.

"Your own?"

"I think so. The one Emma had." Abraham wondered if he could tell her that he was in love with Emma.

"That's Tess. She's a good one. You'll be glad."

"Do you have a horse?"

"Yes, ma'am. It's Cactus. He's the gray in the barn."

They went into the barn together. Sarah listened to everything Abraham had to say about Cactus. It seemed as if their history had been forged together and maybe this was the horse Abraham was on when he went to find Booker, the horse he rode when his name was Theophilus. She loved the boy's blue eyes and quick appreciation. When it was her turn, he listened just as carefully, as if she were twelve and not twice married. Then he had to go, leaving her with Tess.

There were fourteen horse stalls. If there were fourteen horses, now she knew two of them. When she saw the others, she'd have to look them over, find markings by which to remember them. She realized that she knew far more about horses than she wanted to admit.

In Tess's stall, Sarah did as Elijah had done, talking softly, using her hands, feeling the rippling response.

"I'm so glad you're in my life," she said. "I promise I'll take good care of you." Tess nickered in response. This would improve her situation immensely, having something to focus on. Having someone to talk to. She realized immediately how pathetic an idea that was, but so what. She would talk to Tess every day, tell her everything she couldn't tell anyone else.

Finally, she bridled Tess and led her out of the stall. As she was getting up the courage to saddle her, Grady came into the barn.

"I wondered where you went," he said. It was a big house, people could get lost, though she had to admit she'd been in a hurry to get out to the barn.

"I thought I'd try this myself," Sarah said.

"Do you want me to do it?"

"Yes," she said. "But only because I don't want to do it wrong. I did once."

"And the saddle fell off?"

"Yes."

"It happens."

"You're not just telling me this?"

"I've seen it happen. Bad equipment, in too much of a hurry, no sleep, not thinking, all kinds of reasons." Drunk, but he didn't want to add that one.

Grady saddled her horse, then his own, a chestnut gelding. In order to stay on good terms with everybody, Sarah came over and stroked this nose and neck also, then the ears, then sifted fingers through the mane.

"Horse hater, huh?" Grady said.

Sarah ignored him. Fumbling in her skirts, she managed to fit the toe of her boot into the stirrup that Elijah had adjusted. Feeling more confident this time, she pulled herself up and over at an awkward angle, but managed to right herself with hardly any strain. No one could see how many years lay between all her failures and this small triumph.

Grady led the way out of the barn and along a trail through the fields. He set the pace deliberately slow and she was just glad to be out, on this sweet horse, in the middle of a beautiful spring morning. The air was fresh, the fields still and quiet except for the lowing of cattle. Sarah believed that for once, she couldn't ask for anything more.

Grady opened a gate, closed it behind them, and they rode through the cows with their young. They skirted the pasture holding the few menacing-looking bulls, then cantered down the lane along the fields of wheat and corn. Here, the horses all grazed in one pasture while sheep grazed in another. Grady moved among the horses and dismounted. He walked over to where a grizzled old palomino stood in the shade of a tree. He laid his forehead against the horse's neck and the horse responded.

"This is Whiskey," he said. "Took me to Texas. Brought me back. When I see him now I feel way older than I am."

Sarah didn't say anything. What was there to say? This was Grady's life.

He mounted again and they galloped along the boundary of the fields to more open pasture where they found Booker and Jim herding the rest of the cattle along.

"We're going up into the hills," Booker said. Grady nodded. He knew from being told that the grass was tender and greener up there in the spring and Ellen owned the hills as well.

"Abraham said you're butchering a hog today," Sarah said. She hoped Grady didn't mind her getting involved. Well, who cared, that's why she was here.

"We are," Booker said.

"Could we spit it?"

She watched as Booker and Jim's eyes lit up.

"That would be a very fine idea," Booker said. "We could dress it today and get it set up tomorrow."

"I'm pleased that you like them," Grady said as they headed back, riding shoulder to shoulder.

"I do like them," Sarah said. "And I like this horse."

<>

It was almost like a private wedding celebration, the feast with the roasted pig. While Grady rode out with Jim and Booker to mend fences in the old cattle pasture, Sarah cooked her heart out. Abraham stayed with her to keep the slow fire going under the spit and because he liked being around a woman. Sarah made Jace's very private recipe barbeque sauce that required an hour's simmer on the stove and mixed up the batter for spicy hot corn cakes. She sliced a mountain of onions that would sweeten slowly in the pan and a mess of wild greens to be cooked with salt and Bean's vinegar. A chess pie seemed like the perfect ending for such a meal.

Abraham was diligent in his attention to the pig. The spit required a keen eye so that the shrinking pig meat wouldn't fall into the coals. Booker's clever spit also had to be rotated with care and regularity to ensure even cooking. In addition, the coals had to be banked at just the right heat. In between his duties, Abraham sat at the kitchen table and watched Sarah cook.

"That was one of my favorites," he said, nodding toward the kitchen door.

"The pig?" she said. "Oh honey, I'm sorry."

134

"It's just that he was pretty smart, for a pig, that is." He hadn't been called honey ever that he could remember. Sarah didn't call people honey either. She thought she must have picked it up from Grady, but this child was worth the endearment.

"Would you teach me how to cook? I want to know everything. Booker says when you know everything then you've got choices."

"Booker is very wise."

Abraham was going to tell her, even if it was stupid.

"I love Emma," he said simply.

Sarah put down the chopping knife, wiped her hands on her apron and sat down at the table.

"Tell me about it," she said, and he was very relieved.

"I only have a few minutes before I have to check on the pig."

"That's okay. We'll go out and check it together."

"She's pretty and funny and reads books and can ride a horse as good as I can." Sarah felt a pang of guilt.

"And shoot a rifle, too," he added.

"Do you think she knows?"

"She writes me letters."

"She does?"

"Yes and I write her back."

"Does Grady know this?"

"I don't know."

"Did Maybelline get married? Where do they live?"

"She didn't get married, but they live in a nice house on a hill. Emma goes to school."

"Wait. What happened to the lawyer?"

"He smelled funny and he was boring."

Sarah almost laughed out loud. From the mouth of a child came the most startling revelations.

"But Emma's coming back someday," Abraham said. "And I'm going to wait for her."

Then Sarah wasn't smiling. She could see the differences, the gap that would have to be bridged. She wanted to get Abraham into the library, find him his own education or his heart would be broken, which it might be anyway. On the other hand, he was a fine young boy with a history beyond his years and that must count for something.

But still. "Do you read?" Sarah said. "We'll find you some books. It's important. Now let's go out and see about that pig."

As the sun was going down, Sarah set the table in the back parlor. She'd decided that the dining room would no longer see her. Ellen's anger could simmer somewhere else. The candles and oil lamps glowed. The wine flowed and Abraham laughed so hard he almost fell off his chair. The pork fell tender off the bone, the cracklings a thing of wonder, all perfectly cooked by the young chef. Plates were passed around and refilled. When everyone had eaten as much as they could, Sarah brought out the chess pie and cut it into huge slices.

I want this to be my family, she thought. I want these to be my brothers, wise Booker, funny Jim, sweet Abraham. She realized that she was including Grady. He would be a wonderful brother. Then she saw that he was troubled. Instinctively, she felt that whatever was on his mind, it had something to do with the table, the food, the warmth, in other words, with her.

That night Grady couldn't manage anything, still lost in his own private unhappy world. Sarah sat in the candlelit library for a long time, her book facedown on her lap. Then she got up and went to the desk. She took the top ledger off the pile, opened it and began running her fingers down the entries. She shivered, feeling Ellen watching over her shoulder, proud of the endless sums all recorded in a tight, disciplined, forward-leaning hand. There were three other hands after the long span of Ellen's, one just as meticulous, another dark and slanting and the last quite recognizable as Grady's. Logically the one following Ellen's must belong to Maybelline. That left the dark and slanting entries in the middle. It must have been the cook, keeping careful track of the assets and debits, the incredible inventory of goods and supplies. Sarah tried to remember her name.

15

"They should come to dinner as well," Sarah told Grady.

"But we're just married," he said. When she'd been just married to Jacob, they sat down to dinner every night with a house full of people and it hadn't bothered them at all. In truth, it had been a comfort. She considered the fact also that being alone with Grady came too many times in the day and night already.

"They work hard," she said. "Don't they deserve a decent meal?" She wanted to say, Aren't they family?

"I see your point," Grady said, and he was sure he did, but he felt as well that he was losing something.

Sarah served roast chicken for dinner. When the meal ended with a peach tart, she invited them for breakfast. At a breakfast of sausage, eggs and beans, she invited them for dinner and couldn't help but notice the huge smiles on their faces.

"If Jim's truly gonna give up what he calls cooking," Booker said, "then we might all live to see a better day."

Sarah fell easily into her own chores. Abraham, when he wasn't out riding with the men, tutored her in the ways of the pigs and the goats. She took a more careful inventory of the smokehouse, pantry and root cellar. Abraham told her that a neighbor, old Tom, had planted the original acre of kitchen garden for Ellen, then Booker had added to it. Tom and some of his sons helped with the harvests, and sowing the corn and winter wheat, and he had a team of field horses to do the plowing.

Why aren't we growing cotton, for chrissake? Grady had asked of no one, then added bitterly, Might as well be, we're growing everything else.

Sarah walked row after row of the garden, taking mental notes of what to use, keep, plant more of, make room for, and store up for the winter. What to put up, dry, pickle, turn into something else. Such bounty, potatoes, peppers, onions, beans, peas, greens, herbs, turnips, parsnips, watermelons, the list went on and on.

Ellen had surrounded herself with riches that were worth far more than gold, though it was through the gold that she'd acquired them. Her money was put to its best use, Sarah decided, all of it that had been spent in this way.

After the long days of chores, Sarah took to riding Tess in a different direction every afternoon. She had made the mounting and dismounting easier by cutting off several inches of both skirt and petticoats and redoing the long hem with tiny running stitches that she squinted at by candlelight somewhere in the middle of the night. Still not sleeping well? Grady had asked her and she had to admit that no, sleep would not come to her sometimes until almost dawn. She refused to be exhausted, however. There were too many things that needed to be done.

Now that the men had moved the cattle to the hills for the summer, they were in the process of moving the sheep to the fields where the cattle had been. Grady complained that if it wasn't one thing it was another, work that never ended, responsibilities that never ceased. He didn't like sheep, he told her, and there'd been far more than enough cows in his life already. Which didn't even begin to address the goats, chickens, pigs, horses and those damn geese. She'd discovered, however, that Booker and Jim knew more about how to run the ranch than Grady ever had or would.

"Abraham," she called out. The boy appeared at the door to the barn with his shovel. "Where are the geese?"

"Over the hill," he said. "There's a pond."

She followed the trail in the direction that he'd pointed, keeping Tess at a walking pace, almost a plod. That way she could take in the feel of the morning, the slender grasses sprouting delicate blue flowers, the rustle of insects, the scurrying of ground squirrels. She discovered a blackberry patch, perfect for thick sweet pies to be made come late summer. At the top of the rise, the rolling land spread out before her. The prairie ended here, giving way to tree-covered hills. A mourning dove called softly. As Sarah held her breath, a doe and two spotted fawns crossed the path below.

138

Sarah led Tess carefully down the hill to the pond whose calm surface reflected the clouds and blue sky. A flock of noisy geese, storybook tall and white, clustered on the grassy bank. In the middle of the pond stood their sanctuary, a green island beyond the reach of marauding coyotes. The elaborate slant-roofed enclosure on the island suggested another of the architect's gold-plated projects. At the other end of the pond, a thicket of bulrushes hid frogs whose calls echoed in the spring air. Sarah watched a small turtle sunning itself on a log. Wild ducks pecked along in the grass, fighting for insects with a handful of cowbirds.

Sarah rode back out of the hills, along the horse pasture, down the lane to the road. She swung Tess in the direction that Elijah had taken them. Gently, she urged Tess forward, slowly at first, then moving faster and faster till they were flying down the road full out, the landscape passing by in a blur of fields and fence posts, the wind and rhythmic galloping sound of the horse's hooves making her heart soar. After four miles, five, she could only guess, she reined Tess in. Where had this feeling been all her life?

Then she found the orchards. Naturally, every landowner of any account had to have an orchard. Did this woman forget anything? Galloping up over the hills again, Sarah came across the cattle strewn over the new fields, among them many gangly calves. While Tess stood patiently, grown accustomed to these moments, Sarah sat astride her horse with tears rolling down her face. Why? she wondered. What in this lovely scene had caused her to cry?

<>

After days of considering such an adventure, when she'd finished hanging out the laundry, working in the garden, setting pies out to cool, Sarah gathered up her courage and rode into town. She feared appearing scandalous alone on her horse in the skirts that now hit her boot top. She was also afraid of how much might have changed in her brief absence.

Tess seemed alert to the unfamiliar scenery and the lively atmosphere. Sarah tied her to the hitching post outside the hotel and patted her neck, whispered in her ear.

Diego stood at the stove in the kitchen, in exactly the same position as she'd left him. She inhaled deeply.

"Pheasant!" she said. "How amazing!"

Diego looked over his shoulder and smiled broadly. "*Mija*," he said. He put down his tongs, opened his arms and she walked into them. He was warm and smelled of bacon and spices. Don't cry, she told herself. Don't cry, don't cry, don't cry. In doing so, she finally conceded to herself that she was an emotional wreck, though the why still would not come.

"Can I help?"

"Only if you want to. Where's Grady?"

"Taking calves to market."

"How's he doing?" Diego asked.

"Fair, I guess. It's just not in his nature."

"That has always been the truth. Trout needs cleaning, that is the first course. Or preparing the vegetables to roast. I'm making Mexican chocolate in the French way. Your choice."

"I'll take the trout. Where did you learn about chocolate in the French way?"

"I will tell you some day." Or never, he thought, but he was afraid. This possibility weighed on his mind more than any other.

The trout were fat and fresh-caught, still gleaming faintly in the dim afternoon light.

"Bean, I suppose," she said.

"As always."

Sarah tied on an apron, happy to be back in this kitchen. Diego hadn't made any comment about the indecency of her shortened skirts, or even seemed to notice. And he always had room for her.

"Knife, please," she said. Diego handed her one from the rack on the wall. She laid the fish out on the cooking table and one at a time went in through the gills to cut off the head, pulled out the guts, then sliced the fish open along its underneath length. She spread back the halves and sluiced them with water from a barrel to clean out the blood.

"I have a horse," she said.

140

"Your own?" Diego said from the stove.

"My own. But she did belong to Emma."

"That would be Tess."

"Does everyone know everything?"

"Yes. Know always that this is the truth," he said. "Who gave this horse to you?"

"Elijah."

"Ah," Diego said and nodded.

"I've got a question for you and it's one I'm not sure I want to ask," Sarah said.

"This, I can't imagine."

"Who cooks breakfast here now that I'm gone?"

"What makes you think I don't?" Diego said, trying to get around the answer.

"You don't look tired enough."

"You know who it is."

"Justine."

"I have taught her well. And in fairness, on her own she is very good, very capable. The way of it comes naturally to her."

Wonderful, Sarah thought. That avenue of escape had so very quickly closed. It's what she'd been afraid of. Yet she wasn't in truth contemplating escape. Nothing was so bad that it couldn't be overcome and many things were good. So why had she been anxious concerning this question?

Then she couldn't keep herself from asking. "Does John Russell like her breakfasts?"

Diego smiled. "He doesn't say. And he's not around much anyway. They're traveling. Smithy Ryder will be in very soon on his way west to run the kitchen of their new hotel. I would go there myself, first to be on this train when it arrives, and then to taste all of New Orleans in one of his dishes. That would be a special treat." Diego paused a moment. "John Russell did say he missed your coffee."

"That's something I guess, except Smithy Ryder makes the same damn coffee."

"You have a special way you grind it."

141

"You're making that up."

"Maybe not. But how are you?" Diego asked, his voice turned serious.

"I'm good, thank you for asking."

"In every way?"

Do not cry, do not cry! "In every way," she said, glancing everywhere but his eyes.

"It's just a big undertaking, maybe too much all at once," he said. "That's the way it happens out here, but not in the east, I think."

Sarah had finished the trout and laid them out on the board. She covered them with a cloth damp with cool water from the well.

"I'm hardy," she said. "Couldn't you tell?"

"Of course I could tell," Diego said, "that's why I was asking."

It was Sarah's turn to smile and shake her head. She felt about as hardy as Grady's bouquet of prairie flowers wilting in the buckboard.

She wanted to tell Diego that even though he had a lady friend in Justine and possibly a wife on top of that, she loved him and would gladly stand third in line. He was a good man. And he could cook. Instead, she said nothing and hurried off before she became emotional yet one more time.

Addison was out on the sidewalk talking to Tess as Sarah came around the corner from the kitchen's back door.

"There you are," Addison said. "I figured it must be you since this is Emma's horse and Emma isn't here anymore."

"I give up," Sarah said. "Everybody does know everything including the judge's wife who still knows that I got drunk and passed out at the table and had a black eye."

"You were nervous. It's not easy getting married to somebody you just met, especially when that somebody is Grady McGuire."

They all understood, Sarah could see that now. But Addison was the only one who could put it in just the right words, who could cut to the heart of the matter.

"It isn't easy," Addison said. "Is it?"

142

Sarah ran her hand down Tess's neck. Addison wore another stunning outfit and the same diamond ear drops. Her essence, however, was not diamonds but steel and Sarah admired her immensely for it.

"It's an astonishing house," Sarah said, "and so much land."

"I know. I've seen it."

"You knew Ellen?"

"I knew her and believe it or not, I was afraid of her."

"How can that be?" Sarah was stunned.

"She had all that money and nothing to lose. She absolutely did what she wanted, not ever in a bad way, just with this incredible strength and determination that set her apart. She made her decisions and you'd better get out of her way."

"But did you like her?"

"No. That was impossible, she was too cold, too hard, and it's me saying that. But I sure as hell admired her."

"No wonder Grady's the way he is."

"No wonder is right. But how are you?"

"Confused."

"That's a lot better than telling me you're fine."

"I can't sleep. Fortunately, there are about ten thousand books in the library and I'm going through them one at a time."

"It isn't the way you thought it'd be, is it?"

"Looking back, it couldn't possibly have lived up to what I thought it would be." Sarah frowned. "On the other hand, I didn't expect that much." Was she angry, too? That had not yet occurred to her.

Addison patted Tess's flank. "At least you got a horse out of it," she said and laughed her throaty laugh. "And remember, your room's still here. I checked on it the other day. It's sweet, I'd forgotten, with that sleigh bed and the rocker by the window."

Sarah knew she wouldn't forget.

"I'm in debt to you," she said. "For the room and everything else, and especially for standing up with me."

"My pleasure. It was the best wedding I've ever been to. Loved the parrot."

143

"I don't know what I would have done without you," Sarah said.

"I don't either. Now I've got to get back to work, but you go have fun. By yourself. In your sassy short skirts."

Sarah considered that any notion of marriage as a blissful state of affairs was hard pressed to survive Addison's sharp tongue. And fun, what was that? She knew the answer. It was galloping a horse down a dusty road. Who would have thought?

Sarah left Tess hitched and explored the town a little. The post office reminded her that she needed to write to her brothers. From the last letter, they only knew she'd survived the trip. On a whim, she went into the office and asked the clerk at the window if there might be any mail for her. There wasn't, not yet.

In the general store that Grady had chased her out of, she made a slow and thorough perusal of all the goods, barrels of butter, sacks of flour, jars of honey and sorghum molasses, canned sardines, rough jackets, felt hats, quill pens, oil lamps, jack knives, tobacco, mattress ticking, folded linens, dress patterns. Sarah decided that she should start sewing soon in earnest instead of cutting apart the clothes she had. She fingered the bolts of cloth. A small shelf held tattered used books for sale. She stood for a minute hardly daring to admit what was true, that she suddenly had access to a grand library that was beyond anyone's wildest imaginings.

Sarah passed by the bootmaker's shop, stopping only to glance in the window. She didn't have money for new boots. The old ones were fine. Grady had told her to take whatever money she needed for the household accounts and she kept that carefully in a box in a drawer.

The Chinese laundry exhaled a cloud of steam. The barbershop teemed with customers and a line had formed on the sidewalk next to the row of tethered horses. Sarah stared. These were cowboys. She'd heard there was a huge herd of cattle outside of town. She found herself inspecting the horses more than the men, who seemed either rowdy and loud or uncomfortable and shy. Their horses looked worn, as if, given a choice, they'd rather be rolling in the grass somewhere.

At dinner, Sarah told about seeing the cowboys in town and everyone grew silent. Was she not supposed to be in town alone? Booker and Jim covered the awkwardness with their tales of what the cavalry did to cowhands and Grady had his own tales of what cowhands did to the cavalry. When everyone had apparently got past the subject, Abraham took front and center to tell about the books he was reading, ones Sarah had chosen for him, and the men at the table grew silent again, their forks poised over Sarah's tender beef stew, contemplating this new development.

"Why would you want to read about the mammals of Australia?" Jim said. He didn't understand this at all.

"Because it's interesting."

"Where the hell is Australia anyway?"

"I could show you," Abraham said, "in my book."

"And this Robinson Crusoe book," Booker said. "It's right for someone who's still a boy?"

"It's an adventure," Sarah said. "And not easy. He won't get bad ideas from it, but he will get to a whole other level of reading."

"I suppose," Jim said, "the only bad ideas he'll get are from us."

Sarah laughed. "Maybe," she said with some affection. "But I doubt it."

"And what started you on all of this?" Grady said. "There's hundreds and hundreds of books in there and nobody's come asking for them before."

Abraham looked at Sarah uncertainly.

"He's going to tell you," she said, a note of caution in her voice.

Abraham put both hands on the table. "Because if Emma comes back I want her to know I'm educated."

"Emma?" Grady said, and he was echoed by Booker. Jim was speechless.

"I write to her," Abraham said.

"How old *are* you?" Grady said without thinking to ask if she had written back.

The dinner ended in another round of silence that made Sarah glow with happiness.

16

Sarah made sausage and buckwheat cakes for breakfast. She boiled the bed linens over firewood then hung them out to dry, emptied the wash basins, refilled the lamps, set bread dough to rise and felt she had earned some time with Tess. Grady had written into the ledger what the first calves paid and now he and Booker and Jim were out branding the remaining ones. There was also a ledger entry for ten geese to the butcher. Sarah didn't even want to think about how that had gone.

Instead, she went out to the barn. Abraham's horse wasn't there. Sarah considered that he must be out with the men learning the necessary lessons of life, like how to cut calves out of the herd or harvest geese or slaughter a pig. She was glad she could exempt herself from those same lessons. Jace had killed the pigs back home while Sarah ran screaming into the house with her hands over her ears.

Sarah walked past the cat snoozing on a bale of straw outside the barn. The cat watched her with one eye half open, ready to bolt at the least suggestion of human contact. She fed Tess an apple, saddled her up, and walked her out to the clearing. The road into town no longer held any attraction as travel in that direction seemed to invite disapproval. The road away from town led to Texas and was full of dust. They'd never explored the land along the river. Maybe that was a good destination for a sun-filled day.

Sarah mounted and rode Tess over the hill to the geese pond. From there she could see the outline of the river in the meandering line of cottonwoods. The trees' white billowy seeds were already beginning to blow out in the grasses. She led Tess down the slope along a cattle trail and then headed west. The river narrowed in some places, running clear and swift between steep banks. Grady talked about having to ford such rivers without knowing how deep they'd be midstream and Booker talked about how as a scout he was always the one sent to find out. It must be frightening, she thought, to suddenly be astride a swimming and panicked horse.

She rode farther along, to where the river widened and sand bars appeared. The cottonwoods leaned out as if they might tumble into the water. A frog croaked from deep in some watery hiding place. A flock of black ducks winged by swiftly, flying low. Tess's snorts flushed a covey of quail that exploded up in a mad rustle of wing beats.

Sarah sighed and ran her fingers through Tess's mane. She couldn't imagine a more lovely place or a better companion. Everything in the moment seemed just as it should be. She wondered if Ellen had ever taken time out of her relentlessly driven days to enjoy the river, its endless shifting currents, the sunlight cast into diamonds on its surface, the lulling rush of water over rocks.

Sarah dismounted and walked Tess across a narrow beach to the water's edge to let her drink. As Tess stepped gingerly into the water, Sarah turned downriver, shading her eyes against the glare. In the distance, the river went around a bend and the shoreline leading up to it was too heavily forested to ride through. She would have to find another path. As she moved her gaze farther, coming back along the shoreline, her eyes locked onto someone else's and she jumped, letting out a cry of surprise that startled Tess.

Elijah sat quietly on a rock shelf at the end of the beach, his line cast into a dark pool beneath him. He was so still that she could almost have gone right past him, except for his eyes on her. He'd obviously heard them coming from quite a distance.

"Thank God, it's you," she said. "Good grief, what would I have done if it was a stranger out here in the woods? I'd have been scared to death. Why didn't you say anything?"

"It would chase away the fish."

"Oh," she said. "But I did that already, didn't I?"

"A horse in the water doesn't help," he said. He motioned to a skin bag floating in the water. "I've caught about what I need."

"Can I see?"

"Help yourself," he said.

Sarah led Tess gently out of the water and tied the reins to a bush behind the beach's edge. She walked back to the water, her boots slipping in the sand, bent down and slowly reeled in the bag. Inside were six glistening trout. She tightened the drawstring on the bag and let it float back into the small eddies of the current.

"They're beautiful," she said. "I cleaned some like that for Diego just the other day."

"Bean was out here. That's why. It's his favorite spot."

"You know Bean?"

"He takes care of the horses when I'm gone."

"He does everything for everybody," Sarah said. "When you're gone, where do you go?"

"To meet with the traders. Out to the stage stops."

"The stage," she said. "That seems like a hundred years ago." She was quiet for a moment. "Can I sit down?" she said.

She was acutely aware of his capacity for silence and distance from other people. It seemed only wise to ask and not be offended if he said no. She herself had been thinking about peace just minutes before, and was now shattering his. It occurred to her how much she wanted someone to talk to. But then she said to herself, And *this* is who you pick?

"Somehow," Elijah said, "I'm fairly certain if I said no it wouldn't make a difference."

"That's not fair. It would."

"What I meant was, along the river is Grady's land, so I should be asking you if I can sit here."

"That's not fair either, so we're even."

Sarah climbed up onto the shelf. Nothing ladylike about that, she thought. But then as she stretched out her legs and sank back against the rock wall behind her, the sun began to ease into her, warming her skin.

"How is it with Tess?" Elijah said.

"So good," Sarah said. "She's my freedom." She realized she'd spoken too quickly and hoped she hadn't given up anything of what was troubling her. "We ride someplace different every day. That's how we ended up here. But the other day I went into town alone with her."

"And how did that go?"

"You know, don't you?"

"Maybe."

"I think people talked. Of course my mother would have been the first one gossiping around about what a scandal it was. I cut the bottom of my skirts off. I have my own horse. Even Booker and Jim didn't know what to say. But there are worse things in this world, aren't there?"

"Yes, there are."

"I thought this was the wild west. That's what I heard they call it and there weren't supposed to be any rules."

"I don't know about rules, but people's opinions are something you can't ever get away from."

"I guess that's true."

"I want to say something to you," Elijah said. "I'm sorry about your husband."

"Which one?" Sarah said and then immediately regretted it. "I apologize," she said. "I have a mouth. I was raised wrong. I know what you're talking about and I thank you for it. I'm sorry, too." He'd been listening all that time. "What can you do but go on and I'm trying really hard to do that."

Elijah nodded.

"And I want to ask you a question. Can I?"

Elijah still had his line in the water. He moved out and knelt on one knee at the edge of the shelf, sensing a fish.

"I could give you the answer before you ask the question," he said, his eyes still on the river.

"I hope not. That would be scary."

Elijah held out one wrist. "You're going to ask me about these," he said.

"Damn you, how do you know that?"

"It's who I am." He suddenly jerked his hand, bringing the line in a swift arc up and over the shelf with a glistening foot-long bass at its end. Sarah grimaced and quickly pulled her feet in as the fish landed in front of her. Elijah gracefully lifted the fish by its gills, removed the hook, pulled up the skin bag with one hand, opened the drawstring with his teeth and dropped the bass inside. Then he lowered the bag again and sat back down.

"Impressive," she said.

"Helps if you're hungry," he said. "You tend to figure things out faster."

She let a moment of silence go by. "You have to understand," she said, "that you're different from anything I've ever known about."

"You have to understand it's that way for me every day of my life."

The remark cut to her heart. She wanted to touch him in sympathy or caring, friendship, something, but was afraid it would be like touching fire.

He twisted one of the rawhide bracelets to reveal the part she was curious about. At the front, the tight thin strip of leather ran through a hammered silver medallion carved with the image of a turtle. He turned the others around on either wrist. All of them were the same.

"My grandmother was from the Turtle Clan of The Peaceful People," he said. "The People Who Live Upstream, my people, who weren't peaceful, took her in a raid and she ended up as my grandfather's third wife. My mother loved her but I always thought she was strange, maybe not exactly right in the head. Working in silver wasn't our way, only hers. My mother wore the silver turtles from the time she was small and I did too because my grandmother believed they were protection."

"The one Grady wears," Sarah said. "That's why, then."

Elijah would never forget that day, knotting the rawhide onto Grady's wrist while the trail bosses yelled, watching the blizzard come sweeping toward them across the plains, ominous in its fury, blinding as it overtook them, the face of death that they were too young to see. They tied their horses together, lost the herd, lost Grady's dog and yet they survived, looked at each other two days later when the snow stopped and the sun came out, and couldn't believe how lucky they were. He could still feel the pure joy of seeing Grady's tired face again and of both of them being alive.

The memory was hard. Elijah closed his mind against it. "That's why," he said.

She hadn't ever asked Grady about it, feeling as if too much of what she knew came secondhand already. This had been the person she wanted to ask.

"Are you surprised he still has it?"

"No. It was important to him. Besides, the rawhide tightens over time and you'd have to take a knife to it now. I hope he never does, he'd likely kill himself."

"I appreciate that you were willing to tell me," she said.

"It's nothing. It's in the past. I have to go," he said. "I have to find some horses I turned out to graze this morning."

Sarah glanced around. "Where's your own horse?" she said, puzzled.

Elijah let his eyes rest on her.

"I walked," he said.

Sarah took a moment to understand. "Your house is here somewhere." She remembered Grady telling her about the homesteader's cabin.

"Yes, not far through the trees. Walk back with me if you want to."

She wanted to very much. She had a curiosity for everything about him. Besides that, he was calm in the way of the perched hawks or the sleeping cat and now that she wasn't as afraid of him, she could see that she grew calmer in his presence, anyone would. She still feared though that he would turn suddenly and freeze her out, act as if she didn't exist as he had on the stage. She knew he was capable of it at any minute. So grab the opportunity, she told herself. It might not ever come again.

Sarah untied Tess's reins. Elijah retrieved the bag from the river. He led the way up behind the rocks and over a rise onto a wide shady path through what was almost forest. He walked more slowly so that she could stay beside him, leading Tess.

"Will you have the fish tonight for dinner?" she said.

"The bass, yes. I'll likely smoke the trout for later."

"This is another strange question…"

"Not from you."

"…but what do you eat?"

He shook his head.

"What do *you* eat?" he said. "The same things, what's available, whatever I catch, fish, hunt, grow. It's good country here, easy. Sometimes I go into town, see what's there. A couple times a year I'll give Jim or whoever's doing the cooking a deer and trade some things for that, potatoes maybe, or beans. I have tortilla corn from Texas, Diego gets it for me."

"What's a tortilla?"

"What the rancheros live on. It's thin, made of masa, you put meat, beans, rice, whatever you have in it. The *viejas* in Mexico sell them in the street but our old camp cook Rene taught me to make them myself. Grady never misses the tortillas. I do."

"Would you teach me?" She was amazed to find a food she'd never even heard of.

"Someday. Maybe."

"I'm the one in the kitchen now, not Jim."

"Then I'll bring you the deer."

Sarah pictured Elijah at the kitchen door, a huge bloody buck at his feet.

"I know how to cook," she said, "but no one ever gave me anything with antlers and said, Here, make dinner out of this."

"I'll gut it for you."

"Thank you."

"But then it's your job to tan the hide."

"And that would likely take the rest of my life to figure out. Hope nobody's waiting on it for a pair of pants or anything." She hesitated, moving on to other things. "Why don't you come to eat dinner with us? I know Abraham asks you all the time, he told me so."

Elijah was silent. She thought he was choosing his words. "With me and Grady these days," he said, "it's better to keep a

153

distance. He comes down when he needs something or wants to talk."

"There's so much food put up," she said. "It's almost a sin."

"I know, I've seen it. There's too much of everything. Who's supposed to sleep in all those beds or sit in all those chairs?"

"Not to mention the ghost. I feel like I meet up with her some way or other every day."

"That's at least half of what's going on with Grady. You're not difficult enough to make her go away," Elijah said. "And that's a good thing. For you."

They had walked a distance. Though the pace was leisurely, Sarah grew warm in the heat. She was glad when they came to an opening. Tess began to snort with pleasure, sensing the other horses. Sarah realized that she'd only missed the house before because it was set far back from the clearing, on a rise above the river and shielded from the lane entirely by the stables and the trees.

"This is it," he said. The cabin was solidly planked and chinked, with two stone chimneys, a sloped roof and broad porch.

"Not what I had in my mind," she said. "I heard about the homesteaders." She'd seen it run down and leaning, logs filled in haphazardly with mud, wind blowing through the cracks, tarpaper on the windows.

"I wonder sometimes," Elijah said. "Seems like somebody put a lot of thought into the building of it, too much to move right off unless they were paid good money, in gold let's say, to leave. Maybelline could do a thing like that. She likes her space. Go ahead in. I'll stay out here and clean the fish."

The mention of Maybelline made her anxious. Who *was* this woman? But at the moment, this was more important. Sarah couldn't believe she had permission to invade his privacy.

The front door stood open. She didn't dare move more than a foot inside and looked hastily, as if she were trespassing, which in a sense she knew she was.

The house was simple and uncluttered. Bright woven blankets covered the walls. A potbelly stove stood at one end with two chairs in front of it, a fireplace at the other end. She could see a rough hewn half-poster bed in one of the two small rooms beyond. Light poured in from the kitchen at the back. Sarah's curiosity was satisfied, for the moment anyway. She came back out and stood on the porch. Elijah was gutting the fish by the well.

"Where are your books?" she said.

"What makes you think I have books?"

"If you used to read in the library when it rained, then you must like books enough to have your own."

"Grady talks too much. What books I have are back in Texas."

"I sit in the library and read, too," Sarah said. For a moment she was lost in her thoughts, seeing the lamplight reflected off the glass in the middle of the night, remembering the bedroom upstairs. When she recovered, Elijah was watching her. "I could tell you the books I've read," she said bravely. "I could lend you the history of Egypt." Elijah hadn't stopped watching.

"I should go now," she said quickly. "Abraham writes to Emma and he says she's coming home. Do you think that's possible?"

"Anything's possible, but that would change everything."

"Tess?"

"No," he said. "Everything else."

That's what she was afraid of.

155

17

At dinner, Abraham had another announcement to make. He pushed away his plate that had not a trace of food left on it.

"I think it might be my birthday tomorrow," he said.

"You do?" Booker said. "How is that?"

The boy had come to him with nothing, not one piece of paper, no handwritten document giving any particulars as to his identity, his ancestry, his birthing, anything. This bothered Booker sometimes. The boy had made his choices but Booker felt now and then as if Abraham might have lost more than he realized. Booker remembered the father and would never send him back to that man. But the mother, where was she? And wasn't there likely an entire family, kin of all kinds? Abraham never would talk about that and didn't seem bothered himself.

And now he didn't even use his real name for which Booker was grateful. No one searching for Theophilus would stop at a boy named Abraham. Still there were nights when he sat bolt upright in bed and thought he heard the drumbeat of men on horses coming to get him, string him up, claim the boy, take him back. Booker didn't dwell on it too much, he was stronger than that. Just now and then, it came to him that way.

"Mrs. Grady told me tomorrow was the first day of June. That's when we did the planting back home, and that's how I knew when my birthday was."

Booker considered that back home must have originally been somewhere far north for that to be a planting day. "If you've got that all figured out, how old are you going to be when your birthday shows up?"

Booker and Jim had only the vaguest notion of how old they were, so this seemed like an amusing exercise, for the boy to be working at this puzzle.

"Either twelve or thirteen," Abraham said. "But that's a big difference, isn't it? I think thirteen's maybe way better than twelve."

"Well, then make yourself thirteen," Grady said. "That's not hard."

"But do I look going on thirteen?" He didn't want Emma to think he was lying.

"You look going on twelve," Jim said. Both Grady and Booker looked at him in amazement. Jim never had an opinion on anything. Sarah smiled and kept her thoughts to herself.

"Here's this," Booker said. "Why don't you say twelve and see how it goes? Maybe somewhere along the line, you'll wake up and feel like for sure it's thirteen and then we'll change it." Even Booker admitted that was the most ridiculous thing he'd ever heard, but what else were they supposed to do? He didn't want to come too close to the truth that someone out there knew and almost certainly had it written down in one of those big old family Bibles with the worn leather and thin gold-edged pages.

"I wish I had rings on me like a tree," Abraham said.

"What's happening to this boy?" Jim said. "It's all of them books he keeps on reading."

"I'll tell you about the rings if you want."

"That's okay, thank you very much," Jim said. "I'm happy with what I know about trees already."

"But no matter what, we'll have to have a celebration," Sarah said. "A grand dinner and a special dessert. And maybe we'll have dancing." Though she knew that would never happen. The idea of a birthday party, however, cheered her immensely. "For dinner," she said to Abraham, "what'll it be?"

"I get to choose?"

"Yes sir, you do." This was how her birthdays had been and she remembered every one of them fondly.

"Those ducks you made with the stuffing in them." Uh oh, she'd have to find Bean first thing in the morning. He probably had a rack of them hanging somewhere already, just waiting for her.

157

"Roasted onions, too? Maybe squash? Molasses bread?"

"Yes, please."

"And what for dessert?"

"If it's not too much trouble, I would choose custard pie."

"Nothing's too much trouble when it's your birthday."

Jim was beginning to think he would have to figure out a birthday of his own. "And I guess since you've got four parents, we could probably find some way to get you a present," he said.

Everyone looked at Jim again and then Sarah had to turn away.

"If I had to guess," Booker said and put his hand on the boy's head, "it would be a certain very fine white cowhand hat in the dry goods store."

Abraham thought again of Emma and all that he would have to do to impress her. "I wasn't aiming for a present," he said. "I just remembered about June first is all. But if there was going to be a present, that would be the best one I could ever think of in the whole world."

"Just so it's not a dern book," Jim said.

Abraham all at once brightened even more. "And could we play cards?" he said. "We haven't played cards in forever."

"Oh no, you don't," Grady said. "You're not pulling that trick again."

"I believe there'll even be some card playing," Sarah said.

Late that night, Sarah sat in the library in her nightgown, a book closed on her lap, staring out through the darkened windows. Every now and then a firefly rose up from the yard. Then Grady was standing in the doorway, handsome even in his faded summer long johns.

"Can I sit down?" he said.

"It's your house, you know. You can certainly sit down."

"It's our house."

"That notion might take some time to get used to." Especially when it still belonged to the ghost.

Grady sat in the rocking chair opposite her and then regretted it, because when he leaned forward, the chair went with him.

"I think," he said slowly, "that maybe a lot of notions are going to take some time to get used to."

"Yes," she said.

"And maybe you weren't ready for things to happen as fast as they did." His face was so earnest. She considered how easy it would be to fall in love with him, if only a thousand things were different. She'd quit trying to remind herself that she hadn't come here to fall in love with someone. She'd come here to make a marriage out of what was at hand, she'd known a whole lot of what that was, and still she was failing miserably. It wasn't something that made her proud. She wasn't keeping up her end of the bargain at all.

"That's possible," she said faintly, her head bent, concentrating on the cover of the book in her lap. It was a women's novel. She put her hand over the title.

"So I think maybe we should stay away from all of that for a while," he said.

All of what? she thought. Did he know? Of course, he did. It had to be more than obvious.

"I'm sorry," she said. She decided to be honest. "That would be a huge relief. I thought it would be okay."

"I told you he'd be here with you." She let him think that was it, dear dead Jacob. That's all she'd need, Jacob standing by the bed talking to her. She wished him into a far better place.

"It will be okay," she said, and somehow she would make it so. There he was in the rocker, uncomfortable, humble and concerned, with his sadness, his tousled hair, his heart of gold. It wasn't fair. "Thank you, Grady," she said.

Sarah blew out the lamp and they walked back up the stairs together. She would welcome the warmth of him in their bed, she liked the feel of his broad back and his feet when they touched hers. But she didn't have to worry anymore about the rest of it, or use the methods Jace had taught her. That had been most troublesome of all, what brought the tears over and over again, knowing what he wanted, knowing what she was doing. Not now, not with him, she kept thinking, and it made her hate herself.

159

How she would work this out, she didn't know, but she would find a way. He was a good man. They would create a life together, build it, make it good. She just needed time.

18

Sarah began to understand that Tess liked to move. It became her habit after every day's new variety of chores, airing out the quilts, shelling beans, churning butter, gathering eggs and helping Abraham milk the ornery goats, to take Tess out on the road to Texas and let her fly. Sarah prayed for rain for the crops, but only in the night, so that the road would have a chance to dry out before the afternoon and not clot into balls of mud.

She let Tess run as far and fast as she wanted. Then they cantered at an easy pace back toward home with Tess snorting and blowing and even prancing sometimes in what seemed to be sheer happiness. When Sarah became so easy on the horse that she could let her mind drift, she began to notice a familiar-looking meadow. One day, approaching from the south, Sarah recognized it as the overgrown version of the one where she'd first learned to get on and off Tess, and on again.

Despite the maddening frustrations of that afternoon, Sarah saw the meadow more conveniently now as another access to the river, whose banks were in many places impenetrable. She eased Tess through the high grasses teeming with grasshoppers, dragonflies and butterflies. An owl called, a strange and lonely sound for a bright afternoon.

The path opened onto the slope that led down to the river's edge. Out on the shoals, the current lapped up in small waves. She dismounted and let Tess drink. Turkey vultures with their broad dark wingspans circled high overhead. Lowing cattle aired complaints that echoed down the river valley. She bent down at the water's edge, gathered her skirts around her knees, leaned out cupping her hands and drank. Then she splashed the cool water on her face.

This rocky beach was longer than the sand beach. At its end, green cliffs rose into thick vegetation again. The shoreline was restless, not ever wanting to be one way for very long. She tied

Tess's reins to a low tree branch in the shade and walked slowly down the beach, her boots crunching on the water-smoothed stones and pebbles. If she climbed the rise at the end, she figured she might be able to see to the deep bend and maybe even some of where it went.

There was a perfect view at the top of the rise. There was also Elijah. He sat with his back against a tree trunk. Had he been watching her? It was an assumption she made without having to think about it. It seemed to be what he was put on earth for, watching.

"I'm disturbing your peace again," she said. "I have a gift for that."

"What you have a gift for," he said "is finding how to get to the water. There's a blue heron across the river in those shallows. He hasn't moved once."

Sarah squinted across the river. She knew she had good eyes, but she could barely see details of the other side, let alone pick out a blue-gray heron against the blue-gray water.

"I can't see him," she said. "I wish I could." There'd been great blues in the Virginia creeks, beautiful birds, tall and elegant, still and alert, like something from the Japanese silk screens in her mother's art books. "That's what you're doing here?" she said. "Watching the heron?" He could be doing anything and it wouldn't surprise her.

"I'm thinking about a horse."

"What horse? Can I sit down? I know we talked about this, but I'd just like to be polite."

"I gave up a long time ago on what's polite."

Sarah didn't know if that was yes or no, so she sat down in the grass anyway.

"Don't you have a lot of horses to think about?" she said.

"A trader brought this one out yesterday. It wasn't easy even getting him that far."

"Why? What's wrong with him?"

"He's hurt. Somebody tried to break him hard, that's what they do. They used whips. They tied him to a stake out in the

162

heat with no water or food. It's a test of wills and the horse has no chance, he can't win, but this one tried. All he got was damaged."

"Why did you take him?"

"Because you can't refuse if there's any hope at all, but this one I can't figure out. Not yet anyway. Nothing works. That's what I have to sit here and think about."

Sarah picked blades of grass and studied them. "Could you turn him loose?" she said. "Set him free?"

"Maybe. Then I'd have to decide if he could survive. In his condition, if he met up with the wrong circumstances he'd be dead in a day."

"What's your alternative?"

"I don't have one. There's got to be a way, that's all."

"Jesus," Sarah said, sounding more like her father than she would have liked. She shifted her knees and looked out across the river. "I have so many questions," she said.

"About the horse?"

"No, about other things. Where are your people?" She knew she couldn't unnerve him. He alone chose what he wanted to answer.

"It's not something I'd talk about," he said. "Because it's long ago, that's all. But you asked, so I'll tell you. They're dead and gone. All of them."

"What happened to them? Why are they gone but you're here?"

He was silent for a long time. "It's hard to explain to someone who's not from there," he said, "but I'll try. Turning from a child to a man was important. There were things you had to do, sacred ways you had to follow, a path you had to take, always the same. That's where I was when it happened, at that time in life, on that path, in the desert for three days with no food or water. When you fast like that everything changes, gets brighter, stronger, you see in a different way. I was still seeing in that way when I made the long walk back to the village. My family should have been there, my people, but it was only my grandmother running out

163

with a burning branch, shrieking, swinging it at me to keep me away. She said there was the white man's fever and I had to leave. I thought maybe this time she'd entirely lost her mind, but except for her shouting it was so quiet, no smoke from the campfires, no children anywhere. I went back into the desert thinking my father would come because he knew how many days. He never came. A white woman out rounding up stray cattle found me. She had water and saved my life."

"What was her name?"

"Dell."

"Grady told me about her."

"She found Grady, too, in that bad outfit he was working for. We became brothers. She and Conn were our parents and that was our life. She had a son, but she lost him, so I think in a way we took his place."

"How did she lose him?"

"He got in a gunfight over a woman when he wasn't old enough yet to understand what that would mean."

"How sad," Sarah said. And how useless, she thought, how stupid men could be, how much killing there was.

"At least she and Conn got to die of old age," Elijah said.

"I'm sorry," Sarah said. "Now I understand the things you've told me. Did you think you'd be driving cattle?"

"I didn't have any idea what would happen. But they knew I had to learn the white man's ways or I wouldn't survive in his world. They tried the school first, but I could never get used to the clothes, the desks, the teacher, any of it. Being a cowhand was a relief. It gave me a place to be. It gave me back horses. And there was Grady."

"Do you remember your people?" she said.

"Less as time goes by, but certain things you never forget."

Sarah considered this truth. She stared out at where the heron might be, remembering herself the things that she would never forget.

"Do you want to see this horse?" Elijah said.

"I don't," she said. "I cry too much as it is."

164

"I need you to," he said. He got up and held out his hand. She took it and he pulled her to her feet.

"Me? Why?"

"Maybe it won't work, but you'll see."

While Elijah went back into the brush where his horse was tied, Sarah renegotiated the rocky beach, mounted Tess and rode her up into the meadow. It occurred to her in passing that Elijah had tethered his horse where there was grass, and Tess had stones to munch on. But no time to dwell on that. Elijah turned and headed toward home. Sarah was proud of how easily she kept up with him.

They rode through the prairie grass, dismounted in front of the stables and Elijah went into the barn. He came back with a rope bridle. Despite her misgivings, Sarah peered into the corral. The horse was there at the very back, large but gangly, dark and covered in sweat. When the horse moved, the light revealed long wounds down his flanks.

Sarah winced. "Those look raw," she said.

"They're likely only days old. They need to make something back on their failure, so they get rid of the horse quickly, sell at a loss. He may even be sick. I'd know if I could get near him."

"What usually works?" Sarah asked.

"I can only say what's true. My voice and my hands, the same as it was for my father and for his father."

"Then what do you need me for?" she said. "I'm still as afraid of horses as I ever was, and especially that one."

"What is it that you smell of? Is it soap?"

"I hope it's soap."

"It's not a common smell, though." She supposed he knew mostly the lye equivalent cooked up in a vat or the soaproot the cowhands used, or didn't use, out on the trail.

Sarah hesitated. He was right, there was nothing common about it.

"It was part of my dowry," she said, aware that he might be unacquainted with this utterly important concept. "French, hand milled, lavender. It's lavender oil, too. But that's nothing. How could it ever help your horse?"

"If I can smell it, the horse can smell it. Maybe it'll throw him off, change his outlook. It's a possibility." The horse pawed the ground, watching them nervously from the other side of the corral.

Elijah looked at her. "Could I borrow something with that smell on it?"

Borrow something with that smell on it. What was he talking about? Then she thought she knew exactly what he was talking about. "Are you really serious?" she said.

"I don't want to leave this horse out tonight. I have to get him into the barn and that means finding some way to calm him down."

"I only have so much you can borrow," she said.

"Anything," he said, keeping his eye on the horse. The horse suddenly reared and circled the corral in a wild frenzy, his hooves pounding up clouds of dust.

"I'll be back," she said.

At the side of the barn, she hastily untied the innermost of her petticoats and slipped it off. She put the fine cotton to her face and inhaled. It smelled of lavender. She wondered what the soap makers would say if they knew its most notable beneficiary would be a horse. On the other hand, she had just gained the relative freedom that came with two petticoats instead of three.

Sarah returned and solemnly handed the garment with its folds and ruffled hem to Elijah. He never blinked or flinched. A frivolous piece of femininity turned instantly in his hands to just another tool in his horse-dealing arsenal. He had such a way about him that he didn't even seem odd holding it.

"I have one more favor to ask," he said.

The horse threw back his head and bellowed. Sarah looked back at Tess and saw that she was alarmed.

"Anything to stop that noise," she said.

"Sit on the fence with me. Over there where the wind comes from behind."

166

She was in too deep now. She followed him around the corral. When he stopped and climbed the fence, she did the same.

The horse was instantly alert to this change. He pawed the ground and bellowed again. Elijah handed Sarah the bridle. He took the petticoat in both hands and waved it. The horse stopped. Elijah let the garment fall to his knees, then picked it up and waved it again. The horse seemed to be considering this strange occurrence. He didn't charge, as Sarah was certain he would and she didn't even have a plan for how to react beyond falling off the fence. Maybe Elijah was right. Maybe there was something to be had here.

If lavender held the answer, Sarah could draw from another source. She reached up to open the tortoise shell clips and let her hair fall. Much of it had come down already in her ride along the road to Texas. The rest tumbled over her shoulders with what she'd once been told, by someone she loved, was the fresh, clean scent of lavender.

Elijah glanced in her direction, but said nothing. He turned back to the horse and spread the petticoat out on his knees. It could be taken as many things, he seemed to be saying, an invitation, a peace offering, a flag of truce.

The horse appeared to be interested. He came closer gradually, in fits and starts, two steps, then nothing, loud snorts and head bobbing, another two steps. To Sarah, the closer he got, the more frantic he looked. The horse stopped within arm's reach of Elijah, alert and focused, watching for any sudden movement that would send him fleeing back across the corral.

Elijah began talking softly. The horse pricked up his ears. Still holding the length of fabric in one hand, Elijah reached it out. The horse backed up two steps, then came forward again. Sarah held her breath. The horse was nuzzling the cotton. Gently, Elijah touched him with his other hand, stroking down the horse's forehead and nose, still talking. For one stunning moment, this was all there was to the world, the corral, the settling dust, and Elijah holding the horse with his voice, willing the frightened animal to stay.

167

Feeling more confident of the outcome, Elijah came slowly down off the railing and stepped into the corral. The horse didn't move. As Sarah watched, Elijah settled her petticoat over the horse's neck. The horse nickered softly. Elijah began the process she'd seen before with Tess, running his hands along the horse's neck, over his shoulders, along his withers and flanks until the horse finally succumbed, trembling with relief. She saw Elijah exhale slowly. He and the horse were now on the same side. Then she watched as Elijah secured her petticoat in a loose knot around the horse's sweaty neck.

Elijah reached back silently for the rope bridle. She handed it to him. Carefully, he placed it over the horse's head and settled the fit. Sarah started to climb down the outside of the fence, the job accomplished. As Elijah moved toward the barn, he turned back to her with a look that clearly said her role wasn't finished yet. She climbed down the inside of the fence instead, thinking, good Lord, I'm trained like the horses.

In the barn, Elijah backed the soaked but gentled horse into a stall full of clean straw and removed the bridle.

"What do I do?" she said.

"Stay at his head," Elijah said. "Touch him. Talk to him. I need to get something on these wounds."

The horse was bony, nothing like Tess, who seemed wide and matronly in comparison. Sarah reached up and stroked his head, then waited to see what would happen. Nothing happened. His anxious energy was spent. She laid her forehead against his nose. I'll trade you pain for pain, she told him, and meanwhile Elijah will fix what hurts you. The horse suddenly blew through his nostrils and moved against her as Elijah's hands tended to his flanks.

"You'll be all right," Sarah whispered.

Outside the barn, Elijah seemed as if a weight had been lifted from him.

"I'm in your debt," he said. "That had to be the answer, it was all I had."

168

She didn't understand. "Did you already know you were going to try it?"

"Yes."

"What if I hadn't stumbled into you?"

"That's what I was sitting there thinking about, how I was going to ask Grady for a piece of his wife's clothing."

"Oh my God."

"I wouldn't have done it quite that way. I was going to give you the tortilla flour in return, though Grady wouldn't be happy about that either. He got sick of tortillas a long time ago. Since you're here, do you want to know how to make them?"

"Yes," she said without any hesitation.

In the kitchen, Elijah shoved kindling under one of the grill plates on the cookstove and lit it, then went out to the well to wash up and get water. When he returned, he set a crockery bowl in front of her and another in front of himself. The learning process seemed familiar to her. This is how it went with Tess, she thought.

"Take this much flour," he said, reaching for a handful. She held her breath, not quite believing she was doing this. She took her own handful of pale golden flour and tipped it into her bowl. "Then water," he said, cupping his hands in the water from the well and she did the same. "Now mix."

She did, pressing and kneading. The dough was soft, not stretchy like bread dough, more like biscuits.

"Rene could do this in his sleep," he said. "I expected Grady to shoot him one day just to get it over with. No more hot sauce, no more tortillas."

Watching him, she broke off dough and rolled it into a ball that fit in the palm of her hand.

"Here's the hard part," he said. "The *viejas* make it seem like nothing."

"Viejas?"

"The old ones."

"What does Mexico look like?" Sarah asked. She couldn't get an image in her mind of such a place.

169

"Texas only dustier." He began passing his own small piece of dough back and forth between his hands. "To flatten it out," he said. "Make it a circle." In no time, he had a very thin round of dough. Sarah couldn't capture his movements. Her dough didn't make a circle and stopped growing thin.

"Takes time," he said. "Practice. Maybe thousands of tortillas, I don't know. But then one day it just happens. We'll switch. Take mine, the pan's hot. Cooks quickly, you only have to lay it down right in the skillet."

Switching jobs meant changing places at the cookstove, which was more awkward than it should have been. How could they be running into each other? Trading the tortillas was the same, their hands tangled up, unexplainably awkward.

Sarah was suddenly warm, as if the kindling in the cookstove had taken on a life of its own, as if in an instant the seasons had turned to high summer. A memory came to her, of watching him walk across the corral at the stage stop in that other lifetime, thinking then that he was beautiful. That he was so silent it was frightening. And set apart, harder than someone of his years should be. And how she had to look away. Which she needed to do again. Don't be foolish, she told herself sternly. It was nothing. She was nothing, only a woman who kept interfering with someone's privacy and was necessary for a moment because she smelled of lavender. She wished she could cool her face with the water meant for the tortillas, but that would likely make her seem odd.

She was aware that he had put some distance between them. He still held her misshapen piece of dough. Working it back and forth in his hands, he quickly transformed it into a circle. She still couldn't look at him. Please let this be over, she thought. She feared that he must have noticed how flushed she was, the one who missed nothing. It would only add to his opinion of her, a ridiculous woman even, who was afraid of horses and had married Grady McGuire on the strength of three letters.

There was silence. It occurred to her that she should do something with the tortilla in the pan. It was so thin it would

170

soon be burnt to a crisp. She could cook. She shouldn't need someone to tell her how to do this. But that wasn't what the silence was about.

She stood back as he closed the gap between them and reached in front of her. Using the tips of his fingers, he flipped the tortilla quickly out of the pan and onto the board.

Now she had to meet his eyes. "That's it?" she said, confused.

"Not it. Just the beginning," he said. "If I could, I'd say otherwise, but this is the problem that was going to happen."

He was serious. She'd become accustomed to the intensity of his gaze but now there was something different in it, and in his voice as well. She realized what the difference was, and how his words were causing the warmth. She recognized that in some quiet, hidden corner of herself, one that she didn't even want to admit to, she'd been closing her eyes tight to shut everything else out and allowing herself to think about this moment. Maybe even, God forgive me, she thought, hoping for it.

His eyes stayed on her face. She could feel the sudden pounding of her heart.

"I love Grady," he said. "But he's not my brother anymore."

"Why? What has he done?"

"So many things."

"But no one will tell me."

"It's in the past."

She thought of those first long sad nights alone with the books and deep shadows. Still, there was truth to be had.

"He's my husband," she said. Elijah nodded. This was the truth. "He's not at ease in his life." This was the truth also.

She studied the floor for a long moment. "It shouldn't be so hard," she said.

"What shouldn't?"

"All of it."

"Say no," he said.

"That's what I meant," she said, her voice faint. She was horrified that there was no one on her list she could turn to. Even Jace wouldn't understand. She braced for the lightning that was sure to strike her. The heat became a fire in her skin. She tried, shocked at herself, but 'no' wasn't one of the words that came to her. "I'm going to hell," she whispered. "I can't say it."

Slowly, light glinting off the silver at his wrists, he raised his hands. His fingers slid into her hair, his hands warm against her scalp.

"One last chance," he said. "Try. You have to."

"This can't be only up to me," she said. "That's not fair."

"You know already that nothing's fair. It's what life teaches you."

"I don't care anymore what life teaches you," she said fiercely. "I don't want to try."

She closed her eyes and let it happen. His mouth was warm on hers, gentle, as if she were not foolish but valuable, something to be treasured. When he stopped, she opened her eyes and let him see down into her soul if that's what he wanted. She still didn't say no. When he kissed her again, she wakened fully. The kiss was long and thrilling, joining her to him in ways she had never dreamed of. As the world fell away, she moved into him, her trembling hands clutching the front of his shirt. The feeling of finally being alive again traveled all through her in every direction, from his mouth that she wanted more of to the wild pounding of her heart, the tingling of her scalp where his hands still touched her, straight down to her toes curling tightly in their lace-up boots. She prayed that he would never stop.

Without warning, a deeper, almost unbearable, yearning rolled over her like a wave, like nothing she had ever felt before, and she couldn't find any way to fight it. Instead, she felt herself disappearing, sinking beneath the weight and force of it. Drowning in it. Her pulse roared in her ears. She couldn't breathe. There was no air. She refused to let him go, but her fingers weakened anyway. Thousands of tiny stars streaked across her vision. Dizziness buckled her knees. *What I deserve*, she thought in her last trailing gauzy piece of consciousness before everything went black.

When she opened her eyes again, Sarah found herself lying on the stone floor of the kitchen. Elijah sat with her feet lifted in his lap, his apparent remedy for bringing her back to the land of the living. She covered her face with her hands and wanted to die.

The going away had been so peaceful, those last few blurry moments. She vividly remembered the rest of it, though, and the heat rushed back into her face again until she felt she must look like a scorching ember. Which he also couldn't fail to notice, no one could. Now what was she supposed to do? Elijah's expression gave nothing away. He wasn't one to laugh, she understood that, but he also didn't seem concerned that she was ill or dying. Whatever was going on in his mind, she had to face this situation. She couldn't stay on his kitchen floor forever.

"I fainted," she said.

"I know."

"I'm sorry," she said.

"For what?"

"I don't even know."

"How are you now?"

"Embarrassed beyond what's possible."

"I didn't mean that way."

"I'm not done. Mortified. Chagrined. Humiliated for the rest of my life."

She took back her feet, flashing him with her petticoats, not that that mattered anymore either since now she had truly committed herself to everlasting shame and he owned one of them anyway. He stood up and held out his hand. She hesitated, fearing if he touched her it would start all over again and next time possibly lead to God only knew what. Something she couldn't dare think about, that was absolutely certain.

"It's all right. It won't," he said.

"Won't what?"

"Start again." He could read her mind. It was becoming clearer with every passing moment that she shouldn't even be in the same country with him. He took her hand and pulled her up. Though there was no doubt whatsoever in any way that the

173

kissing had to end, nothing could stop her from warming at his touch. It must be what the horses felt, she thought, that energy, that heat.

She straightened and took hold of herself, remembering that she was her father's daughter, a brave woman, but also a law-abiding one. In case she needed extra help with the sudden necessary and required task, she could feel Jace's strong hand on her shoulder, gently moving her toward the door.

Her eyes suddenly filled with tears. "I have to leave," she said. "*Right now.* And for good." She refused to admit what was in fact the truth. She didn't want to leave. Ever. She turned and ran.

Out in front of the stables, she hurriedly untied Tess's reins, mounted and urged her at a gallop through the tall grass. She knew this path well. It led home and home was where she needed to be. She would make dinner, turtle soup, cold meats, vinegar and turnips, fried bread. She would feed Abraham, Jim, Booker and Grady, laugh with them and care about them. She would lie beside her husband and listen for the night heron's call in the darkness, watch the moonlight slant into the room. Somehow, she would quiet the voices in her head, the chaotic beating of her heart.

19

Sarah threw herself into her domestic responsibilities. She scrubbed floors, baked yeast bread, planted an herb garden, cut up meat for the smokehouse, sewed a new petticoat and a soft pale green shawl with roses in it, put up preserves and pickles, made curded cheese and biscuits and honey cake. She started keeping the ledgers, her own hand adding to the others. She sat with Abraham over stacks of books and answered his every question.

"I think Emma's coming home soon," he said. "Can I help you make breakfast?"

"Of course," she said. Cooking had become another one of his options and eggs were his specialty.

"Because they're easy," he told her. "It'll make me look good."

"They aren't always so easy. And you don't have to look good because you are good." And Emma's not coming home, she wanted to say. She was beginning to think of Emma as a temptress, holding out these possibilities to an impressionable young boy to amuse herself from far away in California. Sarah knew how nice it was to get pretty letters that said things you wanted to hear. You could read those letters over and over and make up a whole world that didn't exist. The truth was nobody was fool enough to come back from California. People froze out on the plains or starved in the desert, but California had orange trees and streets that were paved in gold.

Sometimes, she liked to think of Jace in California. If they'd made it that far, they had a chance. Maybe I should ask Abraham to write to Emma and see if she knows anybody named Jace, Sarah thought. She ran the key along the chain around her neck.

<>

Sarah knew she had to avoid the river, but the afternoons with Tess meant too much to give up. She'd just have to go in the other direction, which would bring her along Jacks Creek and then back into town. She'd be more prepared now. In a moment of reflection, she folded the skirts she'd cut short and put them in a drawer. It was the right thing to do. She told herself she had no regrets.

The back way to the creek was a maze of paths, no open road, so Tess had to content herself with galloping across a meadow here and there among the tall grass. The creek itself lay open and exposed, just a lovely meandering byway with grassy banks and hidden pools underneath the cottonwoods. Sarah took Tess along every trail she could find, some made by game, some made by people.

One day, Sarah realized they'd gone past town, beyond the creek, and were now on the road heading back east, the road the stage had come in on. Tess saw the open stretch immediately, snorted and pranced, and Sarah turned her loose, leaning in close as they tore up the distance. But what should have been exhilarating was soon only distress. Sarah couldn't wait for Tess to wear herself out. Why? she thought. What brought that on? I love my horse and my horse loves to run.

Then it occurred to her. Going west was different. Every kind of possibility and unknown lay in that direction, every sort of challenge. Now and then on her rides, Sarah had come across a team of oxen pulling a wagon loaded down with hope and children, the rail-thin mother on the seat, the husband walking ahead with the dog, a horse and a cow tethered at the back. Who knew what stories they would have to tell? Good or bad, it all had the mix of courage and adventure that brought her back to the day she'd left Virginia. That was the problem, then, with the road heading east. It was like going back in time, unraveling the days, undoing the person she'd become, taking away the people who were now her life. There was only relief when Tess slowed and could be talked into heading back to where they belonged.

Along the creek, she came across Bean with a shotgun and a sack of quail. The thought of time with Diego became too hard

176

to resist. She followed Bean, walking Tess along behind him, until he came up beside the chicken coop and the kitchen garden.

Sarah tied Tess to the post outside the kitchen door and went in. Bean had put the bag on the table and Diego was there, a welcome and familiar sight, counting out the money. But Diego's face grew troubled when he saw her. He held up his hand for her to wait. When Bean left smiling, Diego came to her with so much sadness in his eyes. He put his arms around her and held her tight. When he pulled back, his eyes were filled with tears.

"Diego," she said. "What on earth? What's wrong? Is it Justine? Is it something wrong with Addison and you? Tell me."

Diego shook his head. "I have to wait till I can think better," he said. "It's not any of those things. In the meantime, if you don't have to be somewhere else right away, I'm always glad for your hands in my kitchen."

"Tell me what you need," she said. "Who's coming to dinner?"

"I don't know anymore. I just cook. It's the same as when you and Grady ate here, I think." Diego paused for just a moment, then continued. "The oyster stew," he said, "beef steak, grilled onions, dressed cucumbers, even the sugar meringues. That's what you can do if you want, *mija*. Slice the onions then start the meringues."

Sarah went quickly to work. "How is Justine?" she asked.

"I don't know," he said. "I'm exhausted."

"She's still here cooking breakfast, isn't she?"

"Yes."

"Then it will work out when it's supposed to."

"You are more confident than I am."

"And Addison?"

"She is happy. Their new hotel is close to finished and Smithy is there. This is good. Without the train yet, I would ride on horseback for miles, no, I would even walk, for a taste of his beautiful food."

Sarah didn't even recognize anymore what he was talking about, but she wanted to know. Instead, for the moment, she paid careful attention to the onions, slicing them thin and even, thinking how much Grady loved them. She paid the same attention to the egg whites, the making of which could kill a person, beating them hard and fierce in a copper bowl forever.

"My time is up," she said.

Diego nodded. "I love when I look up and you are there," he said. And his eyes filled again.

"What is it?" she said, growing far more concerned. "You have to tell me."

"I can't," he said. "I am hearing things, that's all."

Suddenly Sarah was quiet. "What kind of things?" she said.

"Very bad things. I am so worried, but I keep telling myself maybe they aren't true."

She felt the color drain from her face. "What kind of bad things?"

"I don't even want to think," he said. "Because I know they are not true. Because it is not possible for them to be true, I won't allow it."

"I swear to you," Sarah said, "I didn't do anything wrong."

Diego frowned. "What?" he said. "No, no, this has nothing to do with you. Well, I wish it had nothing to do with you." He choked back a sob.

"This is too much," she said. "I can't bear it. What are you talking about?"

"Nothing," he said. "It will turn out to be nothing." As a distraction, he opened the bag of quail. "Here," he said. "Bean is a crazy person and brings me sixty quail when I need only forty, though I love him to death. I give you whatever you want. How many are you feeding? I'm sure you've taken in Booker and Jim."

"And Abraham."

"Yes, him, too. Take twenty. Have a feast."

Sarah took out the money purse she'd begun keeping with her when she rode in these new directions, just in case she got the courage to go into town. She'd watched Diego negotiate and counted out enough to cover the quail.

"I am giving them to you," Diego said.

"And I am paying you for them," Sarah said, "because you are so generous, always." She put her allotment of quail in a separate sack and hoped the fresh smell of them wouldn't spook Tess.

Diego regarded her again in such a strange way. "Remember," he said, "that you are in my heart."

She shook her head. It was all too serious. "I'll remember," she said.

"You can't ever forget."

"I won't forget." Just please don't let this be about Elijah, she thought. Not anything to do with anything about Elijah.

20

In the morning, Abraham showed up to help cook breakfast wearing clean pants, polished boots, his best shirt and carrying his white hat and the book about Australia. Sarah stopped and stared at him.

"I'm asking," she said. "What's the occasion?"

"I already did my chores," Abraham said. "The horse stalls are mucked out and I did Elijah's, too." Sarah closed her eyes. "I milked the cows and brought in the eggs a while ago."

"I saw them," she said. "You're a wonderful young man, I hope you know that. But we haven't got to the occasion yet. You don't usually show up for breakfast in your Sunday best, not even on Sunday."

Abraham could barely contain himself. "I think this is the day," he said.

"What day?"

"The day Emma comes back."

"Abraham, you and I have to talk about this. If the truth were told, Emma's not likely to be coming back today or tomorrow or probably ever."

"But she is," he said. "She wrote me that she was."

"And when did she say that was going to happen? And how did she put it? Something like, 'I can't exactly promise you, but…'"

"No, she didn't put it like that at all. She said they were leaving four weeks ago and coming by hired wagons."

"What are you talking about?"

"She said it was going to be a great journey, they were crossing mountains and deserts and everything, but she couldn't wait to be home."

"And this is home?" Sarah saw that now she was asking inane questions because she couldn't fathom what he was actually saying.

"Yes, ma'am, of course it is." Of course it is.

"Who's 'they'?"

"Emma and Maybelline."

Sarah found that her hands were shaking.

"What sounds good for breakfast?" she said. "Let's start cooking something." The last thing she wanted was to get hysterical for no reason. She needed to calm down, talk this out, find some logical explanation.

"How about eggs?" he said as if it were a new option.

"Which way?"

"Scrambled, cause I'm nervous and that's easiest."

Sarah had an alarming thought. "She won't be here for breakfast, will she?"

"No, I don't think so. Later on." Later on? What did that mean?

Sarah had to get her mind back on the matter at hand. "But remember," she said, "the eggs need something else. What will you add?"

"Onions." He was good at chopping onions, too.

"And maybe some cheese?" she said.

"Yes, cheese."

"And bacon fat?"

"Yes, bacon fat." The good disciple, the excellent student.

"If you'll do that, then I'll cook up the rest," Sarah said. "How about biscuits and sausage?"

"Sounds right to me."

Sarah just wanted to keep talking, keep busy.

Grady, Booker and Jim showed up when the kitchen filled with the heady aromas of food frying. Grady lay down on the kitchen floor. They'd been rounding up sheep for the shearer the last two days, and this morning were chasing down the renegades.

"Are you okay?" Sarah asked, frowning down at him.

"I hurt everywhere," he said.

"He does," Booker agreed. "You'd think a person who grew up driving cattle could take on a few dozen head of sheep."

"I hate cows with all my heart," Grady said, "but I hate sheep even more."

Booker laughed. Jim seemed deep in thought, as if he was studying the difference.

Grady crawled up off the floor and they sat down to eat. Each reached out for a hand and they bowed their heads in thanks. It was a custom Sarah had insisted on. Maybe it didn't help but it couldn't hurt and besides it was one certain, peaceful, quiet moment in the day. With my family, she thought, and then didn't know what to think.

"Grady," she said, "or any of you, have you noticed Abraham today?"

"He's quite a sight," Booker said.

"Got himself a bath last night," Jim said.

"Grady," Sarah repeated, "do you know why?"

"You've got me, honey," he said. "I don't. But then I don't know why that boy does half the things he does."

Sarah took a deep breath. "He says Emma's coming home today."

Everyone stopped eating, but none of them wanted to challenge Abraham on such a delicate topic. Abraham ducked his head, suddenly shy.

"He does have a brain," Sarah said.

"All them dern books," Jim said.

"He can write letters, which he's been doing. And Emma's been writing him back. She says they're coming home. He thinks it's today."

"Who's coming home?" Grady said. "I don't believe it. What happened to the lawyer?"

"Emma says Maybelline doesn't like him," Abraham said. "He didn't turn out like she thought."

"They're in San Francisco," Grady said. "Who cares if she likes the lawyer? She's got enough of Pa's gold to do whatever kind of crazy thing she wants."

"Abraham says they're in hired wagons coming over the mountains," Sarah said. "Have you ever gotten a letter from Maybelline? Have you ever written to her?"

"Maybelline doesn't write letters, except for that last one about Ma."

"Maybe we should leave," Booker said. This was a conversation he did not want to be part of.

"You're my family," Sarah said. "Sorry, but you're not going anywhere. You either," she said to Jim, who hadn't been thinking of going anywhere.

"When was the last time you were at the post office?" she said to Grady.

"I don't go to the post office. There's never anything there. I learned that the hard way."

"Abraham," she said. "When's the last time you were at the post office?"

"Two days ago," he said. "Booker takes me all the time."

"It's true," Booker said. "I do."

"And Booker gets letters, too."

"We don't have to talk about that right now," Booker said. Wait a minute, Sarah thought, but everything was moving too fast to stop. Abraham put his white hat and the Australia book on the table. "I never considered Emma's letters, though," Booker said. "I guess I should have kept a closer eye on things. This raising-up business is tricky." He expected Emma had said more than she should have. He considered that Maybelline was like the Comanches. Her most successful tactic was always surprise.

"I have to tell you," Sarah said, "that I haven't been to the post office either." That was true also. What was wrong with her? "So if it's okay with everybody, as soon as breakfast is finished, I'm going to saddle up Tess and find out if there are some letters we maybe don't know about but should."

Sarah got through the speech intact, but was glad for Booker's understanding nod in her direction. He was already seeing very clearly the situation, likely more of it than she even knew, that Grady hadn't yet begun to comprehend.

183

"Good eggs," Jim said and Sarah wanted to hug him.

<>

Sarah rode into town without caring about the length of her skirts or the fact of being alone and on her own horse, and she rode fast. She only had one thing in mind, the post office and its shelves full of letters that came in from everywhere on the stage.

She tied Tess to the hitching post and hurried in. At the counter, she gave the clerk Grady's name and for good measure her own. The clerk came back with just one letter. It was for her.

"Are you sure this is all?" she said. He was sure. "No letters for Grady?" None for Grady. Now she was even more confused. What to do about these two who were flesh and blood and couldn't even write each other a letter?

However, she recognized Clayton's handwriting and immediately clasped her own letter to her heart.

Outside, she sat down on the board sidewalk with her boots in the dirt road. There were no niceties anymore. Maybe no one would recognize the woman who had cooked breakfast at the Russell Hotel or chopped off her skirts or got drunk by mistake at Maggie's saloon or got married with a black eye. If they did recognize her, that was their problem.

She pressed the folded out page flat on her knees and read.

Dearest Sarah, We received one letter, that concerning your arrival, are glad for your safety. But did you marry? Good Lord, Sarah, please do enlighten us as to these small details. And after that, how are you?

Here's how we are, at least at present. Miles finds practice of the law bracing, he says, by which he means dry and boring, but he will continue on. He is courting Abigail Owens without much success, and that is fortunate. Father is, I have to tell you, the happiest man on earth. Miles and I know since we live with him. It's rather disconcerting, but I think you would warm to her if you'd been able to stay. Though you know we will always, in every way, painful and otherwise, understand your going.

I am who I am, Clayton from the war, with a bad leg and a worse view of life. I am not courting anyone. I hurt. My dreams are hell. I miss Jacob every day. The only good thing is that he's often nearby and willing to talk. Do you find that? No, maybe not, especially if there's a husband involved.

184

The one thing that gives me peace is riding Stilwell, remember him?, that sorrel stallion so mean that no one could handle him? I can handle him now, we're both miserable and share a notion of the world as a hard place to be. He goes hell to leather fast and flat out and I get to keep my mind on that instead of everything else. What a blessed relief while it lasts. I'm sorry you had such a bad experience with horses. No one could ever understand how you kept falling off, even the saddle coming with you that once, and that you kept breaking your arm. I'm telling you the truth, horses are better company than most of the people I know. But then maybe that's just me.

Enough. I'm tired. Miles will write the next letter after Abigail finally rejects him as a suitor. She's after money and he has none, as Father looks to be around for quite some time yet. We love you, miss you, and really do need to know if you're matrimonially committed. Also, of course, if you are well and happy.

Hoping for both of those. Love you forever,

Clayton

Sarah folded the letter and put it back in the envelope. Her hands were still shaking.

"Was it good news?" a voice above her said. Sarah gave a start and turned to find Addison standing over her.

"It was from my brother," she said.

"Are you doing anything right now?"

"I'm sitting here not knowing what's going on at all."

"Time for a cup of coffee in the kitchen?"

"Yes," Sarah said, still mystified. She'd been so certain she'd find letters from Maybelline. "I have time for that."

"You have to make it, though."

Sarah laughed. "I can do that," she said.

They sat at the table where Diego had eaten his pork chops. Sarah thought it odd to be in the kitchen without him, but he did have to spend time somewhere else, anywhere else in fact, in order to maintain some semblance of sanity.

"How are you?" Addison said, holding her mug with ringed fingers.

"That's what my brother just asked. I forgot to write and tell them that I really did get married."

185

"You look like a woman with something on her mind."

"Abraham's been writing to Emma and he says they're coming home. He thinks it's today. Grady doesn't believe it. I thought there'd be letters for him at the post office, but there aren't any letters. I can't even begin to see what the future is if this happens. Thinking about it makes me want to throw up."

Addison was silent for a moment. The fears she and Diego shared were based on a whole other set of circumstances. This news came completely out of the blue.

"Why would Maybelline do that?" she said. "Nobody comes back from California." Though considering how headstrong that girl was, on the other hand, she could see her doing just about anything.

"Emma wrote that Maybelline didn't like the lawyer she was supposed to marry."

Something harsh occurred to Addison. "Sarah," she said, "did Grady write that he was married?"

"Grady didn't write anything. He's bitter that way. He said she'd never write back so why write to her."

"Good Christ," Addison said. "You believe it then?"

"Abraham's sitting in the kitchen with his new hat and a book, waiting. Doesn't matter how anybody else views this. He's sure about it. And because he's a reliable child, I'm feeling very nervous."

"And Grady's no help."

"No, but in matters of this kind, with his family and all, I wouldn't expect him to be. I knew that coming into it. He told me everything."

Addison gritted her teeth. No he didn't, she thought.

"I guess you just have to ride this one out and see what happens," she said. "I'd give you advice if I had any, but any situations I ever got myself into weren't like this at all. You're still lucky in that regard."

"What's she like?" Sarah said.

"Maybelline? She has Grady's sweet side, but she's tougher. Not like her mother, though, not hard and cold like that. And the thing is, she missed Grady every day. They all did. He should have said the hell with Ellen and come home sooner. Then things would've been different."

"Then I wouldn't be here."

"Then maybe you'd be here with a person much easier to be married to." And one who hadn't managed to get himself into so much trouble.

"At least there are enough bedrooms," Sarah said, trying to feel her way through the rising panic.

"True. I always thought that place would make a good hotel."

"I didn't even ask. How are things going with you and Mr. Russell?"

"Very well, thank you. Mr. Russell's money keeps appearing, that's all I ask."

"Still no to marriage?"

"That's a never to marriage. My life is fine just the way it is. It's yours we have to get taken care of." Addison hesitated again. "If you need anything at all…" she said, and stopped till her voice was under control. "Anything, I don't care what it is. Listen to me, I couldn't be more serious. I'm here. Just ask. I have to know that you will."

The look on Sarah's face was one of puzzlement. "I will."

"Good," Addison said. "I appreciate the coffee. Now go." And please come to me…but her concentration quickly broke. The immediate future was too difficult to contemplate.

21

Sarah devoted all her attention to making lamb stew for dinner. She'd hung Bean's quail in the smokehouse. They could wait. She had no patience at the moment for the arduous task of singeing and plucking. She needed something on which she could fully focus her thoughts with quicker results.

She started by roasting bones to deepen the stock she kept on the back of the cookstove. Then she made up bread dough and set it out to rise. She methodically cut up the lamb shoulder into cubes with Grady's sharpened cleaver. Once tossed with flour and browned, the cubes of meat joined fried up garlic and onions simmering in the stock. Sarah went back to the bread. She punched the dough down and began the second kneading, leaning heavily into the calming rhythm. A lemon cake for dessert was easy. Thank God for the kitchen, she told herself, holding back the fear that everything was about to change and the kitchen would no longer even be hers.

Closer to dinner, she cut up potatoes, carrots, more onions and added them to the pot. The aroma of baking bread filled the room. Even the cat nosed up against the screen. There was nothing left that she could do to make things happen differently. Grady, Booker and Jim came in from the fields, slamming the door and scaring off the cat. Today they'd been moving bales of hay to the loft. Abraham came in from wherever he'd gone hiding so as not to ruin his good clothes. He was whistling. Sarah smiled a shaky smile.

Everyone went back out and washed up, then sat around the table. Sarah ladled out the rich, hot stew into wide crockery bowls. She laid the bread on a board and cut it into slices. They sat and joined hands. Sarah said grace while listening for the sound of horses in the courtyard.

Dinner was quiet. Abraham couldn't talk and the others wouldn't. The air was heavy and humid as if a storm were coming. Sarah hoped it would be a thunderstorm. Even though thunder and lightning spooked the animals, it would suit her mood.

"Best lamb stew I ever tasted in my whole life," Jim said. Grady passed him another piece of bread.

"I'm in agreement with Jim," Booker said. He smiled, but the smile quickly faded. Inside he felt ill at ease. If this all was true, who knew what changes it would bring. He and Jim were each capable in their own way and could find other work, cattle driving if they had to, or ranching of some sort if they could get some land. Maybelline presented a difficult situation for him personally, but on the face of it, she was fair. Abraham was the worry. Booker would want always to do what was best for the boy. Then Booker shook himself awake. Nothing had happened yet, no need to be planning for a made-up future that didn't exist.

Then it did exist, or something like it. A horse, but only one it seemed, galloped at high speed up the lane, the sound easily audible through the open kitchen door. The front door slammed open then shut again. Before anyone could react, Diego was racing down the wide hall, past the drawing room and library, past the long dining room, running full out and breathless into the kitchen. As everyone sat wide-eyed and Sarah rose from her chair, he burst into tears.

"My God," Sarah said. "What's wrong? What are you doing here?" It was the dinner hour. He should have been putting the finishing touches on a meal for the guests in the hotel. There wasn't anything she could see that would make him literally abandon his job.

"I need to sit down," Diego said. He pulled out a chair at the end of the table, put his head down and sobbed.

"*What?*" Sarah said, her voice rising. She was almost screaming. It didn't occur to her that the others had been stunned into silence. They wanted to be expecting something else, not this.

Diego lifted his head. His expression was wretched, his face wet.

189

"Grady," he said. Jim had turned sorrowful, Booker quietly furious. "He's coming. It's not good. I couldn't stop him."

"Who's coming?" Grady said. "How many?" His voice was barely a whisper.

"Five." Diego hung his head. "No, I mean six, if you count…"

"No," Grady said.

And then Diego was angry. "What did you think would happen?" he said. "I told you. I told you about all of it, how it would be. You never listened to me once."

"I tried," Grady said. "I did everything I could."

"It doesn't matter. He doesn't want to hear that. You've been in my country. You know how it is. It is his daughter."

Sarah turned back and forth from Grady to Diego. At Diego's last words, Grady went pale. He folded his hands and bowed his head against them.

"This can't be happening," he said.

"It's not good," Diego said again. Then there were wagon wheels in the courtyard and the clatter of more hooves. Sarah looked questioningly around the table. Abraham hastily put his book and white hat under his chair. Jim and Booker stared hard at Diego. Grady sat with his head in his hands.

A shotgun blast echoed through the house in concert with the sound of splintered wood.

"Shit," Grady said. "He just blew out my front door." Sarah rose in alarm but Booker put a hand on her arm and she sat back down.

The person with the gun stomped heavily down the hall and appeared in the entrance to the kitchen. He was a stout man with silver gray hair and a darker moustache, wearing a black suit and starched collar. "Introduce me," he said to Diego. His accent was heavy, his voice made of gravel.

"This is my father," Diego said. "Hector Juan Garcia."

"Tell them what I did."

"He was a chef in the kitchen of the French ambassador to Mexico."

190

"Did you hear that?" Hector said. "Me. One of the ambassador's chefs. I am known for my food, for my family, for my cultivated ways. And then this. Point him out for me."

"These are good people. They are my friends," Diego said. "First I tell you their names." He gestured around the table. "Abraham, Jim, Booker, Sarah." He nodded toward the end of the table. "Grady McGuire."

"Bastard," Hector said. To make his point, he swung the barrel up and fired a shot into the ceiling. Grady watched as plaster rained down. Sarah began to shake. Why didn't anybody do anything?

Hector brought the barrel down and pointed it at Grady. "Bastard," he said again.

Booker stood up slowly from the table. He wiped off his hands and put down his napkin. As he moved, he started talking.

"Sir," he said. "If anyone was thinking to shoot Grady, it would of been one of us and that hasn't happened, so no way is it happening now." Booker reached out and took the gun without any protest being made. He emptied the shells out onto the floor and threw the shotgun out the back door.

Grady sat as still as a stone. The hole in the front door and the plaster coming down from the ceiling were of no consequence in the larger scheme of things. He almost wished Hector Garcia had shot him. It was the part coming next that was going to kill him anyway. And then there it was.

What was that sound? Sarah thought. Her mind was all tangled up. Nothing made sense. Hadn't they all just missed being killed? Who was this man? If Diego's father was an ambassador's chef, why was he here shooting things? As it grew more distinct coming nearer, Sarah recognized the sound. It was an infant crying.

Hector's traveling companions entered the kitchen together. Diego wiped his eyes with his sleeve.

"This is my mother, Juana Maria," he said, gesturing toward the broad woman wrapped in a shawl and wearing large pieces of silver jewelry. "This is my youngest brother, Hernando." The shy

boy seemed overwhelmed. "This is my next brother, Juan Pedro."
Then Diego was at a loss, but Hector was not.

"I will make the introduction," he said, "though none is
needed." The young woman behind him stepped over the fallen
plaster and into the center of the kitchen. Everyone's eyes were
on her. She had olive skin, dark eyes, black hair pulled back, and
wore her mother's same exquisite pieces of silver. "This is my
daughter, Beatriz," he said. In her arms she held a small weeping
baby girl with dark golden curls. "And my gringo granddaughter,
Maria Elena."

Grady said nothing, did nothing. All those many months, he
had wondered. He tried to send Diego to find out, even offered
to give him a horse if he'd make the journey. Diego wouldn't go.
Diego didn't want to know. He'd had more than enough of
Beatriz to last a lifetime and thought Grady should feel the same
way.

Grady had given up then, thought he would never know. She
left in the middle of the night while he slept out in the bunkhouse.
She had traveled with those damn religious and told them some
story of why she was going to Mexico alone and already showing.
He caught up with them, but they wouldn't let him see her. His
failed dream had been to find the baby if one had come to be
born. His nightmare was to ever meet up with the mother again.
Now here she was in his kitchen and her father had just shot up
the ceiling, and her mother was here, too, and these brothers,
what to do with them? But his eyes could not leave the child.
Maria Elena. Of course, he thought. Shove the knife in me and
twist it.

Sarah took in the sight. She waited to feel something. She felt
nothing. He should stand up and say, This is Sarah. This is my
wife. She wanted very badly for him to make the gesture, afford
her that courtesy, offer her even that small amount of dignity.
Watching his face, where his attention was placed, she could see
that his thoughts weren't turned the least in her direction, and a
vast sadness came over her, a gulf between them that it seemed
would be impossible to bridge. She looked down at the table,

192

trying to remove herself. Clayton came to mind, his letter, the last good thing that had happened to her. For one brief moment, the room began to tilt.

Then two things happened at once. Booker reached out, took her hand firmly in his, and she could feel his strength running through her. And yet another wagon pulled up in the courtyard.

"Jesus Christ," Booker said. Abraham dove under his chair for the book and hat.

"Can it get any worse?" Grady said.

"Yep," said Jim.

"We are going to make some decisions," Hector said. "In which you will have no say."

Grady stood up. "Hold on," he said. He ran his hands through his hair. "There's more coming."

Maybelline stopped at the front of the house. They could all hear her. "What the hell?" she said. "Who shot up the door?" At the entrance to the kitchen, she stopped again. Quickly she assessed the situation, chalking up who she knew and who she didn't know. "Beatriz!" she shouted. "My God, is it really you? I heard you left. Are you back? And who is this?" Maybelline reached out for the little girl, but Beatriz stepped back, keeping one eye on her father. Maybelline was instantly on the alert. She peered at the baby more closely. "No," she said. "Oh please don't tell me. What's her name?"

"I will tell you her name," Hector said, lifting his chin. "It is Maria Elena."

"I can't even deal with that yet," Maybelline said. "Diego, is this your family?"

"It is."

"All of them?"

"Well, all that's here. There are so many more." Thirteen, to be precise, but now was not the time. "This is my father, my mother and my youngest brothers. They have come from Mexico."

193

"Who shot a hole in the ceiling?" Maybelline asked, and then thought better of it. "Doesn't matter," she said. "Never mind." Slowly she moved her full attention to Grady.

"Welcome home," he said.

"I love you," she said.

"I love you, too."

"But seriously," she said. "What the hell?"

"Did you find Pa?"

"We'll talk about that later."

"Maybelline," Grady said very carefully. "I want you to meet my wife." Diego's mother asked what the gringo had said. When told, she gave a harsh laugh and spit on the floor.

Sarah rose slowly. "Maybelline," she said. "Diego." She looked first at one and then the other. Diego burst into tears again. She was moving now. "Jim," she said, and put a hand on his shoulder. She bent down and kissed Abraham's head. "Abraham," she said softly.

The lamb stew sat half-finished in the bowls, the bread in slices on the board. The aroma of both filled the kitchen, along with the charred scent of gunpowder. Sarah took a deep breath. Keeping her eyes focused on her trembling hands, she removed her wedding ring and set it in the middle of the table.

"Booker, can you help me, please, get into town?" she said, her voice faltering. Again, Juana Maria asked for a translation.

"I'll bring the buggy around," he said. Actually, make it the buckboard, Sarah thought, but what would be the use of that. It was too easy.

She walked away from the table, past Diego without another glance, it would be too painful. She averted her eyes from his father, mother, brothers, the woman with the dark eyes, the tiny girl. She exchanged a look with Maybelline that could only bear so much weight, stunned grief on one side, wide-eyed amazement on the other. Maybelline's well-fitted attire, Sarah couldn't help but notice, bore a close resemblance to Addison's. Emma stood out in the hall. She still had the aspect of a child, but her squared shoulders gave notice of the woman she would soon become.

Sarah silently wished Abraham well. Grady might have called out her name but it was faint and from a place very far away.

Upstairs in the room they had shared, she packed only the necessities, what came to mind first. The rest would have to wait. She knew she was numb, carried along on the currency of shock that gave her mind a ringing clarity, framed everything in sharp edges, bright colors. She heard Booker bound up the stairs. She opened the door and handed him a suitcase while she took the valise. She pulled the letters out of their hiding place in the drawer and left them on the dresser. No need to save them with some hopeful future in mind, not unless Maria Elena wanted to read them one day.

In the courtyard, Booker stowed her bags under their feet in the buggy and handed her up into the seat. He climbed up beside her and moved the horses into a fast trot. The rain started when they were halfway into town.

"We're going to get wet," Booker said.

"That's fine by me," Sarah said. The daylight faded prematurely as dark clouds raced across the sky. Sarah remembered the first trip out along this road, putting the top down, seeing the jackrabbit leaping through the tall grass. She thought of the stage and how strange it had been trying to regain her balance after that rough jolting ride. Now she felt as if she'd been run over by the stage, crushed by those iron wheels, trampled by the laboring team of horses. Tomorrow she would surely ache everywhere.

They journeyed in silence. Booker was that way, as good and steady a companion as one could ever want, especially in times of trouble. She knew that whatever he might be thinking, he would not say it.

By the time they reached the hotel, the rain was coming down hard. Booker helped her out and she stepped up onto the covered porch. He brought her bags while the horse stood dripping. Inside, the gas lamps had been lit.

"Where do you want me to put these?" he said.

"Just here for now."

"You have a place to stay?"

Sarah hoped Addison's words were true. "I do," she said. "Thank you, Booker." Her voice faltered again. "I can't bear the thought of losing you."

"We can't come up against that just yet," he said.

"All right."

"You do have a place to stay, now," he said again. Sarah nodded. Only a short time ago she was cooking lamb stew. "I want to see you in," he said.

"I'm fine," she said. "I'll just sit here on the porch a while."

Booker didn't trust anything that was going on with her. She seemed to be in a daze. But he had to get back. There were things he had to deal with as well. He held her hands hard, his anger searing into her soul. Then he climbed into the buggy and was gone.

Sarah watched the buggy's dark, rain-slicked silhouette quickly disappear in the downpour, its driver taking with him every last small bit of happiness she had, leaving her with nothing. She felt run over but also emptied out. Life was a blank wall. She felt the chair she was sitting in. It was one of those that Grady had dragged out back so they could talk and be private. The thought of him made her shudder. He'd gone on to her list that was only two people long and he was first, above the county clerk.

She was glad it was warm and there was no wind. The rain sheeted straight down, making puddles in the street and dripping in a steady curtain off the porch roof. Then there it was, a swift crack of lightning and many seconds later, the rumble of thunder. The heavens were coming apart too. Small consolation, but it was something.

A shadow appeared in the frosted glass and then the brass fittings gleamed as the heavy hotel door opened. A shaft of muted light crossed the porch. It was John Russell, after-dinner cheroot in hand, coming out to smoke in the rain. He frowned, obviously taken by surprise, maybe trying to place her. She wondered if he would recognize this drowned pack rat sitting out here for no reason beside her luggage.

196

"Sarah Mayfield," she said. That wasn't right, but she would never speak the other name again. She hoped this name would jog his memory since he'd been forced to sit through the telling of her life like everyone else.

"The stage," he said.

"Yes," she said.

"I won't ask why you're out here in the rain."

"Thank you."

"Do you mind if I take the other chair? I was going to have a smoke."

"I don't mind," she said.

He tested the seat with his hand. It was still dry. He sat like the wealthy gentleman he was, one knee of his pressed trousers resting on the other, his polished boots shining in the reflected light. The match flared, showing his sharp-planed face and immaculately trimmed goatee. Then the match went out and only the cheroot glowed in the dark. Sarah wondered if there would be conversation. Surely they had not one thing in common.

Just when she was getting used to the silence, he spoke.

"I was in the war," he said. Oh Lord, that's where they were going?

"I suspected maybe you were," she said.

"I'm sorry about your husband."

Everybody was sorry about her husband. Now they could be sorry about two husbands.

"I honor men like him," he said. "I sat in a tent with a staff sergeant to cook my meals and an orderly to polish my boots. I read maps. I gave orders. When I was wrong, do you know how many men died?"

"Sir," Sarah said, "the war's over."

"You of all people should know, it won't ever be over."

"I agree with that. Especially where I'm from, you're right, it won't ever be over." She had to deal with him quickly or lose her sanity.

"I don't mean to be rude," she said, "but I've got so many things to cry about right now that I don't think I can take one more."

"Understood." There was more silence. "Wait," he said. "Forgive me. You make the good French coffee."

"And cook with bacon grease." She considered that to someone like him the help must often be faceless.

He exhaled a long, satisfying stream of smoke. "Ah yes," he said. "Those breakfasts. Who would have guessed?"

Anybody in Virginia, she wanted to say, but didn't. He pitched the end of his cheroot in an arc out into the street where it would be trampled into the mud. Sarah could feel his hesitation.

"Is there anything I can do for you?" he said. She must look truly pathetic, she considered, if she'd pushed John Russell to the point of sympathy.

"I imagine sooner or later I'll need to talk to Addison," she said. "Is she here?" Then it occurred to her what a stupid question that was. Addison could only have the privilege of spending John Russell's money if she kept him nearby. Another flash of lightning lit up the frame buildings of the town, with thunder close behind it, echoing out over the dark hills.

22

Addison led her up to the small room at the back and opened the door. The room was ready and waiting for her. Sarah couldn't think clearly enough to read the implications in that fact. The night porter brought up her bags and at Addison's bidding hauled up enough hot water for a bath. While Sarah got out of her wet clothes, Addison went and fetched soft towels and her own silk wrap.

"Do you want to talk?" she said.

Sarah shook her head no. While Addison realized she held the strongest of emotions concerning this situation, she never could abide silence. There was no information in it. She'd feared, they all had, that this would occur. Keeping the possibility in the back of their minds didn't prevent the shock of hearing from Diego that the day had come. But she couldn't rest until she knew what had actually taken place, who'd said what, whether Grady had survived. Sarah obviously had not. Could she at least ask a question about Maybelline? No, she told herself, she could not.

Sarah found nightclothes in her valise and welcomed the warmth of Addison's wrap. She sat down in the rocking chair by the darkened window. Addison perched uneasily on the edge of the bed, elegantly dressed as always. She wouldn't tell Sarah that when a rider came with a message for Diego and he bolted from the kitchen, she finished cooking the meal herself. She was very proud of that. John Russell, usually oblivious to all crises but his own, had even helped her a little, though the kitchen was a very foreign place to him. She'd been glad for the addition of Elmira's familiar, boisterous presence. Otherwise, the domesticity might have stuck in her throat like a chicken bone.

Sarah took in the room. Everything was familiar. She distinctly remembered being happy here, with all of her life ahead of her. That's what she kept reaching for but couldn't grasp, that she was back, in this same room, and every understanding she had, every person she believed she knew had disappeared, leaving her with only ideas and people she didn't know at all. We said vows, she thought. I slept beside him and none of it meant anything.

She watched the rain stream down the panes of glass. The window was open just a fraction and the air smelled fresh and clean. A deafening crack of lightning broke immediately into thunder that shook the building. The storm must be directly overhead. How would she sleep? How could she pull up the covers and pretend this was just another day? Surely at some moment all the details would come flying back at her and she would cry. But not now. Now there was only the rain and this room and the scent of grass and no thought of the future because there was no future.

Addison waited. She was not adept at ministering without words, or even with them, for that matter. An arm around the shoulder? What good could that possibly do? She'd gotten through plenty without those meaningless gestures. What she dealt in were unvarnished truths and harsh realities. However, with the pain clearly visible in Sarah's face, she could see that unvarnished truths would not, at the moment, be useful.

"Do you want some wine?" she asked. That was her only other solution. "Mine's French, won't knock you off your feet like Maggie's."

Sarah flinched and Addison realized that she would have to be much more careful. Even that reference was a mistake.

"No wine then, I guess."

Sarah shook her head no. "Thank you, though," she said, and Addison considered it a hopeful sign, the voice, words spoken.

"Did you know?" Sarah said. "Did you all know?"

Addison wondered what she could possibly do with that question. There was no answer that wouldn't cause even more pain.

"We'll talk about that later," she said, and was amazed to find that her voice had a note of true gentleness in it. "It's better than what you're thinking." It was what she had to offer, not a lie, hopefully not artful or deceiving. We were all on your side, she could have said, and that would be the truth. "I'll be in my room if you need me." She considered a moment. "And John Russell won't be there, if you want to be assured of that, if it makes a difference on whether you'd open the door or not." He was meticulous, almost finicky, she reflected with some distaste, didn't like the scent of her perfume on the sheets.

"All right," Sarah said, but it was just words.

"Can I send Diego up with breakfast?"

Sarah almost jumped out of her chair. "No, please," she said. "You've been so kind, but please don't let that happen."

This careful business was going to be more difficult than she'd imagined. But then Addison considered that she was careful around John Russell all the time, so that's what she'd have to learn to do here.

"I won't let that happen," she said. "I promise. Get some sleep."

"I have no way to pay you back," Sarah said. This was the woman who had saved her at every turn.

"That's fortunate," Addison said, "because I wasn't ever expecting one." She closed the door softly. Bastard, she thought. She would kill him if she could, tear out his heart of gold and feed it to the dogs.

<>

Sarah was tired but had no desire to give herself up to sleep, to dreams that would be as bad as wakefulness. She sat and rocked as the storm moved on, thunder rumbling far off in the distance. The rain faded to a gentle patter on the windowsills and downspouts. Hours passed. The room was pitch dark. She got up and felt her way to the bed. She slid in under the down duvet, cushioned in Addison's luxurious linens. She pulled up her knees, folded her arms, tried to make herself small. But as soon as she closed her eyes, as she had feared, she was back in that room with all those people. She lay on her back staring into the darkness until the sky began to lighten.

She remembered standing out on the back porch and watching the sunrise, bringing in the warm milk that Bean left, frying up ham with onions and gravy. None of these things would ever happen again and she wished them back. But then she would be in the same situation as now, come so far with nowhere to go. She decided that she didn't regret any of it, right up to when Hector Juan Garcia shot apart the front door. She regretted everything after that, all of it.

She seemed to have grown heavy. Her limbs were a weight she could hardly bear. She felt weak just trying to move around. She crept back to her seat by the window. As she watched, the chickens burst out of the coop all at once in the odd way they had, squawking, feathers flying. She wanted to laugh, but instead her eyes welled up with tears. Was this the way it would be, everything that had made her happy would now only cause her sorrow?

I have dealt with this before, she told herself. But that hurt was entirely different, an unconscionable loss, irrevocable but at least understandable because it was from the very beginning half-expected. This loss had blindsided her. Even in her moments of doubt, she clung to the trust she'd placed. Here she was now, trust shattered, her life turned completely inside out, yet she had no comprehension of the surrounding events. She curled up in the rocking chair, cradled her head in her arms and longed to disappear, dissolve into nothingness.

Sarah looked up at the knock on the door. She had to believe in Addison. Maybe it was not Diego but John Russell. Maybe he had thought to cook her breakfast but would retreat at the sight of her wild tangled hair and the bruised dark circles under her eyes.

"Come in?" she said. Her voice was raw. The door inched open with a small sound to reveal Justine, her huge eyes uncertain, tentative with the tray of food she was carrying. The tears rose up again unbidden. There was nothing Sarah could do to hide them. Justine set the tray down on the tiny table next to the rocking chair. On it were a plate of bacon and eggs, cornbread with butter, a bowl of strawberries and a small jug of fresh coffee.

202

Sarah pulled the silk wrap more closely around her. She bit her lip, not knowing what to say. She was afraid if she tried to speak, the tears would become a torrent. She couldn't keep pressing this sadness on other people. It was hers alone to carry. Instead she stared into those amazing dark eyes and hoped that a love for Diego could be found there. Justine, strong as she was, blushed at the scrutiny. She's too young, Sarah thought again, younger even than the seventeen-year-old she herself had been when she fell in love with Jacob.

After a silence that seemed full of confusion and understanding at the same time, Justine smiled slightly then backed out and closed the door behind her. Sarah got up, and because she didn't trust herself to carry the whole tray, moved the plates one at a time to the dresser where they would stay, the eggs growing cold, the bacon leathery, the cornbread dry. She poured the coffee and sipped it, appreciating the strength and bitterness.

At midpoint of the morning, Sarah got dressed. Why, she didn't know. She had no intention of going out. Likely, she acknowledged, her mother's views came once more to bear on her behavior. None of the people in her mother's circle of friends sat around in their nightclothes. They could spend the whole day writing inadequate poetry or playing the piano poorly, but there was always proper attire involved. With the window opened wide, Sarah returned to the sanctuary of her rocking chair.

Glad for the distraction, she focused her attention on the pigs. They ran wild, rooting along in every direction, but never venturing very far afield. Maybe they had met up with a coyote or a bobcat at some point and learned from that hard lesson. The chickens scattered randomly, foraging in a wide path. Justine came out and worked in the kitchen garden. Sarah waited to see what she put in her basket. Onions and mustard greens.

The sun crossed overhead, the shadows re-forming east to west. A flock of white-crowned sparrows chittered in the meadow grass. Sarah thought she saw a family of deer out of the corner of her eye, but mostly she didn't see anything, looking inward, trying to find her way through the layers of thick gray fog.

In early afternoon, when the heat began to rise, she drank the last of the coffee cold and ate crumbs of cornbread. In the late afternoon, she rocked with her head against the back of the chair while a mild breeze blew over her. No plan would form. No destination would come to mind. She was so tired, but she kept seeing the shot-out door and plaster falling down in the kitchen.

As the sun descended, while its rays still held from the west, bright and blinding, Addison pushed open the door. She'd brought more food, beef roast, greens, fresh-baked bread. She saw the uneaten breakfast on the dresser and sighed.

"I'll be back in a minute," she said, as if Sarah might get up and go somewhere in the meantime. Addison returned with a slipper chair to fit into the tight space by the table.

"Eat," she said. She picked up her heavy silverware and placed it correctly, unfolded the white starched napkin.

"I can't," Sarah said. "It would come right back up."

"That's not what anybody wants to happen."

"No, it isn't," Sarah said, turning her head away from even the smell of the meat.

Addison reached over and brought the silver back to her side of the table. "If you won't then I guess I will," she said, taking a bite of the sliced roast. Sarah considered that she'd never known a more pragmatic woman. "But a glass of wine is mandatory."

"I'll pass out."

"Worse things have occurred," Addison said, sidestepping at the very last second the realization that it had, in fact, actually occurred in that other time they weren't talking about. "That's what the bread's for. Bread and wine, and thou something. It's poetry. John Russell reads it when he's feeling moody, which is always." Addison could see that she was not proving beneficial in any way.

Sarah couldn't drink the wine but she broke off a piece of bread, chewed it slowly and swallowed. It would sit in her stomach like lead, but Addison had been kind. Addison drank her share of the wine more quickly and put down her glass. She reminded herself again about being careful.

"Diego wants to see you," she said. Make it simple and swift.

Sarah closed her eyes against the thought. "I can't see Diego," she said. She couldn't even begin to list the reasons why.

Two to go, Addison said to herself. Then her role as messenger would be over, though the second was more curious.

"Elijah was here," she said.

"Elijah?" Why not? Who else was left to find out about the disaster that was her life? No one.

"He wanted to know where you were and how you were and you know me, I'm more honest than most folks would approve of, so I told him. What's that all about?" Addison couldn't imagine but didn't mind asking.

Sarah waded back through her various miseries to the answer. "It's about the horse," she said.

"What horse?"

"He gave me a horse that belonged to someone else, remember? He's coming to tell me I have to give her back."

"Oh," Addison said. Now she did remember and had finally gained one small possible piece of information. Maybelline had seemingly arrived with Emma as predicted.

"It doesn't matter," Sarah said. "She was never really mine. I knew that."

Somehow, Addison thought, despite her best intentions, the conversation continued to go straight downhill. And she still had one last mission to accomplish. She took a deep breath.

"I'll tell you this quick and then I'm going before I make matters any worse," she said. "Grady was here."

Sarah stiffened. Her heart was cold. She said nothing.

"He paid for your room, even though I told him there was no bill, nothing to pay. He just kept putting down money till he figured that he'd got to a month's worth. Then he put down some more. I've got a sack full of it. I'll give it to you."

"Not to me," Sarah said. She had her savings hidden in her valise. She would pay in full on her own when she left. This reminded her in an agonizing way that she did have to leave. But where would she go? It was the most impossible question she'd ever had to ask herself.

A sudden rush of heartache overwhelmed her. "I don't want anything from him," she said through her tears.

Addison was again confronted with the problem of comfort. She was more familiar with the let-them-cry-it-out method. She decided to go with what she knew and stood up to leave.

"First," she said, "take some advice. I'm leaving the money here. When you get angry enough, and you will, then it'll come in handy for all sorts of things. And God knows he won't miss it. Second, I'm just letting you know again that I'm down the hall. I'll take the breakfast and leave the dinner." She hesitated. "There's always a tomorrow," she said. "I know. I've seen thousands of them." It was the best she could do.

"I'm grateful to you forever," Sarah said.

Addison nodded and walked out the door thinking, Elijah?

23

Sarah sat through the evening. At dusk, mist rose up from the creek. The faintest sliver of moon rose in the east. A whippoorwill called mournfully from the meadow. Later, a hoot owl added its haunting notes to the peaceful night.

Sarah removed the tray to the dresser. She washed in the basin and put on clean nightclothes. She was still afraid to lie down, to close her eyes. She preferred the sleepless numbness, the fog. But she had to make the attempt. She crept into bed and curled up into a ball again, trying to find comfort in the down pillows and crisply laundered sheets. The hours passed and there was no sleep.

In the dark, the door opened with just the faintest creaking sound. She pulled herself wearily up in the bed to confront whatever might be there, but something in her recognized the shadowed figure instantly.

"Elijah?" she said.

She dropped back down on the pillows. She was too tired to consider how he'd gotten there or what he was doing. Nothing was normal, why would he not walk into her room in the middle of the night? She closed her eyes and tried not to think about it. She heard the snick of his belt as he stripped the hard-edged silver-buckled leather out of his pants. She heard him take off one boot and then the other.

When he eased into bed behind her, she was still not surprised. In fact, she felt drowsy, as if nodding off was suddenly a possibility. He slid one arm underneath her and folded his knees against the back of hers. He wrapped his other arm around her. She could feel his breath in her hair. She closed her hand on his wrist, over the thin rawhide with the silver turtle medallions from The Peaceful People.

"Is this about the horse?" she mumbled.

"No," he said, his voice quiet and calm. "It's not about the horse."

<>

When Sarah woke, the sun was halfway up the sky, the birds had conducted their full chorus then quieted and Elijah was gone. She wondered for a moment if it had all been a sleep-deprived hallucination, though she knew it was not. He would never do anything that was expected, and did everything that was completely unexpected. But she couldn't think about that right now. Her main very essential concern was banished. She'd slept, deeply, and was now refreshed, prepared to take on some of the task before her. Thank God, she thought. I'm stronger. I can do this.

She wondered if she dared brave the kitchen to find some breakfast, or if she should manage with what Addison had left of the cold beef. People couldn't keep bringing food to her on trays. She wasn't an invalid.

She decided on going to the kitchen. She washed, dressed, and took last night's tray with her along with the half empty bottle of wine. The kitchen was deserted, breakfast long over. She washed the dishes in the sink, then went through the shelves and cupboards. It wouldn't require much. She took the leftover bread and fried it with bacon and two eggs. She ate quickly and cleaned the pan. Remembering her first days here, and her brothers, she poured a small glass of hard cider and drank it down.

With enough sleep, she wasn't afraid of the town or anyone in it, their eyes on her, what they might know. She brought her drawstring purse and the documents she needed. She knew exactly where she wanted to go. She could even face the judge's wife. Getting married with a black eye wasn't the worst thing ever. What about that parrot? she wanted to ask. She felt as if she were on fire.

The judge's wife was nowhere to be seen. Sarah wondered if it was Thursday. It might be. She'd lost all track of time. The judge was in his office, a small cluttered room off his chambers. She didn't hesitate once, walking through the main room. It occurred

208

to her at the last minute that an appointment might be needed, but the judge's caught-out expression said he possibly hadn't seen a visitor in weeks.

"Hello," he said. "And who are you?"

First problem, Sarah thought, not wanting to use that name ever again.

"I got married here," she said. "It was not so long ago. In the early spring."

The judge squinted. He wasn't very good at remembering women.

"It was a very small wedding," Sarah continued. "There were just the four of us."

The judge looked up suddenly. "And one of you was..."

Don't, Sarah thought. Please don't.

The judge got hold of himself. "You're married to Grady McGuire, aren't you?" He'd come around to who she was, the story his wife had told him, all of it.

"Yes," Sarah said. "And I don't want to be. Isn't there such a thing as an annulment?" She'd grown up in a house full of law books. She was fairly sure of herself on this, but not completely certain of the details.

"An annulment?" The judge was shocked. He'd never in his life come up against such a question. His experience of bad marriages was that the husband either took up and left town or the wife shot him. Once he'd had a husband try and shoot a wife, but without success. The defendant claimed he was cleaning his gun at the time, but it was widely suspected that the wife was smarter by a mile and he'd just plain missed. And who would want an annulment from a marriage to Grady McGuire? Now that his mother was gone, he had that ranch and all that gold. And besides, he was such a nice young man.

"Isn't there such a thing?" she said. The judge's furrowed brow was making her less sure.

"Yes there is. I just don't have much experience of it. Or any, if you really want to know."

"But I have to get one," Sarah said. She looked the judge squarely in the eye. "I *have* to," she repeated emphatically, just so he understood. He seemed completely befuddled.

"Let me consult my books," he said. He went straight to one shelf. At least he knew where to start.

He took down a volume, thumbed through an index, and opened it to a page. He glanced up over his reading glasses. "There are requirements," he said. He returned to the page. "Yes, definitely, conditions to be met. Circumstances, you might say, that need to be involved."

"And what are those?" Sarah said.

"Well," he said, running his finger down the list. "Adultery's obviously the big one. Then concealed intent, failure to engage, fraud..."

Sarah jumped on the term. "What kind of fraud?"

"Let me see, what kind of fraud, here it is: *Fraud that goes to the very essence of the marital relation. This includes concealed sterility or pregnancy...*"

"Concealed pregnancy." That's not quite what had happened, but she forged on. "So would this apply, if someone you married had a child and you didn't know they had a child and this child entered back into the situation along with its mother, creating what might be looked at as three people in the same relationship? That might be grounds?"

The judge looked up sharply from his book again. "Young woman," he said, "are you saying that's what has occurred?" Lord in heaven. He would have to talk to his wife about this.

"I am saying that's exactly what has occurred."

"There will be papers to fill out and sign," the judge said. "In the practice of law, there are always papers to sign. My dear, do you have the originals from...from before?"

"I do," Sarah said, and laid them on his desk.

"Then I believe we can take care of this right now. Have a seat."

"He doesn't have to be here?"

"He does not. If his signature is needed, I'll get it later." The judge began searching through his heavy wooden file drawers for something that would pass for forms.

When Sarah left the judge's office, she carried with her two copies of the admittedly unusual-looking document. But it stated, in no uncertain terms, that her marriage had ceased to exist. She'd read it several times with a dizzying sense of disbelief. At the same time, she experienced a deep satisfaction, which was compounded by Grady's money having paid for it. Addison's advice had been completely right in that regard.

She'd also paid for a legal notice stating as a court order that the entirety of her remaining belongings be packed in her trunk and waiting outside on Grady's porch by sundown. She wondered about calling it a court order, but the judge was just gearing up and disappointed that she didn't have any more issues to which he could apply his creative legal mind.

Next, she needed an emissary, which required a hopeful walk down by the creek. As crawfish season was over, she went out a farther distance than usual. She spotted Bean near the river. He was down on his haunches watching a clutch of turkey vultures in the distance feed on a dead deer. Bean didn't have a gun, and she hoped a cougar wasn't lurking nearby. Just in case, she peered up into the low-lying branches where she knew they sometimes hid. That was one of the more spectacular and frightening ways she'd fallen off a horse.

She talked and Bean listened, nodding. When she was done, he took her hand and drew a number in her palm. She realized this was how he not only existed, but apparently prospered. He was a natural businessman. She doubled the figure and paid him on the spot for the mission, which had to be concluded with Grady and no one else, and also for the horse and cart he'd need to hire. Then she gave him the documents to take with him. His clear blue gaze intrigued her. *Who are you?* she wanted to ask.

Last, with time on her hands for once and the proper length skirts, she walked slowly through the town, stopping to study every window and go into every storefront. How strange, she thought, that on what must of necessity be one of her last days as a resident, she was actually discovering what was here.

Sarah began to understand Addison's role in life. Since Sarah couldn't picture a future, she also couldn't picture what she might need in that future, if anything. But still, in the general store, she became a consumer attracted to all sorts of small luxuries, sachet, a length of satin ribbon, hat pins for the hat she no longer even owned. She used Grady's money to purchase a box of writing paper, a pen set and a bottle of ink. There was still a great deal of money remaining, but the mood had left her.

Sarah waited with a small amount of anxiety for sundown. Preoccupied, she forgot about dinner till Addison arrived with yet another tray of food and another bottle of wine. She began to feel that Addison was enjoying the clandestine nature of this routine, a break from her usual role as hostess to rich and boring guests.

"Last time," Sarah said. "I'm up and on my own."

"You are," Addison said. "To what do we owe the recovery?" Certainly not to my soothing reassurances, she thought.

Sarah's cheeks brightened, something she was sure Addison didn't miss. Her interest fatally piqued, Addison redirected her attention to uncorking the wine. Now was not the time to pry. Everyone dealt with a crisis in his or her own way

"Just promise me you'll eat and have some of this French wine I keep opening. It's not fun drinking alone. Not that I ever do of course, but it isn't."

Sarah already had her fork in hand. The heavenly dish they would share was instantly recognizable. It was Diego's exquisite coq au vin, built on a base of rich stock and sinfully laced with Cognac. His exotic cooking skills made far more sense now.

Sarah took the glass Addison offered and sipped the wine. It tasted of the fruits of the earth, intricate and luscious. It must be nice to have such expensive tastes. Even her father didn't have wine like this. God bless John Russell. She forked up a morsel of tender chicken, savoring the vibrant flavors.

She took another gulp of the wine for courage. Then she put down her fork and took in Addison sitting so carefully groomed and perfect across the small space, beautiful in the light of the warm late afternoon sun. Sarah began again the conversation she hadn't been able to get through before.

"I have to ask now," she said. "Did you know about Grady?"

Addison put down her fork as well and smoothed the napkin on her lap. "How blunt do you want me to be?" she said.

"I don't have anything left," Sarah said. "So it doesn't matter."

"You have everything left and it does matter."

"Very blunt. I need that."

"Then the truth is, we all knew."

"Why didn't someone tell me? Why didn't Diego tell me?"

"Maybe Diego hoped it was all done and gone. It was for Grady. He knew he'd been made such a fool of. He wanted to start over. And there you were, the best thing that ever happened to him."

"I'm not the best thing. That child is. I wish you could have seen him. He couldn't take his eyes off her. I don't think he could actually grasp that she was there and real. But she looks just like him."

Addison shook her head, her earrings catching the light. "I'm so sorry you had to go through that," she said. "I can't believe they just showed up out of nowhere."

"From what I can tell," Sarah said, remembering the scene painfully, "the father's crazy, but I think he was also very angry with his daughter, with Diego, Grady, everyone. Strange man, he had a shotgun. He blasted apart the front door, then shot a hole in the kitchen ceiling before Booker just walked over and took the gun away from him. What he really wanted to do was shoot Grady."

"Jesus," Addison said. She wished she'd been there.

Sarah steeled herself. "Who is she?" she asked. "What happened?"

"It's not pretty," Addison said. "Diego was so ashamed. Beatriz was the wild one her father couldn't control but maybe with thirteen in the family those are the odds. She fell hard for a poker player named J.D. Leggett. He had a reputation

213

everywhere, even here. When he'd had enough of her, he left Mexico and she tried to follow him. He put her off, sent word to meet him in Sweetwater. So she ran away from home and her father made Diego go after her. Naturally when they got to Sweetwater J.D. Leggett was nowhere to be seen. Diego got a job cooking at the boarding house so they wouldn't starve, but Miss High and Mighty wouldn't work a job like that. She asked around who was the richest person in town. No secret there, it was Ellen, who was dying by then. Beatriz just went right up and knocked on the door, said she was there to do the cooking. She had so much brass, Maybelline loved her. And she could cook up a storm.

"But then Ellen died, Grady came home, everybody else left and there were the two of them alone in that big house. I have to tell you, Grady was helpless, like a cute little furry animal grabbed up by a sharp-clawed hawk. She was so bad and he'd never come up against anything like her, he didn't even know what hit him. It was just mean fun for her, a game until she found J.D. again. The two of them started playing cards at night, drinking all day, and then of course everything else went on. Diego wanted to die. To try and make it up to him, one day when Grady was half-sober he talked me into taking a chance on Diego as the hotel cook and you can see how that worked out, I've been thrilled ever since.

"Then, who couldn't guess it, she got with child. Doc Morrison was called out to confirm because being ignorant like she was, she wouldn't believe it. Oh my God, she was furious. What was she going to do, poor thing? J.D. wouldn't want her anymore, not that she was ever going to see him again. She flew into a rage every day over everything, broke all the china, used words in two different languages that would make a cowhand blush, made Grady's life a living hell.

"The final insult, it almost takes your breath away, she kicked Grady out of his own house. You know Grady, or maybe you don't want to, but he is a good person. By then, Lord in heaven, he hated her, but I can't tell you how much he wanted that baby. I think partly he just wanted to have something in this world to call his own, someone who loved him and he could love back. She killed him with all the things she said about that.

"And the worse thing, the stupidest thing is that she was doing the ledgers and stealing him blind, building up a stockpile for when she took off. If Grady'd ever looked at them even once, he would've known. It took Booker and Jim to figure it out.

"One morning, she'd begun to show by then, he went into the house like he did to check on her and she was gone. He went crazy. He got his horse and he rode and rode, back and forth and into Texas, everywhere, asking everybody. When he found her, she'd hid herself in a bunch of religious, told them some big lie, and they wouldn't let him near her.

"Then he figured she must have gone home, because that's where those folk were headed, they were halfway to the border already. I think maybe she got scared of everything she'd done. He tried to get Diego to go and find out how she was, said he'd give him a horse, but Diego wouldn't have any part of it. Good riddance is what he thought."

"Are you still all right?" Addison asked.

"I am, please don't stop," Sarah said.

"I'm almost done." Addison poured them both another glass of wine. "In that time after Diego wouldn't go," she said, "Grady died a little. It was like one more thing taken away from him. He couldn't go himself, it wasn't his right, and he was afraid he'd be shot if he showed up anyway. Took a while, but when he got over the worst of it, he lived simple, it was funny to see, had that whole big house but stayed with Jim and Booker, accepted his responsibilities and started doing work on the ranch, decided to get the newspaper from the east one day and find a better kind of woman, put in an ad that he wrote from his heart and the rest is what you know."

Sarah stared out the window. So this was the missing part. She waited to feel sorry for Grady, but couldn't. She wondered if she would ever forgive him or want to see him again.

215

There was a knock at the door and Sarah jumped. It was the night porter to tell her a messenger was downstairs with her luggage.

"Who is it?" Addison said.

"Bean," Sarah said. "I sent him this afternoon with a letter from the judge. I had the marriage annulled this morning."

Addison's eyebrows raised. "Good Lord," she said. "Hell hath no fury…"

"Hell seriously hath not," Sarah said, but when she got down to the front porch, it was not Bean standing there with her trunk. It was Grady. She should have known.

"Go," she said. "Now."

"I brought your things," he said.

"I can see that. Bean was supposed to bring them."

"I dropped him off at the stables. I've got my horse."

"I doubt he was pleased."

"No, he wasn't."

"I have nothing to say, Grady. Not now, not ever."

"Everything that happened, I didn't know, I didn't ever think…I just wanted to be happy. And I was happy. I was glad to be married to you."

"If you don't leave, I'll get the sheriff."

"You didn't take the letters."

"Give them to your daughter. They'll help her understand how thoughtful and trustworthy her father is."

Grady had to quickly get past that remark or he would fall apart. "I left money to pay for the room," he said.

"Addison told me. She wouldn't take it so she gave it to me. I used it to pay the judge and to buy writing paper. I'm going to write to Uncle Henry and say what in the name of God were you thinking?"

"Stop," Grady said. "Please. I know you could go on for days. I'll leave. I'll get out of your life. Just don't forget me, okay?"

"Believe me, I won't forget you."

"I meant in a good way."

216

"That's asking too much."

Sarah watched him go. He was still handsome. He still had that familiar walk, though at the moment his shoulders sagged. He mounted his horse, his face a map of troubles. She thought she would cry, but the tears didn't come. She couldn't even begin to fathom what his life must be like now. She couldn't bear to think for even a minute of the three in the bunkhouse who had been her family.

The night porter dragged her trunk up the stairs to her room. Addison was still sitting at the small table by the window, fingering her wine glass thoughtfully.

"That wasn't Bean, it was Grady," Sarah said. "And here I am. I'm fine."

24

At dawn, Sarah sat in a chair out by the creek under the cottonwoods. The morning was cool, dew still on the grass. She wrapped herself in a shawl and gazed out over the silver water. She knew she had to be like Addison and face reality even if it was harsh. She had nothing to her name, no house or cookstove, no cows or chickens, she could only claim her clothes and a trunk full of useless linens and quilts. She considered that instead of giving her a dowry, they'd have been better off trading her for goats. What was she supposed to do now? Homestead like Elmira and starve to death? Find company to travel with and try her fortunes in California? Move to the boarding house and take in sewing like Bean's sister?

The truth was, she had only one place left to go and that was home. No matter how much her heart ached, this time she would have to get on the road headed east and make that long journey back to Virginia. She would return to her father's house not only widowed, but divorced, or annulled, whatever she was now, and sleep again in the room with Jacob's uniform. It was not something she welcomed, but given the circumstances she had no choice. The wild west had conquered her, even when she secretly thought herself strong. Maybe now she would cry.

"Hola," Elijah said softly from behind her and she jumped out of the chair as if it was on fire, still not used to how silently he moved. She was so taken aback by his presence that she forgot to be tongue-tied and flustered, the condition she'd assumed would naturally occur if she ever saw him again. She had spent the night with him, or some part of it, she didn't distinctly remember which part since sleep had dropped on her like a brick. But she had to shrug off any imagined embarrassment or false modesty. Those were things she knew he put no stock in.

"We should walk," he said.

"We should?"

"Yes. I have something to show you." Sarah didn't even try to come up with an idea of what it might be. She followed him along the path next to the creek, far behind the storefronts and alleyways of town. He waited as she stopped for a family of quail to cross the path, the smallest ones scurrying along in a line. She stopped again to watch an oddly colored duck in the creek, cinnamon with brilliant edges to its wings. The hem of her skirts grew damp. She glanced up at the violet hills just exploding into green as the sun hit them.

When they had almost reached the outskirts, Elijah moved onto another path heading back to the edge of town. They came out behind the feed and grain and started across the dusty street toward what Sarah recognized as the livery stables.

Suddenly she came to an abrupt halt. There, on the other side, tied to the hitching post, was Tess. Sarah fought back the tears. If she let them come, they would be a torrent, a floodgate opening. She walked over and buried her face in Tess's neck. Tess nickered softly. Sarah took a long moment to compose herself, then turned to Elijah, the question plain in her eyes.

"She's still yours," he said.

"But how? Why?" It didn't seem fair that this would be happening now, when the next stage left in two days. On the other hand, please don't tell me how, she prayed. No details. Don't take me back to that night.

"She just is. I promise you." Sarah was relieved. However it had worked out, she believed him. "But she should be ridden," he said. Tess was saddled up and ready to go. "No one has and it would do her good."

"No, it would do me good," she said. "But where's your horse?" He must have ridden one in. "You'll come with us, right?"

"Only if it's what you want."

Good grief, she thought. "It's what I want," she said. Then her eyes went to one of the other horses tied to the hitching post, the one Elijah was moving toward. The one dark and sleek, hooves stamping in impatience.

219

Sarah was stunned as the recognition came. "That's *him!*" she cried. "What have you done to him? He's beautiful!" He had filled out, grown sinewy and proud, only the faintest scars still showing on his flanks. Sarah understood the enormous amount of patience and skill it must have taken to bring him to this point. He was almost new, reborn.

"He'll let you ride him?" she said incredulously.

"Only me," Elijah said. "He's still half-wild but there's no question about it, he's the finest horse I've ever had."

"What do you call him?"

"Caleb. Abraham named him. He said Caleb was in the Bible and he was fearless, a survivor."

The child she loved had named his difficult horse. Someday long in the future, she told herself, after years and years had gone by, she would hardly care about either one of them at all.

"Where do you want to go?" he said.

"Anywhere as long as it's that way," she said, pointing west.

Sarah wrapped the shawl around her waist and tied it in a large knot. Then she lifted her boot into the stirrup and swung into the saddle. As quickly as she moved, Elijah was already up and waiting for her. They rode out of town, leaving the storefronts and saloons behind. Out on the road, Elijah settled the horses into a comfortable rhythm. When he sensed that Tess was eager, he opened up the pace till they were galloping, tearing up the road. Sarah's skirts blew out, her hair came undone and she laughed for the first time in what felt like an eternity.

They went farther than she'd ever been on the road out of town. The winter wheat fields, lying fallow now, disappeared behind them, to be replaced by an endless horizon of shifting prairie grass. The river gleamed in the morning light, then it too disappeared. Elijah slowed when Tess had run herself out. For a length of time they rode easily, leather saddles creaking, while the sun rose in the sky. Sarah watched the dark horse prance sideways and snort, his energy not nearly spent. She would never forget seeing him come painfully across the corral, so frightened, but giving in to Elijah in the end.

220

Long lines of white fence suddenly marked the land. An opening in the fence produced a lane. Elijah reined in his horse and gazed out into the distance. The sky stretched out wide and blue to an endless horizon in every direction. Sarah was moved again by the enormity of the open vistas that swallowed up trees and hills, erased every landmark, leaving only a blaze of white sun.

"What are you looking at?" she said.

"Can you see out there?"

Sarah squinted. "It's either ants or buildings, I can't tell. What is it really?"

"John Russell's horse farm."

"His horse farm?" she said. "What are you talking about?"

"It got finished last week."

Sarah squinted harder. "But I don't see any horses."

"There aren't any, not yet."

"Elijah, how do you know all this?"

"He came and asked would I work horses for him. He wants champions, trotters and pacers both."

She was shocked. "You're talking to John Russell?"

"He's talking to me. I'm not necessarily talking to him."

"How did this ever happen? I mean…"

"It's just who he is. He can wipe out anything, what might have been said or done, it doesn't exist. He wants to make big money and he needs what I know about horses."

"What did you say?"

"I told him no and he said he wasn't in any hurry, he could wait till I changed my mind."

"Doesn't that make you angry?"

"It's not good to be angry with men like John Russell. Makes you less able to see them." The dark horse began snorting and tossing his head. "El Loco doesn't like it here," he said. "With good reason, I guess. Are you ready?"

Sarah looked longingly down the road. "I suppose we have to turn back," she said.

"We could keep going. There's not much out there."

221

"No, I know." She was running away from decisions again. "We'll go back."

They rode in silence at an easy pace that was still quick enough to bring up a trail of dust behind them. Sarah was lost in her thoughts and felt Elijah was, too. Now and then the dark horse tossed his head restlessly and bolted. Sarah stroked her own horse's neck and was glad for Tess's steadiness, her reliable nature.

As they passed the meadow, Sarah reined Tess in. Elijah went around in a circle and came back to her. The path was right there. "Out to the river?" he said.

"Please," she said. She didn't want any of it to end.

Down on the rocky shoreline, Elijah tied up the horses in the shade and climbed to the top of the rise. Sarah sat down beside him and was just glad to be there. It was all she asked.

"I love this place," she said. "I love this river."

"The heron's over there again," he said. "In case you wanted to know."

"You realize I still can't see him."

"I can tell you what he looks like."

"Thank you, but I know what a blue heron looks like. In Virginia, they stand right there in the creek. You don't need to be the People Who Live Upstream to see them."

Elijah was silent for a long while.

"The river turns south up there," he said finally, nodding in the direction of the wide bend.

"And that's a bad thing?"

"It's not anything for the river. But then it runs through disputed land."

"And is that a bad thing?"

"Can be. Cattle drivers on one hand, farmers on the other and the two don't mix."

"What brought that up?" she asked.

"You said you loved the river. I haven't seen where it comes from, up in the mountains, but I've seen where it goes."

"To Texas."

"To north Texas, which is almost a different place."

She considered that maybe he was also making decisions. Then it was certain she would never see him again.

"Can I ask you a question?" she said. "It's personal."

"Everything you've ever asked me is personal. You don't know how to ask anything else."

"Do you mind?"

"No."

"Then, how did you get your name?"

He looked at her. "What makes you think these things?" he said. She wondered how she could ever explain her need to know everything and there was so little time left.

"It didn't seem like a name from your people."

"It isn't. Dell gave it to me. She said Elijah was a prophet and blue was the color of the grass in Texas in the spring. I didn't think Dell had religion, so that's a mystery, but she did love Texas and that made as much sense to me as anything."

"Did you have a name before that?"

"Yes, but it was a child's name. When I came back from the desert, it was up to my father to choose a new name. He could even give me his own name if that was the right thing to do. There were questions he'd ask me. He'd listen to everything I said, because that's what your father did for you. But I never saw him again. So Dell gave me this name and I'm glad for it."

Sarah sat quietly for a while herself, moved by everything he'd said. A fish leaped, one quick flash of silver in the middle of the river, and left widening rings that slowly disappeared. A flock of ducks flew swiftly by, their wings whistling in the stillness. "It's a good name," she said. "It suits you." She wished she had gotten to meet this woman who found a boy alone in the desert and made him her son.

"I have to go," she said then. "I have to sit down and figure things out."

"That's what you were doing this morning?"

"That's what I was trying to do. Mostly, it wasn't working."

"It's strange," he said, "how different it is in my two worlds. In this one, there's time, divided up into hours and minutes. Who

223

thought to do that? In the old one, there was only the sun rising and setting, the stars moving across the sky, the moon changing shapes."

"What are you saying?"

"There are no hours and minutes, only the sun," he said. "Stay a while."

She wanted to, but knew she couldn't. "I'll get anxious," she said. "I need to be responsible." Didn't he understand that her entire life had just been shattered into a million pieces?

"I'll make the tortillas to eat, with something inside them," he said.

"You will?" She was afraid of being in the house.

"You can stay outside. I'll bring them to you." He was reading her mind again.

She stood up and peered down into the water. Nothing stirred in the circling pool below. "Will it be fish inside?" she said.

"Do you see any?"

"No."

"Then I don't think it'll be fish."

They rode the horses in a line up the narrow path and into the trees. Sarah took in the towering oaks and elms, the rustling grasses, the hollow tapping of a woodpecker.

Crossing the clearing toward the meadow, Elijah pulled up his horse and stopped. "We should talk about Grady," he said.

"Why?" she said.

"Because it might be a good thing to do."

"It wouldn't be a good thing to do," she said. "Not now, not ever."

"That's what I needed to know."

They rode out of the meadow, back down along the road and through the tall grass to the stables. Elijah tied the horses in the shade and brought in kindling and water. He stoked two burners of the cookstove. Sarah walked around the kitchen nervously, touching everything. He was too close. She had to occupy herself some way.

224

"Let me cook," she said. "You're the only person I haven't done that for."

"We'll both cook."

"Do you have a root cellar?"

"Out back."

She returned to the kitchen minutes later with her skirts held up. One at a time, she took out eggs and laid them on the counter.

"How does this work?" she said. "You have eggs, but no chickens. You have onions and potatoes, but only squash planted in your garden."

"It's like the deer. Same thing."

She held up a string of odd little green pods. "What are these?"

"Green chilies. They're from Smithy. They're more mild than hot. The ones in your other hand are scorching hot, be careful."

"And what is this?" She held up a mason jar full of something sloshing, seeded and dark red.

"Hot sauce."

"Bean makes it, I'll bet any money."

"You would be right, but the only people I've seen bet money are fast to lose it."

Grady, she thought. Something else occurred to her. "You didn't know my Uncle Henry, did you?"

"I met him, that was all."

Sarah sighed and put her finds on the table. A can on a shelf next to the cookstove caught her eye. "What is that?" she said.

"I usually don't think this much about what's in here," he said. "It's bacon grease."

"Why?"

"Why is it bacon grease? I don't know. It just is."

"Bacon grease never 'just is'. You have to work at keeping it. You have to want it. I cook everything in it. I can't cook without it. Nobody in the South can. Isn't that odd? Who ever decided to use it in the first place? And then it gets to be the only thing that makes a difference, the one thing you can't do without. And

John Russell notices it. And some people even put it in their hair, but that's not something I would ever do." Sarah quickly began chopping up the onions and peppers, aware that she was talking too fast and not making any sense.

She almost choked when Elijah got out the masa flour and began mixing dough again.

"What are you doing?" she said. "I'm making eggs."

"I told you, for the tortillas. It's the way in Mexico, with the hot sauce, they go together. Easy for the rancheros, out on the trail you don't even need a plate."

Standing beside her at the cookstove and working fast, Elijah piled up a stack of the round thin tortillas, deftly turning one after the other out of the pan.

"Stop," she said. "They're lovely, but there aren't five hundred of us here." She had produced a small mountain of fluffy eggs scrambled in bacon grease and laced with onions and chilies.

"What do we do now?" She pressed her trembling hands together.

"Here," he said. "Like this."

He held out a tortilla flat in his hands. "First put in the eggs."

Sarah picked up a spatula full of eggs. She couldn't hold it steady. She took a deep breath. "I can do this," she said. But she couldn't.

She put the spatula with the eggs back in the pan before it all ended up on the floor. Her hands went to her face. She was on high alert, reacting to the sound of his voice, his every move, her mind going where she didn't want it to go. It was hopeless trying to convince herself that last chances didn't matter. Elijah slowly set the tortilla back on the board beside the cookstove.

"What do you see when you look at me?" she said, unsure of anything.

"The woman holding up Doc Morrison."

She stared at him. "From the stage stop? All that time ago?" That couldn't be. She felt herself blush furiously.

"Not everybody tries to hold up Doc Morrison."

"He was drunk."

226

"He's always drunk."

She couldn't stop herself from talking. What difference did it make? It was all a disaster anyway.

"I was afraid of you," she said.

"There's a person I have to be in that world."

"John Russell's world. I prayed you wouldn't have to shoot the rifle."

"Because of your skirts," he said. "I prayed too. But that's how I knew you'd ask about the silver."

"I spent all that time staring at it. You don't exactly read minds then."

"No."

"But you watch. You're watching me right now." In a way that she could feel down to her toes.

"Because you're here."

"What are you thinking?"

"I'm trying not to think," he said.

She was making herself crazy. "One last question," she said. "How do you know about these things?"

"The things we're not talking about? Much can happen in a place like Mexico when you're young and far from home."

An unwanted image came to mind. "Is that where Grady learned about women?" she said.

"That's where Grady learned about tequila."

"I need to sit down," she said. There were chairs at the plain table. Hastily, she pulled one out and sat in it with her hands folded in her lap. She tried to breathe, but was having trouble with it. She thought about Jace and her confederate soldier. Be brave, she told herself. All of a long sad life lay ahead, dreams dead and forgotten. Lightning was going to strike her down this time for sure. If only she could make herself calm.

"I'm taking off my boots," she said. If this was unexpected, he didn't show it. She brought her boot up and braced the heel against the chair edge, but her hands betrayed her and she could only fumble with the knot.

227

"You're serious?" he said. She nodded. "Then let me do that."

"It's eighteen holes," she said. Why couldn't she just stop *talking*? "It takes a while."

He sat opposite her with her foot wedged between his knees.

"It's like the hours and minutes, who thinks to do this?" he said, stripping out the laces. She reflected on a world without eighteen-hole lace-ups to take her mind off this other world she was very willfully entering.

When one boot and sock were gone, she switched and gave him the other boot, then closed her eyes to just be aware of his hands. The second boot came off, the second soft wool sock that Jace had knitted, and her bare foot was in those hands. Quickly she pulled her foot back and stood up.

"Your boots," she said, motioning for one of them. Was this *really* her plan? He still acted as if everything was perfectly normal. His boots were worn and creased. She almost had to work up a sweat, yanking on them. Finally, one after the other, they both came free, along with his own hand-knitted socks. She held one up and frowned. Who would knit him socks?

But she couldn't get sidetracked and lose her courage. What next, she thought. She reached up and took the clips out of her hair, letting the rest of it come down that hadn't already blown out on the ride. And the shawl still tied around her waist. She undid the clumsy knot and let the shawl slide to the floor.

Elijah stood up. He waited, his eyes never leaving her, and it seemed as if he was weighing a decision. He reached out and laid a hand gently on her arm, a tentative gesture. There was the heat again. She considered that he might be expecting her to turn and run for the door. She had been known to do that. Or faint, she'd been known to do that, too. Instead of either one, she moved a step closer, willing him to see that the boundaries between them were down, all reservations on her part gone. And then it was simple. They moved into each other at the same time, stepping urgently into the embrace that had been so long in coming, holding on tight. Muffled into his collar, she was aware of the

228

scent of him, pine and horses and wood smoke. The soft fabric of his shirt. His warm, smooth skin. The edges of the silver belt buckle he'd taken off for her once, somewhere in the night. She could hear his breathing and feel the steady beat of his heart that was in such a sharp contrast to her own. Don't move, she thought. Let me store up each detail in my mind, to take out and savor when I have nothing left.

But they were in their bare feet. That was strange, though she was the one who had done it. She shifted, fitting even closer against him, stepping on his feet, feeling him shift, too, his arms hard around her, his face pressed into her hair.

She lifted her head and leaned back just enough to look at him. If his eyes showed something different, misgivings or doubt, she would put her boots back on and go home. His eyes said everything, gave back every one of her own emotions. Still holding her, he released one hand and raised it to her face, running his fingers tenderly along her brow, her cheekbone, coming down to touch her mouth. Again, it was as easy as that. Though she was still trembling when he kissed her, she kissed him back, wrapping her arms more tightly around him, feeling him strong and lean against her.

The heat rose again in her face and she could hardly believe that she was *still* talking. "I shouldn't have taken off my boots," she said. "Or I didn't, you took them off, but I tried to at least. I shouldn't have taken off yours. I don't know why I did any of that, it seems like maybe not the right thing to do. Someone else would know better. I don't know anything."

"Are you still afraid in some way?"

"No." Now she was back on track. It wasn't close to true, she was afraid of everything, but that wouldn't stop her. "Are you?"

"No," he said. "This is all I ever wanted."

"The woman holding up Doc Morrison?"

"That one only, not any other one. Ever."

She gave him that woman, kissing him with the same fierceness that had caused her to faint before, no fainting now, only holding on more tightly when he picked her up. The sunlight creating a pattern on the wall, the fact that it was before noon, though not an experience she'd ever had before, never entered her thoughts. They fell together onto the bed, still tangled up, bound to each other as they sank down into the blankets, mouth on mouth, wanting, searching. She turned in his beautiful hands as he undid her slowly, with reverence and care, his fingers easily working through all the knots and ribbons. Then she was arching, rising, moving with him again and again until he filled all her senses, he was everything, the lost boy, the shotgun rider, the silent one, all belonging to her for just this one moment, a small and sacred window before the darkness closed in. Of course Jace had run off with the soldier, of course her father had chosen the county clerk, if this is what they'd had.

Afterwards, he brushed the damp hair back from her face and held her. They were quiet for a long time.

"Now I know," she said.

He found her hand and moved his fingers over her palm. "It was always there," he said.

"What about Grady?" she said. "I was there to marry him."

"And where was he? The way I saw it, he had already lost you."

"By not saying the truth?"

"By not coming near the truth, not any of it."

"And being passed out in a wagon."

"That didn't help."

Sarah hesitated. Then she asked the question she so much feared asking any of them.

"Were you all just waiting for her to come back?"

"On her own, no. Not even for all of Ellen's gold, which is fairly unbelievable considering who she is. But Diego worried. He said his father could never live with what had happened and he'd be the one to bring her back, get her a husband."

"And he did."

"Yes, he did. I need to talk to you about how it is up there," he said. "I've got a reason."

"It hurts."

230

"It can't hurt forever."

"I'm glad if you think that, but go ahead."

"She used to scream and throw things, but now she's quiet, won't talk to anyone, won't say anything except to tell Grady every day how much she hates him for doing this to her. Her mother curses him in Spanish, she's very good at it and he understands all the words. The rest of them just work at staying away from each other. The father cooks. That's something, I guess. Maybelline's the only one who gets along."

Sarah couldn't bear to think about Abraham and what this all meant to him.

"How could Maybelline like her?" she said.

"Maybelline's her own kind of woman. They maybe see something in each other. And no one can say what comes next. Grady got the family he had in his mind, just not how he ever wanted it. Now he has to live with it."

"No matter how awful it is," Sarah said, "the child makes up for all of it. I saw it in his face. I'm glad for him having her, but that's when I had to get as far away as possible."

A stillness filled the room, dust motes floating in the shaft of sunlight. Sarah could feel her heart beating. Now it was steady, like his. He was still tracing her palm.

"What's as far away as possible?" he said.

"Back home. Virginia."

"When would you go?"

"The next stage leaves in two days."

He was silent again.

"There are some things I want you to know," he said.

"If there are more serious things to say, it should be with food then." And dressed, she thought.

She sat up and began to put her clothing back on, finding items lost in the bedclothes, working the small buttons and re-doing the laces. She watched him thread the belt back into his pants and her heart sped up again.

In the kitchen, he watched as she quickly managed the eighteen-hole lace-ups, her fingers nimble now, remembering

231

what they were supposed to do, her brain unclouded. Everything clear. Everything, him.

She wrapped the tortillas in a cloth to warm them, then moved the pan back over the fire and gently heated the eggs. They wouldn't be at their best, but that didn't matter anymore.

They sat across the table from each other. His plates were English china, the same as the ones in Grady's house. Ellen's reach was everywhere.

Elijah ladled hot sauce, folded over a tortilla. Sarah lingered over the process, more intent on taking in the sight of him, his hands, his wrists wrapped in leather and silver, his dark eyes going through her again.

"There's nothing more I can do for Grady," he said. "So I also need to be far away. It's the same feeling."

Sarah thought she would look at him for as long as she could bear it and then her heart would break. "You're going home. To Texas."

"Yes."

"But what's there? Grady said you closed up the house."

"I did, but that was for him. It's all still there and watched over. I'd never give up Dell's ranch. Anything Grady needed to believe to get him home is what I did."

"Tell me about the house," she said. "I want to know what it's like."

"Just a house the same as anyone's. Except not Ellen's. Dell didn't have all that gold or any need for it. Built around a courtyard, the way it's done there."

"This size?" she said, nodding at the small confines of the cabin. She wondered if he would let her take one of the blankets.

"More rooms and a kitchen at the back like Diego's. When the trail riders came in, Dell was the one who fed them."

She took a deep breath. Not much to go on, but enough. The eggs were soft and burning at the same time. The tortillas helped, though in reality, nothing helped. Just keep talking, she told herself. Till it's time to go.

"What about your horses?"

232

"They'll go to Booker. And the land for a dollar the way Maybelline sold it to me."

"Booker?" she said, surprised again.

"Booker knows horses the same way I do, with his hands and what's inside him." She would never get over his eyes when he was watching her. He was considering his words again. "The thing is," he said, "they should get out of the bunkhouse soon and they need a place to go."

"Because of Maybelline?"

"Because of everything."

She realized what he was saying. "They'd live here?" That couldn't even be. Sarah tried in her mind to put Jim at the cookstove, Abraham at the plank table with his books. She couldn't do it, it was too strange. But she could see that it was already settled.

"You've talked this out," she said.

"It was necessary. Things are changing for everyone."

"What do you do then when you get to Texas?"

"Find more horses. Start over. Maybe some day Booker and Jim would come."

"And Abraham."

"And Abraham, though he could be grown enough by then with ideas of his own."

Emma, she thought. "They're all agreed is what you're saying. It's practically done."

"Almost."

The eggs were finished. A stack of tortillas remained. Anything else was pointless.

Sarah stood up. "Now I have to go," she said.

"Where?"

"The only place there is to go, my room at the hotel."

"Not yet."

"I have to, Elijah. It's important. And if I stay here, people will talk."

"I'd get used to the idea that they're already talking."

She sat back down. That hadn't occurred to her.

"Don't say that," she said. But they had ridden out of town together. Did any of the town gossips, say the judge's wife perhaps, choose to speculate on where they might be going? Or how they knew each other in the first place?

"It's nothing, don't think about it."

"You don't care, so it's easy."

"You're right, I don't care. Let's get the horses. I want to take you somewhere you haven't been."

Since people were already talking, why not? She hoped the judge's wife had one eye on her watch, or was keeping track of the sun crossing the sky. And sitting in Addison's sweet hotel room wasn't going to accomplish anything anyway. Her trunk was packed. What else did she think there was to do?

She picked up the plates to wash them. Elijah took them from her and put them down. The brush of their hands against each other almost did her in. She quickly reached for her shawl.

They rode in a new direction, around the corral and then far out, past a different meadow where the other horses were turned out to graze, and beyond it along a well-worn trail. At the end, Elijah led his horse into a narrow path that wound through the woods. Sarah followed, noting a pungent scent. Tess stepped carefully and snorted as a pheasant flushed from the understory and beat its way up through the trees. All else was quiet. The sunlight lay dappled on the ground, filtered through the softly rustling leaves. She considered that everywhere Elijah went, there was peace. Then she heard the rush of water.

Elijah dismounted and she climbed down beside him.

The sound came from a narrow spring that splashed into a deep green pool, then flowed over the edge in a small cascade rushing headlong downhill to the river. The trees leaned in, a sparrow's song rose from somewhere in the brush, and she couldn't have dreamed of a more perfect place.

"You can't tell anyone about this," Elijah said. "It's Bean's secret. I don't know what he gets here, but he protects it with his life."

234

"Wild greens and rosemary," she said. "And garlic. I could smell it coming in. And roots. Does he do medicine?"

"He does everything."

She bent down. "Here are nettles right here," she said. Another time, she would have gathered them to make tea. Transporting a handful of leaves all the way to Virginia made no sense, however. She stood up. The surface of the pool was ruffled by the breeze and scattering the light. Shading her eyes, she peered up into the branches. A mourning dove called out softly. The solitary notes were how she felt. There was a reason for the name. "It's all so beautiful."

"We need to go farther," Elijah said. "Over there." He nodded in the direction of an escarpment on the other side.

"How?" she said with some alarm. "Swim?" The vegetation all around the spring was dense.

"This way." He followed the faint path that led to the flat rocks at the edge of the pool. It would require a balancing act to cross them, with the prospect of a misstep ending either in the pool or following the waterfall down the hill. He held out his hand and Sarah took it, her fingers closing tightly around his, walking after him one careful step at a time, one long stride to span the rushing water, and tiptoeing over the rest to safe ground.

"Now up," he said and her eyes widened at the steepness of the ascent. A switchback and a scramble over loose shale and boulders brought them to the top, and then she was standing on a narrow ledge looking out over rolling land that went on forever.

"It's the bend in the river," she said, staring out into the dazzling sunlight. "Seems like you can almost see Texas." She glanced over at him. "Do you come here often?"

"No. Just every now and then."

What was out there in the distance? She thought of all he'd said, the desert and blue grass, cattle drivers and farmers, wind and snowstorms and houses built around courtyards.

He sat down on the warm stone and she sat down with him, her legs dangling over the ledge, listening to the soothing splash of the falls, watching a hawk float in lazy circles, either hunting or just drifting on the wind currents. The sky was a faded blue, the heat rising.

"If Texas means that much to you, you must have missed it all this time," she said. "Is there a town?"

"Just a ranchers' town, small."

"Not Ellenville."

"No, not Ellenville."

"Is there a mayor?"

"A mayor, a dry goods store, a bank. But it's not about the town, it's about the land. The best there is for horses."

"That's how you have it in your mind then," she said. He was watching the hawk, too.

"It is how I have it in my mind," he said. "Except I see you there."

Her heart stopped. "Where?" she said, not daring to let his words register.

"In Texas."

"How would that ever happen?"

"Come with me."

The shock of it ran through her from head to toe. "What?" she said. "Elijah…"

"I mean it," he said.

"You can't mean it. You haven't thought about it the right way." It's just the day, just what happened, that's all, she told herself.

"I don't have to think about it. I told you it was there."

"You were talking about something else."

"I was talking about everything. That woman in black with dust all over her. I looked up from the horses. I said, if she's gone when I look up again, what I felt just then was nothing. I turned away, turned back and you were holding up Doc Morrison. Only this one woman, ever."

"How could you know that it wouldn't work with Grady?"

"I couldn't. I could only wait." Which he was good at, she thought. But *Texas*.

Many months ago, in another lifetime, she had answered a notice in a newspaper, put away the roses and her wedding gloves, packed her quilts and lavender soap and transformed her world entirely. That's the only way she found herself now sitting on this ledge with a huge sky overhead, a waterfall at her feet and this person from the People Who Live Upstream beside her, a part of her, the air she breathed, every longing she had ever had.

She steeled herself. How long had she known Jacob? All her life. How long had she known Grady? One week, plus the voice in three letters and a recommendation from her drunken uncle. "That's crazy, Elijah," she said. "No matter how I feel, no matter what's inside me, I can't. I've made too many mistakes, I've hurt people, and now I have to go home. That's the only place where I belong."

"What would happen to you and Grady?"

"You mean with the marriage? I got an annulment yesterday."

He took his eyes from the hawk. "What is that?" he said.

"I told the judge everything and he filled out a form that he said, when I signed it, made it as if I'd never been married at all."

"How can that be?"

"It just is. I knew there was such a thing, that's why I went searching for it. It's got stamps and official seals, and it's what the judge said. He was not happy."

"Does Grady know?"

"Bean took it out to him yesterday. Grady brought my belongings to the hotel and we talked. It didn't go well."

Elijah narrowed his eyes, focusing on the horizon, and Sarah knew he was seeing Grady's pain.

"Then I'm saying it again," he said, "and I mean it even more, if that's possible. Come to Texas with me."

"Elijah, you're not hearing me. You're just imagining that woman in the black dress. See me for who I really am, someone grieving over two husbands, one I loved and one I shouldn't hate, you shouldn't hate anybody but right now I do, staying in a hotel room that I'm not paying for, depending on kindness that no one owes me. I'm just like Grady, I can feel Ellen laughing at me. I should never have gone near that house."

"Come with me," Elijah said, his voice never wavering.

"You haven't seen me cry," she said.

"I have seen you cry." He had, she thought, the first time with Tess.

"I was hysterical, remember? Sitting in the dirt and sobbing over a horse."

"It wasn't the horse and I knew it even then. Come with me." They were sitting close. He held out his hand and she took it. "Come with me," he said again.

She needed the strength of his hand to keep her from flying off the ledge and out into space, falling through the trees, crashing onto the rocks. She wished she knew if Jace had made it to freedom, to safety.

"I'm not imagining anything," he said. "The person I saw was real, the same person who's here."

Maybe she hadn't always done the right thing, but in her heart she knew she was still strong. She couldn't kill a pig, but she'd been raised to do everything else, whatever it took. Jacob was never far away, but the room in her father's house was receding.

"It would be starting over with nothing," she said.

"I lost everything once," he said.

"So starting over is not new to you."

"No."

"I never expected anything like this," she said. "I expected I would go home. I don't know how to answer what you're asking."

"If you still decide to go to Virginia, I'll ride back with you to where the boats come in."

"Go with me on the stage?" she said. "Oh my God no, I couldn't bear it. To have to leave you somewhere with a crowd of people around to witness when I fall apart?" When I'm devastated? When I start crying and can't stop? When my life officially ends? Listen to yourself, she thought. Listen to what you're saying.

"That was unfair," she said.

"It's only the truth," he said. "Because it would mean that much to me, it's what I would do."

She was the terrified horse in the corral and that odd white thing was waving, the calming scent wafting out on the wind, the promise being held out, the trust being asked for and offered. Texas was so far away that she didn't even know the exact location of it, only the direction. What might await there was equally unknown, a blank, a dream that could become something good or, an equal chance, something awful. Her feelings for this person were irrational, they could turn her inside out. Already the pieces that made her up had changed. But she kept hold of the truth that cut like a knife. The fates gave and took away with the same hand. Sometimes she felt the only thing she'd learned was how little you could ever really count on.

"I can't make this decision now, not sitting here," she said. "This time I do need to go."

He helped her up and she followed him down over the rocky slope, holding his hand one more time as they edged across the falls. On the other side, she stopped in the grass beside Tess.

"My hair," she said, reaching up to touch the wildness of it. She'd lost the clips and she knew where and why. She wondered if her face would ever stop being hot. "I'm worried about the judge's wife. I don't want any trouble with her. She already knows I got drunk at Maggie's Saloon before the wedding. That's how I got the black eye. Did you have questions about that? You didn't, did you?"

"Have questions? No."

"Because everyone knew. See what I mean? How humiliating."

"I'll fix your hair," he said. "I would do that for my grandmother when she was too old."

She shook her head. Nothing made sense anymore. She turned her back to him and he worked his fingers through the tangles, pulling gently to straighten them out.

"Was she truly crazy?" she said.

239

"Yes. And she didn't like my grandfather."

"He was a hard man?"

"That's how I remember him." She pictured him and shivered.

"Important, though?"

"Yes."

And then in no time he had braided the unruly mess, tied the braid off with long strips of grass and her knees were weak again. She was afraid if she got on her horse, she would just fall off the other side. But she had to make herself think straight.

"What do I do with Tess?" she said. "Can I ride her back?"

"Go to the stables. They'll keep her."

"And then what? Will I see you again?" She had to, this couldn't be the end.

"Tomorrow morning, early," he said. "I'll be out by the creek."

"I'll know by then," she said. She hesitated. "Elijah, what if I can't see my way straight to doing this? What if the answer is no?"

"It isn't morning yet," he said.

She knew it took so much more than what they'd already shared, that even if they managed to survive, every understanding and affection between them would be tested. The mourning dove called softly. Far up in the sky, the hawk shrieked and a squirrel chittered out its alarm call from a branch above their heads. She would think about the waterfall, the smell of rosemary, the beating of his heart. Everything else was too frightening, too real. The tears came, streaming down her face.

"I told you I cry," she said, using her sleeve to try and wipe them away. She wondered if that would be his last memory of her, the woman who couldn't stop crying, the woman whose fevered kisses tasted of salt. But she had to go.

"Tomorrow then," she said. She took his wrists and ran her thumbs over the silver. How much she had wanted to do that, and now she could. For one more day. Still basking in his heat, still loving the way his eyes held her, she put her boot in the

240

stirrup, swung up onto her horse and eased Tess onto the trail that led into town and then out again, to the east, back to the past, if that's where she decided she had to go.

25

Sarah entered the hotel silently, aware that Diego might already be in the kitchen cooking up an exquisite half-French dinner for whichever noteworthy guests were in residence today. She couldn't allow herself to see him. That night came back to her with perfect clarity, the father with his shotgun, the broad wife covered in silver and spitting on the floor, Maybelline, the dark-haired young woman and crying child, the truth that seemed to have come agonizingly late, that made her feel completely blind and foolish for not having seen it before. How could she live with the idea that they all had known, wished her well, cared for her but participated in the deceit, held the truth at bay, hoping that it would never come to light, that what happened in the end would never actually happen.

In her room, Sarah rocked by the window, overcome by a flood of emotions. She couldn't stop herself from going back over every room in the house, every word Grady ever uttered, every meal she'd cooked, every time they touched each other. The absurdly long dining table took on a different aspect, as did the palatial chicken coop, the outhouse, the burned-down candles on the mantle, the meats hanging in the smokehouse. Had that woman, that girl really, run her hand down the same rows of books in the library? Had she been the one who lit the candles on the mantle and polished the dining room table? Had that been her venison in the smokehouse, her stores of spices, her jars of exotic preserves? And where had they slept, in which room, which bed? Or maybe, drunk, they'd slept in all of them.

I can't be doing this, she thought. It was too much, making her as dark and threatening as the prairie thunderstorms. She got up and went to the trunk Diego had dragged into the corner of the room when she first arrived. She upended the contents until she found what she wanted, the leather bound journal that Miles had given her, what he called his going-away-forever present.

Miles was the intellectual among them, the one most likely to approve of using words to sort things out.

Sarah remembered that now. She'd been very moved at the time, but was moved by everything back then. She wished she could tell him what she was doing at this moment, cracking the spine, smoothing out the first page, taking out the ink jar and pen she'd bought, setting the jar on the window sill with the blotting paper and starting to write.

Miles had been right. It all poured out of her in no order, anxieties, concerns, details, names and places, hurt, anger, embarrassment, confusion, happiness, affection, gratitude, all mixed up together. She gave over several pages to Ellen, whom she'd never even met, and several more to Jace, before starting in on the heart of the matter, Elijah. As the sun was beginning its downward arc, she sat back, every ounce of energy spent. Satisfied, she put the pen down and watched the afternoon soften as the bright light filtered through the trees. Bless Miles, she thought. He was so wise. It was almost as if he'd known how soon she would have the need for his gift.

Having examined everything in an admittedly illogical way but from every possible angle, she at least knew where to start. She went down the stairs and through the dining room where newly acquired gilt-framed landscapes lent yet more richness to the atmosphere. Diego was in the kitchen, standing exactly where she knew he'd be. He looked halfway up, then looked sharply up, realizing what he'd seen.

Sarah held up a hand. "Don't say anything," she said. "Please. Just let me hug you." She could see him fighting back much of the same anguish she'd just consigned to her journal. When he opened his mouth to speak, she cautioned him again. "Not a word," she said. "You have to promise."

He found his voice. "I promise," he said, though he wanted so badly to pour out his heart to her. It was his father, his mother, his sister. How could she ever forgive him?

She walked swiftly up to him, hugged him hard and they both cried. He wiped his tears away with his apron.

243

"Good," she said. "That's done and it was more important to me than you'll ever know. Now let's talk about something else. What's for dinner? Are there a lot of people coming?"

"There are twenty-two, *mija*, the most so far, a delegation of some sort. And a man making photographs for the history of the railroad before it is even a railroad, what is that?"

"My God, how are you going to do this? Why isn't Justine helping you?"

"She is," Diego said and Sarah noticed right away that the flame still burned. "She's out in the garden. I'm serving a buffet, it was so much easier, fish and roasts and ducks, greens, six desserts, those are done, maybe I'm forgetting something. Ah, I am. The French potatoes."

Sarah had seen him do the French potatoes before and knew what this meant, the required intensive handwork, careful thin slicing, delicate layers and pools of melted butter. He opened the oven, revealing the copper pans Addison had ordered for him from France, piled high with the lusciously browning potatoes. He was beaming with uncharacteristic pride.

"What?" she said.

"I am still afraid of your pain, but I wanted to tell you that Justine made these and they are perfect, I couldn't have done better myself." It was all so complicated, he thought, being grateful to Grady, sorrowful for him, furious with him. Not to mention how Diego felt about his sister. She was the one his father should have shot. And now here he was in the middle of all of this, trying to be happy.

"They're amazing," Sarah said. "And your face says everything else I needed to know." She hugged him again. Before Elmira arrived to do the serving and likely ask questions, Sarah slipped quietly out into the yard. Justine looked up, nodded shyly and went back to her work. The chickens scratched around in the bushes. The pigs squealed in their enclosure, tired from a day of foraging and now awaiting the kitchen scraps. A mockingbird sang seventeen different songs from the top of one of the cottonwood trees. Sarah listened. It was just what she needed.

244

<>

At dawn, having slept soundly, Sarah woke, bathed in the wash basin and brushed out her hair. It was time.

Elijah was already out by the creek as she'd known he would be. Sometimes she wondered if he ever slept. Seeing him quickened her pulse. She'd been so calm and now she was all nerves.

"Let's walk," he said. It was always his solution. She nodded and followed his lead, which took them back along the creek to where it joined the river. Weeping willows and cottonwoods hid large sections of the path from view and she saw now how he kept her out of harm's way when he could, shielding her from the town's idle talk. They walked close, touching. The pieces had shifted again. They knew each other differently now. She only had to make up her mind what to do about that.

"It's very far from everything I know," she said.

"You're right. It is."

"Is it green or brown?"

"Mostly green, like here. More familiar than you'd expect."

"There'd be chickens, cows, a goat?"

"All of that."

"A garden?"

"There was a good one. It'd take some work now, I think, to get it back."

"How would you intend to travel?" she asked, going down the list she'd composed in her mind.

"We'd need to talk about that."

"The stage? A wagon?"

"Or horseback."

"Horseback?" she said. "Why?"

"Safer."

"There'd be trouble?" She thought about the cattle drivers and farmers. God only knew what else lay out there.

"We'd go out of our way to avoid it." Nothing he said was making it easier.

"How long do you think it would take?"

245

"Two weeks. Maybe more."

Two weeks on a horse? The stage had been bad enough. No bed, no cookstove. No shelter. She considered under those conditions they could end up hating each other in about a day. Then she would be in trouble.

"We'd travel along the river," he said, as if anticipating at least some of her concerns. Bathe in the river? She'd never done that. Fish in it? What about thunderstorms? And rattlesnakes?

"You and Grady managed it," she said, trying to make the idea sound better. But that missed the point. It was *Texas*. And that also missed the point. She was taking her life into her own hands, but also putting that same life in someone else's hands. Elijah's.

"I spent some time with him yesterday," Elijah said. "We talked."

Sarah stopped. "Grady? You did? What did you talk about?"

"I'm leaving. I needed to tell him that. If you were coming with me, or if I'd even asked you, I needed to tell him that too."

"Good Lord. What did he say?"

"He said, 'What else can happen?'"

"Is he all right?"

"No, but he has Maybelline now, and besides that, he's never turned his back on whose fault it was. He gave me this." Elijah dug into a pocket. He pulled out his hand and opened it. In his palm was her wedding ring. "He said it's yours and he wanted you to have it back. He said it was still good since it was hardly used."

Sarah pressed her fingers to her temples. Grady. It was never-ending. "What am I supposed to do with it?" she said.

"I don't know. Save it as something to tell your children."

She paused for one long moment, then started breathing again.

"Tell them what? That I was married for five minutes to someone who was unfaithful before I even met him?" She reached out and took the ring from his hand. "I grew up with 'waste not, want not' drilled into me. I know the value of a dollar. I want you to be aware of that. Do you have a knife?"

"Not with me, if that's what you're asking."

"Then I'll have to use a stick." She picked up a sturdy dead twig, stepped off the path, leaned on her knees and gouged a rough hole in the dirt. She dropped the ring in, covered the hole back up, topped it with a few small stones, then broke the twig in two, lashed it into a cross with several long blades of grass and stuck it in among the stones. She stood up again.

"I guess you're not keeping the ring," Elijah said.

"My apologies if that's awful, but no, I'm not."

"To go back some," he said, "I would have been talking about the children we could have."

"I realize that," she said, her voice growing quiet.

"If we go to Texas…"

"I know, but it's too much, when you bring that kind of thing up, I can't even think straight. We're not anywhere near that part yet."

He opened his hand again. A second gold band lay in his palm. Sarah stood very still. "There's this," he said. "Booker got it for me. He said it was important to have."

Sarah put a hand on his arm, not out of her feelings for him, but because she was trying not to faint again. She closed her eyes. At a still very young age was she really going on marriage number three? When she opened her eyes, he was there, and she found herself profoundly grateful for that fact.

Sarah understood in her head the thousand ways in which her decision could just add to the wreckage, but she was listening to her heart. Whatever the outcome, it was of no consequence. Only this held any importance at all, this moment, this one daring step forward into the rest of her life.

"I'll take that ring," she said. "Elijah? I swear, I wouldn't do this again for anyone else in the world but you." She let her eyes rest on him, seeing the expression on his face flash for just a moment from its customary watchfulness to something more emotional and deeper. And then he was back.

"You need to be sure," he said.

She nodded. "I am. Very sure." She stood up straighter, gathering her resolve. This was her new life, the one she'd just

247

chosen, and she needed to get used to how it would be, and then get on with it.

"When do we leave?" she said.

"Now?"

She wasn't getting used to it fast enough.

"Now?" she said, completely taken aback. "That's impossible. Isn't it?"

"Why?" When she considered it, the question had some validity. Her trunks were packed and the stage didn't leave for another day. Where else had she thought she was going?

"I guess I don't have a reason why," she said. "But if it's today, I can't even get an idea in my head of what that means or what needs done or anything. Tell me where to start."

"How we get there."

She thought for a minute, studying his face. "Every time I got Tess out on the road to Texas," she said, "all I wanted was to keep going. There was something very strong in me that said I'd be doing that some day and I believe in those strong feelings. That's how I want to go."

"You have to be sure of that, too. Once we get out there, doubts aren't going to do anybody any good."

"Two weeks?"

"Maybe less. Maybe more. Depends."

She suddenly found that she had another list already in mind.

"Bedding?"

"Blankets from the cabin."

"Food?"

"What seems right to you, beside what's out there. I don't need much."

"Do you have a skillet?"

"A tin one if you want it. Has to be light."

"And a knife?"

"Always. You should have one, too. I'll get you one."

"Matches or a flint?"

"Yes."

"Okay," she said. She closed her hand over his, with the ring still in his palm. The heat was there, but for now it needed to go somewhere else. "It means so much to me that you did this," she said, "but hold onto it because if you're serious I have to go looking for the judge. Marrying requires one."

"I know. I was there, remember?"

"Oh, Lord, you were."

She thought of something else. "There should be witnesses," she said. "How would you feel about my bringing Addison? The judge's wife can be the other one."

"As long as you're there, I don't care about anything else. I have a wedding present, though," he said. "I'll give it to you later."

"A wedding present?"

"That was just in case."

"Just in case. What is it?"

"A shotgun."

"A shotgun?" Sarah said. Suddenly everything he did was unexpected. "Does this say anything about Texas?"

"It's just that you should have one."

She was studying him again. "Ellen shot the buffalo hunter," she said.

"Grady told me that story about a thousand times. Can you use a gun?"

She smiled, thinking of her father. "Yes, I can," she said.

"I thought so."

"We're agreed about the judge, right?"

"Yes."

"Then I have to go. I have so many things to do."

"I'll be with the horses," he said.

"I'll find you. Elijah?" He waited. "Are *you* sure?"

"Same as your strong feelings about the road to Texas," he said. "From the very beginning. I'm sure."

She watched him as he walked away, watched his back till he turned into the street, then moments later, she saw the dark horse flash across the openings between the buildings. That person was suddenly her intended. She prayed to God she'd made the right decision, that he would be the one she belonged with, the one that held and lasted, didn't have secrets, wasn't going to get killed in a war. Otherwise, she couldn't take it.

26

Sarah took Grady's money and went to the boot shop. No respectable rider out on the trail would ever wear eighteen-hole lace-ups. They required a great deal of work to get on and even more of a struggle to get off. Standing in front of the shelves she felt her color rise, the sensation of Elijah's hands on her having come unbidden.

She got the lace-ups off and tried everything that fit, but the boots were all too new and stiff and hard. That was the last thing she needed. Custom boots were out of the question, not enough money or time. She put her own boots back on and was standing out on the sidewalk when Addison appeared at the door of the hotel and seeing her, quickly crossed the street.

She embraced Sarah and kissed her cheek. "You look so much better," she said. "Rest, that's the key. And my God, what I hear...but you don't want to know about that. Better that you don't. Anyway, what are you doing standing in front of the boot shop? Were you in there? They have nothing. Even custom-made. Nothing. Though I'm in love with the cobbler, he's very sweet." Addison leaned in the door and smiled.

"I was hoping for a pair of riding boots," Sarah said. She wanted to take this carefully, one piece of information at a time. "Is there such a thing? You can't ride a horse forever in these." She lifted her skirts and held out her foot.

"How much riding of a horse?" Addison said.

"Lots."

"Sit down." Sarah sat on the edge of the board sidewalk and Addison took a place next to her. "Hold out your foot again," she said. Addison held hers out as well and measured one against the other. "We're the same size. I can give you a pair of mine. But first, you can understand that I might have some questions."

Sarah studied her hands in her lap. She wondered how to do this and not make it seem like she'd gone entirely out of her mind.

"Actually," she said, "first I've got a question to ask you."

"Ask away. I'm dying of curiosity."

"It's not a request you'd ever expect, so be aware of that."

"Okay, I'm aware. Hurry up, ask me."

"Will you stand up with me one more time?"

Addison's eyes flew wide open. "What?" she said. "Why don't I know about this? Oh my God, who is it?"

There was only one way to do it, straight up and fast. "Elijah," Sarah said.

"Elijah? Our Elijah? I can't believe it. How is this possible? And when did it even happen?"

"After Grady," Sarah said. "I want everybody to know that. But he was always there, even from that first day on the stage. I was afraid of him, but he was there. I thought about him."

"Where have I been? I missed everything. He's not even around that much. How did you ever come across each other?"

"Grady said I had to have a horse."

"Ah, Tess," Addison said. She narrowed her eyes. "There's a lot of room to roam out there in the woods. I've been out there. Have you been with him?"

"Good grief," Sarah said. "Don't. You can't do that."

Now Addison was watching her even more closely. "You have!" she said.

Because she was completely flustered and blushing furiously, Sarah made a tactical error. "But it was after Grady," she said again and regretted it immediately.

Addison threw back her head and laughed. Then she grew serious. "Was it what you wanted?" she said. "Don't go doing this if you're uncertain for even one minute about that."

Sarah pulled herself together. What was done was done. Her look held Addison with its intensity. "I never knew…" she said.

"No need to say anymore," Addison said. "Lucky you to find out. Since that's all settled, let's get on with it. Now what's this about horses?"

"He's going back to Texas," Sarah said.

"And you're going with him?"

"I am."

"When?"

"As far as I can tell, this afternoon."

"Wait a minute. Are you saying you and he are going to ride horseback all the way to Texas?"

"Well, north Texas. Not quite so far, but I know it's hard and long. He gave me the choice. It was what I wanted to do."

"Then you're completely crazy, but sometimes it seems like everybody is," Addison said. She had another thought.

"Do you trust him?" she said. "That's the next thing you have to watch out for. Or maybe not you, but I always did."

"I do trust him." Sarah waited a moment, riding an emotion. "I trust him with my life."

"Some day you'll have to tell me about that," Addison said. She stood up and brushed off her skirts. "Come up to my room. I've got a whole damn wardrobe full of boots."

The room was as elegant as Sarah had pictured it, fit for a queen, lavish, luxurious, with a bow window and an adjoining sitting room, a canopy bed, the biggest armoire Sarah had ever seen, and an exquisite copper bathing tub right there in the corner. Addison opened a polished door and exposed what was in fact a wall of boots.

"Let's see," she said, going along the rows. "Here. These. Strong Italian leather. Beautiful but very kind to your feet. Heel for the stirrup. Perfect."

"You have so many. I didn't know you rode."

"At one time or another in my life, I've done everything, I swear. Now I just like collecting boots."

Sarah unlaced her own boots one more time. She pulled Addison's boots on and sighed. Her feet fit into them like gloves.

"These are perfect," she said. "I've got Grady's money to pay for them."

"Good Lord, Grady's money. It's all over the place and done everyone good but him. Put it away. These are my wedding present to you. Now, I can't believe there aren't a thousand other

253

things you need. We'll go shopping, as much as it's possible in this town. And keep talking to me. I want to know everything."

Sarah was thankful for Addison's company and glad to confide in someone. It was hard trying to keep it all inside. By the time she was talked out and heard all of Addison's wise and irreverent opinions, they'd bought medicinal herbs, bees wax, Milk of Roses lotion for sunburn, ribbons to tie back her hair, more socks instead of stockings and a hat of felt with a wide brim, not a cowhand hat, that was too much, but one that would serve the purpose.

"You have to be able to carry water in it," Addison said. "That's the test." To the shopkeeper's horror, she went out and filled it from the pump. It passed. "Sold," Addison said. "Plus it's actually quite attractive on you."

"Now we have to find the judge," Sarah said. "I can't forget about that."

Addison looked at her, thinking. "Are you certain about the judge?" she said.

"Why? What's wrong with him?"

"Nothing, really. He's harmless and doddering, can't remember a thing. I'm more uncomfortable when it comes to his wife."

"What are you saying?"

"Mostly what I'm saying is I don't like her. I'll come right out with it. She's the town telegraph."

"Oh," Sarah said. She hadn't thought of that. The town telegraph wasn't something she wanted. "But who else is there? Isn't the judge the only one?"

"Not necessarily," Addison said, and smiled. "Come with me. This should prove interesting."

"We're still talking about getting married, aren't we?"

"Most definitely. The party in question just has to be available, in so many ways."

Addison crossed the street again with Sarah in tow. They stepped up onto the sidewalk and continued past the tailor, the sheriff's office, the Tin Goose Saloon, and the Chinese laundry to a small hole in the wall with the blinds half-drawn and dying plants on the windowsill. Addison opened the door before Sarah had a chance to read the peeling gold lettering on the glass.

Inside was a small stuffy room filled with wooden chairs. How strange, but Addison seemed quite familiar with the space. She knocked on a door behind which must have been a second room.

"Hello!" she shouted.

Sarah heard a commotion then footsteps and suddenly Doc Morrison appeared in the doorway, looking more than usually disheveled. His vest was unbuttoned, his collar loose and hanging from his shirt. Sarah noticed with embarrassment that even his pants were buttoned wrong. He blinked sheepishly and peered at his two guests.

"He sometimes naps on his examining table," Addison explained. "They kick him out of the boarding house at nine, way too early for his sensibilities." She regarded the person in question. "Doc," she said, "how are you this fine day?"

"Actually," he said, "I'm quite good, thank you, Mrs. Pruitt." It took Sarah a minute to register what he'd just said. Mrs? Then she remembered it was the name Addison had used on the ride in on the stage, how she'd introduced herself.

"You were married?" she said.

Addison smiled. "I was," she said. "I keep forgetting until people call me that, though I am also the one who puts it out there. Just another little needed bit of respectability."

"Who was he?"

"A criminal, if you really want to know. Charming, but he kept shooting people. He died in jail, but that was a long time ago. He'd laugh, knowing what I've done with his name." Sarah watched as Addison's thoughts went elsewhere for just a moment. "But to get on with our reason for calling," Addison said.

"I have to say I was wondering about that," Doc said. "It's not every day that I have the pleasure of your visit, Mrs. Pruitt."

"Doctor Morrison," Addison said. "Is there someone else here? Do you have a patient that we're keeping you from?"

Sarah couldn't understand what Addison had heard that would lead her to say this. Doc, on the other hand, seemed to understand very well.

"Here we all are," he said. With those words, Elmira appeared from the back room, apparently not the least bit flustered.

"Addison," she said, nodding. "Sarah Mayfield. Good morning to you. I'll be going now."

"Elmira will be staying now," Doc said, holding her back from her exit with his arm. "Let us all sit down and discuss the delicious possibilities for what has already been called a very fine morning."

Sarah couldn't begin to conceive of what was going on, but she took a chair.

"Doc," Addison said, summoning her no nonsense voice. "This young woman, do you remember her?" Doc's smile was gentle as his eyes lit again on Sarah.

"Of course, I do," he said. "You were on the stage. I'm so sorry for the loss of your husband."

"Thank you," Sarah said.

Then she saw Doc remember the rest of that day and his brow furrowed. "Ah, yes," he said. She was touched by his sentiments as well as his recall abilities, especially considering the state he'd been in.

Addison broke back into the conversation. "Much has happened since then. Maybe you've heard."

"Possibly," Doc said. Elmira squirmed uncomfortably in her chair. "But I try not to listen."

"There is then a task of a certain nature that has come up and requires your moral, not to mention legal, authority. Do you still have all the necessary papers?"

"For an annulment? Good God, no. I'm not allowed to be anywhere near those sophisticated legal maneuverings."

"No, that's already taken care of. I was referring to a marriage. As a retired justice of the peace, you do still have that certificate, don't you? That's what I meant."

256

Sarah thought Elmira was going to fall off her chair. Doc raised his eyebrows just slightly, trying to divine the situation without offending anyone. "A marriage?" he said. He turned to Sarah, buying time. "You see, Mrs. Mayfield, my checkered past has unfortunately proved itself both brilliant and dreadful. I tragically lost my law degree but have in this glorious forgiving land we call the West retained my retired justice of the peace credentials along with my rather, if I may say so, undistinguished medical degree. I'm not quite yet understanding the request, but I am fully validated in every way and at your service."

"You do have the proper papers," Addison said.

"I do, and provide them on such occasions, of which there have been few, but every one lovely, I have to say."

Addison waited for Sarah to enter the conversation, but Sarah appeared to have been struck mute. "Would you be available," Addison said, "to officiate at the marriage of Sarah Mayfield to Elijah Blue? Likely in the next hour or so?"

Doc held his breath for just a moment. Elmira let out a small sound. Addison realized the town telegraph would keep on churning, but at least the news wouldn't be coming from the chattering judge's wife with her spiteful parrot. Then the good doctor regained his powers of speech.

"I would definitely," he said. "Just please kindly provide me with a location."

"Sarah?" Addison said. "You have to say something."

Sarah couldn't think of the words. The momentous decisions of the morning were catching up with her.

"Mrs. Mayfield," Doc Morrison said. "Are you certain that you're free and willing in this enterprise?"

"Yes, sir," she said fervently. That was as much she could get out.

"Then in an hour," Addison said, trying to speed up the process. She thought fast. "At the hotel." How that was going to happen, she had no idea. She would just make it happen.

Out on the street, she tried one more time.

"How are you?" she said to Sarah.

257

"My head's spinning."

"No wonder. But does this all meet with your approval? Doc Morrison? The hotel? I'm not one to stand around. I get impatient and make the decisions myself."

"Oh no," Sarah said. "You were right about the judge. It would have been very uncomfortable there. It's just that it's all coming so fast."

"Go sit down in your rocker," Addison said. "Have some wine, you know where it is. I'm excusing myself. We've had fun, but I've got work to do."

"Wait," Sarah said. Finally, it had come to her. "In the garden," she said.

"In the garden what? To get married? With the chickens?"

"Yes." Sarah smiled. There couldn't be a better place.

"Whatever you want is fine with me. Consider it done."

Sarah went slowly down the boardwalk in a daze, trying to fully comprehend the last hours of her life and at the same time assemble the next hours of her life. She crossed the street and went up to her room one last time. There, she opened the trunk and carefully felt through it until she found the cut-off skirts and petticoats that she'd pressed into the depths, thinking she'd left that person behind forever. Now, instead, she pulled them out and put them on. Addison had agreed that when the day porter arrived, he'd remove the trunks and baggage to the porch, and from there to the stage office to be loaded on the next coach heading to north Texas.

Next, gathering purpose again, she went to the general store. She'd cooked in lean times, sometimes making do with nothing, and knew what was possible. Still using Grady's money and thanking him silently for it, she purchased cornmeal, a side of bacon, salt, dried apples and onions. With these meager staples, plus greens and even one fish or quail now and then, she could get them to Texas.

Hesitant in her daring clothes, carrying the small amount of possessions she'd chosen and her purchases, she walked to the stables at the edge of town. Elijah looked up and saw her coming.

She waited while he took in everything about her from the uncertain expression on her face to the cut-off skirts and the boots that were no longer eighteen-hole lace-ups.

"How is everything?" he said.

"Everything is very strange," she said.

"In what way?"

"Well, about the judge…"

"You didn't find him?"

"I've been with Addison. As it turns out we didn't go looking for him."

"Does that say anything?"

She realized what he was thinking. "No, no," she said. "It's not like that. Addison doesn't like his wife, that woman with the parrot?"

"Because she talks too much." There he was, she thought, right again. But it was becoming one of the things she most appreciated about him, how aware he was.

"Exactly. But then we went to see Doc Morrison. He's not only a doctor, he's a retired justice of the peace, so he has whatever there is needed to marry someone. We'd get married at the hotel. Is that all right with you?"

"I don't care if we get married right here with the horses."

"I'm glad I didn't wait to ask you."

"How much time do we have?"

"An hour."

"Good," Elijah said. He whistled and Bean appeared around a corner of the building. Elijah went over and talked to him. Bean nodded, mounted a horse and rode off.

"What was that?" she said, only slightly alarmed.

"Some things you can't get in the way of because they're going to happen anyway. Not bad things. Good things. Necessary maybe."

"That's less than straightforward."

"There's no other choice. But come with me."

Elijah took her to the back of the stables. Tess and the dark horse were both there, calm in the shaded interior. Sarah stepped

259

back. The sight of Tess brought home the reality of what they were doing. The horse was completely outfitted now with a saddle she didn't recognize, a collection of leather bags and a bedroll. She reached out and stroked her horse. Tess whinnied softly, as she always did.

"We're really doing this," Sarah said.

"As long as you're willing," he said. "Here, try this first. I was seeing how well it fit." He took the bedroll off and untied it on the ground. The outer layer was a thin waterproof, the next layer a blanket. "Put your clothes in here."

Sarah was reminded again of learning about Tess. Elijah wasn't going to help her. She'd have to do this by herself. She knelt down on the hard-packed earth and laid out what she had. He could watch if he wanted. He'd already had some experience with these items of clothing. She smoothed out cotton drawers, camisoles, two shirts, one petticoat and rolled everything back up tightly. Then she settled it behind her saddle and cinched the straps.

Next she put her women's necessities and socks into the smaller bag wrapped around the saddle horn. Without consulting him, she undid her purchases and filled in the saddlebags with food. He handed her a canteen. She regarded it for a moment, then found a place for it in the saddle bags. Maybe they were finished. He handed her a box. She opened it and nodded thoughtfully. Ammunition. She took out the canteen to make room for the box. He handed her a knife in its sheath.

"I'm getting the message," she said. She rebalanced everything, stroked Tess gently and brushed off her hands. "Done." He handed her the shotgun.

"My wedding present," she said. "Thank you. I love it. Where does it go?"

"There's a holster on the off side."

"The off side of what?"

"Your horse. You should try it, see how it feels."

She thought about her brothers. "I don't have to do that now, do I? Not here in town?"

"No, it can wait. But sometime. Soon. The rifle, too."

Which put the buffalo hunter back in her vision. As far as the guns, it had been a while. She wasn't as good as Clayton, but she was better than Miles. Then she wished they hadn't come to mind.

"I'm here," Elijah said. She'd forgotten just for a minute about the watching. She closed her eyes to clear away the images. She'd miss them, but though he was his own person, he had so many of their best qualities, and that alone would keep them close.

"I know," she said and smiled, aware that he saw the sadness.

Sarah hung her hat over the saddle horn. It was a good hat, much more useful than the one she'd thrown away. She wondered what else there was to do, how they would occupy the nervous time left. Elijah handed her a horse brush.

"They've already been hard-brushed," he said, "but the soft brush calms them down. Calms people down too."

"That's what you say," she said. And then found out that he was right.

27

It was so peaceful in the stall with Tess, brushing her and talking to her, that when Elijah touched her, Sarah jumped.

"It's time, I think," he said.

She wondered how he knew. They were under a roof and couldn't even see the sun. It didn't matter.

"I'm wearing Addison's boots and my cut-off skirts," she said. "Not quite what you hope for your wedding." But this is the third one, she reminded herself. "And that suit looked so good on you." Wait, what was she doing, that was at her second wedding, don't bring that up again.

"I gave it to Jim," he said.

"You did? Why?"

"He liked it better than I did."

In that way, she thought, he was definitely not like her brothers at all.

Out in the middle of the dusty street, making their way to the hotel, after dodging several carriages, Sarah stopped. Her feet wouldn't move anymore.

"Elijah..." she said.

"I'll wait," he said. She knew he would, even if she stood out here all night, and she was grateful for him all over again. "Think about something else," he said. "Tortillas. The heron. Rattlesnakes. John Russell."

"Are you doing this on purpose?"

"Yes."

"At least you're honest." She hesitated. "You and I are getting married," she said.

"Only if we can get across the street."

"The ceremony's in the garden."

"With the chickens? Perfect."

"I don't think you mean that."

"I sincerely mean every word of it."

"I'm still scared to death."

"That'd likely be anyone's feelings about now."

"That's not helpful."

Behind them, a group of riders suddenly kicked up dust and slowed their horses to a walk.

Elijah took a deep breath. "Don't turn around," he said. "Just keep walking."

"Why?"

"Why's not a good thing to ask right now."

Sarah turned around and her hand went up to her mouth. The three riders were Booker, Jim and Abraham.

"They wanted to come," Elijah said. "But they respect how you might feel."

How much could she cry? But they were here. She would get to be with them one more time.

They tied up their horses and stood so quietly that she would have laughed if it wasn't for the crying. She hugged each of them in turn and the gap was closed, that night gone, everything painful that went with it put away. These three were her family, her heart, the good in all that had happened.

She wiped her face with the back of her hands and went back to Abraham. "How is Emma?" she said.

"Tall," he said. And then she did smile.

"I've missed you all so much," she said. "Thank God you're here. Now everything's right."

"We're glad for you," Booker said.

"It got a little confusing," Abraham said. "There were people coming back that'd been here before and people here that hadn't ever been here before and people that had been here weren't even here anymore. And then they said people you wanted to be here were going really far away."

Sarah thought it was hopeless, she'd be crying for the rest of her life. She couldn't keep hugging him, but she did love this child.

"Whatever he's saying," Jim said, "the confusing part's for sure. And the going away part."

Booker sighed. "We agreed to just say we were glad."

"Elijah says you'll have the horses," Sarah said haltingly, using her sleeve now.

He nodded and looked at Elijah. "I believe those horses will end up in Texas," he said. "God willing."

Addison appeared at the hotel door and was seemingly unfazed by the new arrivals, as if from experience she'd been expecting them. "I wondered where you all were," she said. "Booker, get that boy some new pants, he's about outgrown those. Would you all be considering coming in? Nobody's getting married in the street that I know of."

As they walked through the hotel, Sarah realized that every part of it held memories for her, the porch where Booker put her suitcases while the thunderstorm drenched them both, the chair John Russell sat in as he talked about the war, the dining room aglow at night, Grady's pleasure over a thick beef steak served with onions on good china, the stairs Elijah had climbed in the dark.

Although it wasn't yet noon, Diego was in the kitchen. Sarah frowned. The fire in the oven was banked, a large pot simmered on the stove and the smell of fresh baked bread filled the air.

"What's this?" she said.

"Just a small wedding lunch," he said, smiling. He glanced at Elijah. "Peace, *mi hermano*. Texas will still be there. It is duck breast and oyster stew and the ceremony should begin before Doc Morrison dies of either hunger or fright, that's what he told me to tell you."

Jim leaned over quietly and peered into the deep pot. "Never had oyster stew before," he said. "Should of worn my suit."

"Enough," Addison said. "I can't keep Doc out there forever. He's afraid of the chickens." She shot a look at Sarah. "Justine and Elmira are there to help him out. Okay with you?"

"Yes," Sarah said. Everything was okay with her. Elijah had stayed beside her from the time they left the stables. Now as they went out the kitchen door she reached for his hand and wound her fingers tightly through his. Stay calm, she told herself, even as she felt the trembling start.

The view before her was the one Sarah loved, the fields spread out, the waving prairie grass, the willows lining the creek, the green hills and enormous sky. At the edge of the kitchen garden, Addison had set up a pedestal that suspiciously resembled the judge's and on it was a huge bouquet of flowers. Other than that, the only sign of a ceremony was Doc Morrison dressed in black without stains and holding a book out of which stuck folded notes. Elmira and Justine stood on either side of him with flapping dishtowels at the ready.

"We chased away the pigs entirely," Addison said. "They probably won't get back here till a week from Sunday."

"There you all are," Doc said with obvious relief. "Please forgive me if I rush the preliminaries, or possibly eliminate them entirely, but if everyone's acceptable to the notion, and I for one certainly am, then I believe we should turn our attention to the necessary formalities in a suitably hastened fashion." He glanced around behind him for wayward fowl, then smiled nervously at his two protectors.

He opened the book in his hand. When he looked up, he realized that he had failed to create a proper assembly. He forgot sometimes that good people out west did not attend an official event every day of their lives, or ever. He directed the rearranging, Addison to the left, Booker, Jim and Abraham to the right, Sarah and Elijah in the middle.

He went back to his book. He considered that this marriage business was more exhausting than he'd remembered.

"Elijah? Sarah Mayfield? Are you prepared?"

Who was ever prepared, Sarah thought.

Doc ignored the question he'd just asked, reminded himself that he had to stop calling her by that name, and cleared his throat. "Kind and gentle folk," he said. "Stay with me." He checked his notes and raised his eyes again. "We are gathered here together," he began, "in the company of witnesses, to unite this man and this woman in what most would hopefully consider to be the joyous state of holy matrimony. It is the widely held belief among those few of our citizens deemed to be reputable that marriage is a solemn institution, the enviable cornerstone on which the community is built and around which the family revolves. God knows it is not to be entered into lightly." He paused, gathering his listeners to him.

"If there is no notice of reason why this union should not take place, we will now continue on. Speak up or forever hold your peace."

In the silence, a noisy jay set up its raucous calls.

Doc Morrison turned to Elijah. "Do you, Elijah, take this woman to be your lawful wedded wife? Do you promise to love her, honor and cherish her, keep her in sickness and in health, forsaking all others, for as long as you both shall live? The answer, if you shall choose it, is I do."

"I do," Elijah said. Sarah took a deep breath. Then she heard a sound, something odd. She leaned out and looked past Elijah. The sound she'd heard was Jim crying.

"Oh Lord," she said. She shut her eyes tight. "No, no, no," she said, but the tears came anyway.

Doc felt the best way forward was to proceed. "Sarah," he said, working hard to forget the rest of the name by which everyone knew her, despite, he was quite aware, her more recent matrimonial state. "Do you take this man to be your lawful wedded husband? Do you promise to love him, honor and cherish him, keep him in sickness and in health, forsaking all others, for as long as you both shall live? The answer, if you shall choose it, is I do."

Finally, Sarah had found something certain. To this question, she knew the answer. "I do," she said.

"Is there a ring?" Doc said. He had learned from experience not to have expectations, to always ask.

"Let go for just a minute," Elijah said.

Sarah let go. He took her shaking hand. Carefully he slid the ring onto her finger.

"Repeat after me," Doc said. "With this ring, I thee wed."

"With this ring," Elijah said, watching the tears stream down her face, "I thee wed."

Doc breathed a sigh of relief. He felt an inordinate amount of happiness wash over him with only the smallest amount of breakfast whiskey involved. "By the powers vested in me," he said, "I now pronounce you man and wife. You may kiss the bride."

Elijah turned to Sarah again. He took her face in his hands and in public, in front of the white man's God and everyone they knew, he kissed her. Elmira sighed. Justine wheeled just in time to swat an oncoming chicken. Doc wiped his brow. Diego felt he, for one, could finally stop crying. Abraham lent Jim his handkerchief.

"Done," Addison said, finding that she was somewhat overcome herself. "Please let's all go in and eat."

Sarah left Elijah and kissed everyone else, Jim, Booker, Abraham, Doc, Justine, she even found herself in Elmira's bosomy embrace.

In the kitchen, Addison had set chairs all the way around the table. Diego put out the dishes, the duck breast and oyster stew, with fresh bread on a plank, and three jugs of wine, and then sat down himself.

When all the seats were taken, Sarah knew what would happen. Abraham held out his hands. This was how it was done in his family. As hands joined around the crowded table, Sarah felt Elijah suddenly look down. She wondered if he was seeing other hands, other faces, hearing the sound of lost voices. They would talk about it later. She would ask him and he would tell her. Together they would talk about everything.

She bowed her head. "Bless the food before us, the hands that prepared it, and those about to receive it," she said, no more than that, her father's simple grace.

"Amen!" Doc said loudly. "Could someone be good enough to pass the nearest jug of wine?"

The meal came to a satisfying end. The bowls and plates were wiped clean, the wine jugs nearly empty and the wedding guests smiling. Sarah's breath caught as Elijah put his hand on her thigh under the table. Despite the warmth, she recognized his touch as a quiet signal that they needed to go.

When she stood up, everyone stood up, chairs scraping on the stone floor and the kissing, hugging, and tears commenced again. Even Elijah was forced to submit. It was after all, Sarah thought, his wedding day too and these were people who had cared about him long before they even knew her. She said goodbye and thank you until her voice was hoarse with emotion. Overwhelmed by the finality of the moment, it was only with a fierce amount of willpower that she managed to tear herself away. When she did she was carrying bread, sausage and hard cheese from Diego, always the gift of his food.

She was glad she'd survived, but she saw how everything had changed. Life as she'd known it was gone. From here on, so much of what happened would be a complete surprise, she was certain of it. But the future suddenly held more than she ever could have asked for. Crossing the street, Sarah reached out her hand again and Elijah took it. No need for concern over other peoples' opinions anymore, not here at least. They were so close to being gone.

At the back of the stables, Sarah leaned her head against Tess and cried silently one last time for all that she kept leaving behind. Then she straightened and took herself in hand. If she intended to be a reliable person, she should be doing what Elijah was doing, checking his horse's shoes, re-cinching the saddle, making sure the fittings were tight, the saddlebags in place, the rifle tied down, the bridle secure, waiting for her.

She went to the pump and splashed cold water on her face.

"Where's the brush?" he said. "You'll want it later."

"What brush? The horse's?" She searched until she found where she'd left it, on the top corner of the stall. Every time she moved her hands the slim gold wedding ring caught the light and startled her. What if she'd kept going on that other difficult path? What if none of this had come to pass, the good and bad, all of it? Then she looked over at Elijah. He was there, he was the good, and it had come to pass. She felt like the luckiest, happiest, most frightened woman on earth.

He handed her a bandanna. "It's one of my old ones, broken in," he said. "It's useful like the shawl." She'd thrown the shawl over the saddle and was glad to see it there.

"Thank you," she said. She opened the top of her shirt and tied the soft bandanna around her neck. Her hands were shaking again. She reached up and carefully undid her hair, letting it fall to her shoulders. From the leather bag slung over the saddle horn, she retrieved her own brush. Working in strong strokes, she brushed out her hair until it found some kind of order. Then she tied it back with one of the ribbons she and Addison had bought, noting that Elijah had to look away.

Sarah wished he would speak, say something to get them moving, but she understood that he wouldn't. At every point, this decision needed to be hers. She hesitated, one hand on Tess, stopped again by the enormity of what they were about to do, what she was about to do. The hand on Tess was the one with his ring.

"Who will our children be?" she said.

"Whoever they want to be."

"But strong," she said.

"And beautiful."

She realized he was talking about her. Overwhelmed again, she went to him. He wrapped her into his arms and held her tight, as if the enormity of everything had occurred to him as well, then kissed her as if they had all day and night and this was all he wanted to do.

Breathless, she stepped back, trying to put some distance between them so that she could steady herself for what came next. This was Elijah of the silver turtles and Dell and the People Who Live Upstream and she was going to Texas with him. And he kissed her like that. She smiled to herself at the thought.

Tess seemed even taller now. "All those saddle bags and the bedroll make it harder," she said, aware that this was only the first of many obstacles. "But if you and Grady could manage it when

269

you were hardly grown then I can surely manage it as a woman who's been married three times. The married three times was the hard part. Getting up on this horse will be the easy part, I know that, it's just I have to think about it, I have to get it figured it out." She stopped. She was talking too much.

"Elijah," she said. "It's my wedding day and to be honest with you, I don't want to figure it out. If I asked you, would you help me?"

"Yes."

"You didn't help me before."

"You didn't need help."

"That's what you say. That's your way, you know. You've got a lot of things that are your way."

He locked his fingers together under her foot in Addison's Italian leather riding boot and lifted her easily up over the bedroll and into the saddle. "Not so many," he said.

"We'll see," she said, "and I have my ways too, but thank you, and don't say 'any time' because it won't be the truth." Because he hadn't moved, she leaned down to kiss him one more time. He kissed her back, slowly, his hand running gently up and down her leg.

"We'll never get to Texas if we keep this up," she said.

"No, we won't," he said. Before she had time to think about that, he swiftly mounted his own horse, led the way through the stables and they were out on the road.

At the very edge of town, just before she knew that he would open up the pace, Sarah turned again. She sat quietly on Tess, settling into the calm he lent her, and looked one last time at the familiar town, its broad main street, mix of sagging and fine buildings, the beginnings of the new stone courthouse that would fit perfectly with a railroad and a high class hotel. Beyond the prairie, far off in the distance, the green hills met the cloudless sky. She reached up to touch the silver key. This was what Jace had been preparing her for, she was sure of it, Elijah and all that life with him would be. There were no secrets in the box. They were in the knowledge Jace imparted to the three of them over all those years, a constant source of fierce wisdom, a means of survival and protection, a labor of love.

Elijah brought the dark horse around. Sarah's eyes were filled to the brim but her face was shining.

"I am truly, seriously, afraid of rattlesnakes," she said.

"Me too," he said. She'd learned it didn't matter whether she looked at him or not. His expression would never give anything away. He held his restless horse in check until she eased Tess up beside him. Then they flew. She saw in her mind how they would rein back in when the road was played out and find their way more slowly, from sun to moon to sun, hunting rabbits and greens, fish in the river, heading south into the wild strange land where her heart and her husband wanted to be.

<>

Dearest Clayton and Miles,

Clayton, thank you a thousand times over for your letter. It came at the most important time imaginable and meant everything to me. I love you both more than words can say. Miles, I think of you every day and know you will write soon, but please don't send the letter to Sweetwater. I'm not there anymore.

I have so much to say that a letter can't possibly hold it all. I don't even know where to begin. But first, let me tell you about Elijah...

Made in the USA
Las Vegas, NV
11 January 2021